M000041242

Also by John Rolfe Gardiner

Great Dream From Heaven
EP Dutton, 1974

Unknown Soldiers
EP Dutton, 1977

Going On Like This
Atheneum, 1983

In The Heart Of The Whole World
Alfred Knopf, 1988

The Incubator Ballroom
Alfred Knopf, 1991

Somewhere in France
Alfred Knopf, 1999

Double Stitch
Counterpoint, 2003

The Magellan House
Counterpoint, 2004

NEWPORT RISING

A NOVEL

JOHN ROLFE GARDINER

STRAFFORD & UNISON 2017

ISBN 9780692839812

FIRST EDITION

To Helen, Arthur, and Fred

With special thanks to Russel Baker, Christopher Benfey, and Jill Lepore for their critical readings of the *Newport Rising* manuscript

Cover Art
Newport, R.I. 1730 J.P. Newell
By permission of the Newport Historical Society

Book Design by AJVS Books

"Newport, Rhode Island,
the most thriving place in all America"

Bishop Berkeley, 1730

ONE

WOULD THEY HAVE ME?

Cotton Palmer on the masthead, Inkfinger in the town, I was a pest to royalist and patriot alike, and a nagging puzzle to the clergy. Known from high Jew Street to the wharves as the eavesdropper and tattle-mouth of the *Newport Mercury,* mistrusted on all sides. If we'd published half what I knew about the handsome port's corruption or a fraction of my doubts about scripture, we'd have had no more rags for paper, and seen our type thrown to a three-thousand letter anagram at the bottom of the harbor.

Still, men and women plied me with their schemes and complaints, hoping I'd be a crier to their trade, or healer to the community's ills. From the mills on the high ridge to the counting houses at harbor-side, from the alms house to the ferry wharf, from the hiding place under the synagogue's aisle dais that gave secret passage to Barney Street, and down to the auction block at the Brick Market, I raked through every shop and sail loft, every ropewalk, distillery and warehouse with ears snapped forward like a mule's, my eyes alert to every craft and dodge.

Newport was thriving when I arrived in 1762, home to three-hundred ocean-going ships, and as many coasting vessels - sloops, shallops, longboats and barges, moored at wharf, laying out at anchor, or drifting away, pennants stretched leeward in a sassy freedom. On a normal day I might have seen sixty or more brigs, a half-dozen of them dropping over the edge of the world, and as many home-bound, rising to that profitable nest of slave-trading merchants and craftsmen.

<>

The town was having a marvelous good run, in practice almost a free port, taxing itself on the slave profit to keep the streets cobbled if lotteries wouldn't answer. Hardly more than a village if you paced the streets and counted buildings, but easily a state in wealth and variety of enterprise and craft, something of a miracle, unlike any other on the long Atlantic shore.

I came there on the same ship that brought Sally Warren, a tender blooming vision of twenty-three, with no man at her side but a letter of probity from a pastor against evidence of a child showing. We were making the short passage from New Haven on John Bannister's slave ship, the Piety, under Captain Lester Clarke.

On that last short leg of his slave voyage I was Clarke's superannuated cabin-boy, far too old for the job at thirty-four, thoroughly schooled in letters, though ignorant of slave ships and the sea. I was the chance substitute for a miscreant who, on the ship's Guinea-reach, got at a rum barrel with a gimlet and was found at his makeshift bung with liquor trickling onto his tongue. He was sold off the deck of the ship to a captain on his way back to Africa.

"The feet of a fool like him might never touch land. I've got irons to fit your neck too," Captain Clarke warned me, in case I should think ungratefully of his forbearance and command, his gracious tutoring of a fool at sea. He'd only taken me by default, in a hurry to be away from New Haven where I'd recently been fired for editorial insubordination at the *Gazette* newspaper.

Stepping aboard behind me came the swollen woman Sally Warren. "The throat distemper took my husband," she told the Captain. Nothing more in my hearing. Her raven hair and half her face she kept hidden behind a scarf, determined in her diffidence, turning away from any conversation.

On the deck as well were two Narragansett pacing mares for return to Rhode Island, tied at the rail, stomping at each shifting slant of a new tack. Below was our cargo of molasses and two blacks in a yoke of neck irons, leftovers of the ship's Jamaica sale. Through most of three days and nights in a light breeze, or none at all, I was obliged to stand by Clarke while he damned the contrary air and my uselessness.

"Wouldn't know mist from mast," he grumbled, while I stole quarter glances at the young woman who paced mainmast to stern, back and forth, ignoring the crew's vulgarities thrown her way from the ropes. She flinched only as she passed the angry howl from below, the complaint of the two slaves. Sound but unwanted in Jamaica or Charleston. I supposed they'd been shunned for the wild thrashing of their arms and indelible hatred in their eyes.

It was my duty to lead them up to the deck by a rope attached to their joined collars for exercise and evening bath under a bucket of sea-water, and to bring them their watered oats. The man was short and powerful; the boy as tall, though he looked no more than twelve. I had to feed the two mares as well, oats plus molasses. It was the livestock on his ship Clarke hated most, not so much the shrieking of the iron-coupled man and boy below.

It was mid-March and dawn of the third day out of New Haven on what should have been a trip of a day and a half, unseasonably calm, sails flapping, and the crew taking ease in the still air's gift to their indolence. Clarke angrily turned on me and my remark on the flight of geese overhead, how their shifting course suggested the slow turning of the world. To Clarke it seemed all nature with my connivance and maybe the black cargo's curse were conspiring against him. "Why did I trouble myself with you?" he said. "Too gibberty by half, and don't know a sheet from a block. Bring up their duty bucket, Palmer. Bring them up too for their exercise."

My hands wide, palms up, were meant to say 'How would I do that?'

"If you can't blow a penny-pipe, twist your gob into a whistle. They'll trot to any tune."

The bright day left me blinded on my way under the low ceiling of the slave deck. By then I knew to breathe through my mouth when I went down. They said all evidence of the earlier cargoes' urgencies had been scrubbed away with lye in Jamaica, but a lingering miasma could still gag me. Keeping low on the way down I saw nothing toward the bow where the two had been lying on my last trip under. Bent over to less than half my height, my feet had only touched the planking, when two hands grabbed my ankles through the stair-steps behind me. My legs were pulled sharply backward, I pitched ahead, forehead to joist, and the floor came up to meet my chin at the full speed of gravity. When I regained mind and vision one of the spar monkeys was kneeling over me. My shirt had been rolled up into a bandage and tied around my forehead.

"Reefed your blouse," he said. "You were in a fair way to having your head stove in, you idiot."

This red-headed rover who had jumped below to save my life wanted nothing more to do with "a rogue college snob." What? It was 1762, twenty years since my aborted season among scholars. That's how sticky my reputation was, that someone could come along who knew a bit about my past for good or ill. I'd knocked about north and south since my half session at Yale, all over the lot with a ripe history, and twenty years of the telltale stain on my palms and under my nails, the residue of that sharp mix of flax oil, resin and carbon that betrays a life in print shops.

This man who came to save me was no ordinary sailor, but one of those lately gone to sea disguised in ignorance and a full beard to observe and tell what he sees and hears to the Crown. Still, it was strange I should be known to that day for my youthful disrespect for the Rector of Yale. Since then a half-dozen printers had hired and let me go, raising me from apprentice to journeyman on the way. My opinions were more dangerous than useful to most of them. I amazed them with my printing and composition skills, but I was never long at a press before my ideas found a way into print, delivered surreptitiously as letters to the editor. No one was fooled for long. I was the victim of my own vanity.

<>

My rescuer pled an aching head from his exertion, and asked a morning in his hammock; not granted. I'd made my way back up the stairway, where Clarke and his Mate Crawford were standing over the two slaves, who waited, still as lizards, for their punishment. The Mate was all for the single-tailed horse whip in preparation of shark meat. Gradually, he was calmed by Clarke, who kept repeating the value of the living cargo.

"Seventy pounds Sterling, Mr. Crawford, I'd guess no less. Seventy pounds Sterling," lamenting the new lesions where the struggle in neck irons had opened flesh down to the older slave's collar-bone. The twin yoke made the tandem attack from behind the stairway more remarkable. The boy, so young, looked up at me in a way to memorize my face or maybe fix a hex. There was silence, save for the easy creaking of mast and spars against their rope harness.

For the rest of the trip the red beard took every opportunity to provoke me, blocking my way on the deck, or pushing me into the rail, maybe hoping I'd raise a hand against him. "A spider-legged traitor," he called me. “Hands all black with sedition. They won’t have you in Newport. They know all about you.

"NEWPORT RISING!" rang out from the topmast.

The black man struggled to raise his head, and screamed back at the lookout in mocking imitation, "MUPHART RIGEING!" Unresponsive to prodding by the Mate Crawford, he and the boy were tugged below as they'd been pulled up - by their iron-collared necks.

Captain Clarke had us dead center in the harbor's roadway. Without boasting of the cunningly achieved landfall, he nudged me, pointing to the tallest steeple on the distant hillside.

"Trinity," he said. "Sixty pounds a half year for a front pew with the Tories. You couldn't afford it. For that matter, what is your faith?”

“Haven’t chosen.” I confessed my fear of a nightmare in eternity. I was quite certain a body never left the grave, not sure whether the mind went traveling without it.

“The red beard says you’ve been to college."

Yes, years earlier I’d been one of Rector Clapp’s Yale freshmen. ‘An unlikely scholar,’ my father had always said, turned likely by an early facility in reading and recitation. Not just the required King James, but any printed matter I could find. Mr. Butler’s *Hudibras* for example with its rhymed mockery of parliament and religious excess. Chastised for laziness at age eleven, I’d broken free of a timid silence and begun to recite:

Call fire, sword, and desolation,
A godly thorough reformation,
Which always must be carried on,
And still be doing, never done;
As if religion were intended
For nothing else but to be mended...

and thirty following lines, surprising even myself as each word seemed to propagate the next, from a visual slate that hardly taxed my concentration.

"Can he do more?" my astonished father asked. I could, but having excited his attention, I retreated into stubborn shyness. He and my mother talked about me as if I weren't there, supposing I might secure their future if my talent could be turned to account.

"There'll be a seat for him in the college.”

"For a blasphemer? Won't you get him a proper book?"

My parents began to imagine a church of their own led by a boy minister, me. I was to memorize one book at a time till I had all scripture by heart. They could already hear coins in the collection basket. I wouldn't cooperate. I was driven this way and that by my father's willow switch, but never toward their dogma or any other.

<>

NEWPORT RISING! The town spied from the crow's nest, but our way so slow the sun was falling before we passed the Custom House on Conanicut, and slid under Goat Island. Clarke ignored the Collector's bleating horn. He knew he'd had a royal spy with him since Jamaica, the Red Beard, who moved his charade from port to port, watching piers and ladings, and keeping book on traitorous sentiment. Clarke had taken him on just to waste his time and insult him with duty behind a mop.

Nothing to hide this trip, Clarke assured him, nothing, that is, but a bit of Spanish lace in his trunk, several kegs of powder. These and 70 full hogsheads of molasses at six pence per gallon tax by an edict thirty years standing and yet to be honored! Good luck collecting it! Why heed the Collector's horn? That grafter's silence already paid for by Mr. Bannister.

"Let Bannister deal with the red devil," Clarke said.

Candles glowed in the windows. The town showed a generous face of light as if a bright spermaceti extravagance was no more expense than a tallow glimmer. The grand silhouette of life and commerce against the landscape at nightfall, from windmill to hillside roofs down to the masterful weave of rigging and stays, that intricate harness of Newport's trading navy that could make any man wonder, even a heretic, at the gift of craft and gentle genius that walked and floated there in defiance of the King and Parliament. Parliament, the name of half the print-shop privies in New England.

In its shadowy delineation, the town was everything I'd been told, but less. Less, because so compressed, so many homes and enterprises on a small flatland behind a pier-sectioned cove, and street-squared hillside of limited acreage. How could it hold them all? Thirty distilleries? A half-dozen cabinet shops? The Meeting Houses of ten faiths? The shops of forty-odd trades and services? A hundred and more warehouses on the waterfront, sail lofts, State House, Promenade, a dozen coffee houses, eighteen taverns? I could make out several shipyard cradles. The streets followed down the hillside to a wide shop-lined avenue along the shore where wharves sat in the harbor like wooden teeth in an overcrowded mouth.

The ships, sprouting a forest of masts and spars, might have been bees hovering at the hive, certain of their duty as they confused the watching. Who was inbound, who bound away on the next favoring wind, and with what nectar in the hold, custom-cleared or contraband?

I wouldn't give them cause to chase me out, I promised myself, and the words blew back in my face like so many intentions sworn before. But maybe the place I'd chosen this time was of a size and persuasion that I'd capture its kind regard. Clarke interrupted the reverie.

"If you don't go bleating your doubts, they might tolerate your talent. If you have one. Take your eyes off the young woman, Palmer. You can see she's in no need of more cock."

Could a man's innocence suffer ruder inference? Though my attention to her endless back-and-forth deserved some part of his suspicion. We were drifting under Goat Island, then to starboard of the town's long central pier at slack-tide with the nudging help of a dozen oarsmen in a little craft and then by ropes from the dock.

"Is it Bannister's Wharf, or Banister's?"

I spelled my confusion for the moody Captain, because I'd seen it both ways on the rum barrels.

"If we could spell we wouldn't be colonists would we? Who'd care anyway?"

The red-headed sailor had his sea bag over the side and dropped himself with it into a long-boat before I could see how he managed the trick. The men on deck whistled their scorn at his hasty escape. He hadn't even waited for Clarke to pay him, unmasked and harried by the despising crew.

<>

Off the ship, gathering my legs under me, I watched the unattended Sally Warren discourage would-be helping hands, and disappear up the Parade with her bag. I was thinking, if you know so well where you'll sleep tonight, won't you take me with you? Just gathering wool in my admiration, ignorant of her life. For all I knew, no widow at all. Following her off the ship, I called, "fair night for our landing."

Over her shoulder she threw a muffled reply. "What good is fair weather to a ship that's so foul?"

Just off the pier, two young boys were throwing pebbles at a ragged fellow staggering along under a rough-lettered sign:

IT PAYS TO SHOOT AN ADMIRAL FROM TIME TO TIME, IF JUST TO ENCOURAGE THE OTHERS.

They threw a sing-song of muck at his name as well "Walter Shfflett, shit, shit, Shitlett," ducking away as he took an awkward swipe at them.

I was pointed toward the town's cheapest rooms on the waterfront as the well-pleased Bannister led Clarke off to a tavern for the full story of the voyage. The Captain had just made the ship-owner a bountiful Guinea run while other vessels of the Newport fleet were sailing after French prizes, making small fortunes of their own.

I gave ten pence for a double bed shared with a mulatto, who said our landlady had the easiest heart on Thames Street, that we could lie in till eight in the morning. Though if we abused the lenience we'd be bounced from our damp sheets into the harbor by her black houseboy

<>

I was up early the next day, wandering Thames Street for the first coffee shop in my path, where I made a thorough and disheartening inspection of the latest issue of the *Mercury*. Then on to the paper's office under the School House on the Parade, where Samuel Hall told me he had no need of a pressman. The place was a thorough mess with half-light coming from street level window boxes. Hall was at his paper-strewn desk, sipping a cup of tea, reading the London Gazette, fresh at six weeks old, marking the columns to be reset for his own.

How could I tell him all the things wrong with his paper? It was a dull sheet, poorly composed, ink-splashed, and written as if by a list-making schoolboy. And why bother at all if he was so politically timid. Why not just pose behind the pseudo-prescience of an ordinary almanac fraud, just be another Esquire Bickerstaff?

I hadn't warned Hall of my coming, but he knew more than a little about me. Every print shop in the colonies did. I'd been fired from half of them.

"Cotton Palmer, is it?"

Cotton suggests ashen blond, and misleads. My hair was black, wet-looking, and too sleek for my own taste. With that, I was lean and there was something in my face not acceptable to Hall, who'd been running the print shop for most of a year.

"Do you have a little of the Jew in you, Palmer? We've got a synagogue in the works, just up the hill. You must know your reputation arrives before you."

"Maybe half of it true."

There was no use lying to him.

"No particular church. I'm the sort to try them all. I favor a preacher who can find some truth outside the book. But I believe."

I didn't say what I believed in - my guilty conscience and the nagging possibility of an eternal bad dream. He stared so hard I was forced to remember my mirror's reflection, the nose a bit long though without bump or twist, cheeks as high as an Indian's, eyes the darkest kind of brown.

Hall said "just this morning a hasty man in sailor's trou' walks in with information that Cotton Palmer will be coming my way. Off the Piety with Clarke, he says, a treasonous goat of a stalker who made trouble under the deck, and went sniffing along the rail after a swollen petticoat."

"Wouldn't you ask for a name to go with gossip like that?"

"Didn't have time to tell me, did he?"

Right off, heading into the wind, I'd have to drop sail, before making way in this suspicious place. I asked Hall, not to be hasty himself, to let me account for myself at some leisure. I might tell him things that could save him some money, and make him more. This only annoyed him, but a short while later he was treating me to a second breakfast, biscuits and java, sitting in a coffee shop at the foot of the Parade.

Not in town a day, and already I saw two familiar faces at the counter. I turned in my chair, not to be seen, or recognized, by either. I'd come here in spite of the older one, Ezra Stiles, whom I knew had come to live and preach in Newport; and partly because of the younger one, William Goddard, just turned journeyman, trained in my last shop in New Haven, a clever boy of twenty-one, who had been offered my job there, but had bigger plans.

Little use to tell Hall how Ezra Stiles raised my hackles, Stiles who'd been another of Rector Clap's Yale freshmen with me and ten others way back in 1742. He was the little snipper-snapper scholar-king and linguist among us. While I, feckless at the time, was lazy and fly-about, conveniently influenced by that growing horde of New Lights, grateful to hear that mental exertion in parsing texts would be of no use in avoiding the horror of hell.

Hall wouldn't approve of the way I used to chafe Stiles with all his piss-pretty learning, his Greek and Hebrew. What good were they if God had already decided where he was going? Stiles despised me, and I regarded him in kind. Easy enough to tease him; he was so full of precise calculation. The world: 'Five thousand seven hundred and three years old.' The celestial population: 'one hundred and twenty billion corporeal souls on the right and left hand of the Lord,' on the assumption that ninety percent were being admitted through the gates.

"Why are you here?" Stiles had asked me back then, a question I felt no need to answer.

Hall was waiting for me to defend myself, but my thoughts were back in New Haven, at a long table with the other Yale freshman, Clap at the head, going on about error and salvation. Worn down by his enthusiasm, I'd bent slowly forward until my head was resting on the table, thinking this might be taken for concentration rather than drowsy indifference.

"Mr. Palmer, what did I just say?"

Head still down, I replied, "You said, What do we make of the variety of Christian doctrines abroad in the land. Has God chosen one of these for salvation, and consigned the rest to perdition? Should we allow Mr. Whitefield's New Lights to rule by their strength of numbers?" I'd obliged Clap with his exact words and a far too accurate imitation of his voice and emphases. There were indignant exhalations from Ezra Stiles and my other classmates.

I wasn't the only one guilty of occasional drunkenness in that class of raillery and insolent sporting, but I was the one who broke the Rector's patience beyond repair with a chalked line on the lecture hall slate:

THE FEMALE QUIXOTE ARABELLA, SUPPOSING HERSELF UNDER ATTACK BY AN ENGORGED SATYR, CALLS ON THE LORD TO EQUIP HER WITH A CHASTITY BELT. THE LORD RESPONDS.
EXPATIATE.

That would have been Clap's command when he called for composition. Expatiate. Boys who hadn't seen me at my mischief began to write for the Rector.

I was thrown out of Yale. Easy enough for Stiles to say then that he was sorry to lose a worthy adversary. And here he was across the room, so many years later, unaware I'd come to town, where I might disturb his peace again.

Hall, annoyed by my silence, began: 'Well, Mr. Palmer, I suppose you followed here on the news that James Franklin died, and his widow wanted help. You're late, you see? I got here first. And what use would I have for a man of your history, anyway? Which of your employers would you give for reference?"

So bitter! A journeyman like myself deserved some portion of brotherhood in the trade. I suppose he meant to insult me before sending me on my way. I thought of telling him the sorry rag he published had better been left for dry-rot linen, never soaked for paper. But I was in Newport without friend or shelter, with only my life's kit of clothes and savings, and thinking this might be the last hope for me. The town was still the fine harbor it was the night before, bustling in daylight. Maybe best to bite my tongue, and start again

I asked that he call me Cotton, and let me use his surname in due respect.

"Respect as you will, Cotton. What would I gain keeping you under foot?"

I told him I was not just a composing machine with deft fingers, but a mind as well. Yes, I had opinions, which I hoped would not be at swords with his. Here I took a chance.

"Who is it you serve, after all? Aren't the most of your readers Tories in the pew and pirates of any flag at sea? I suspect they like their political stew at a boil now and then." No boil in his pages, and precious little stew.

"What's all that to a pressman?" he asked.

"Mr. Hall, you know I'd want to do more than set your type and pull your pages. What's your survival run; eight hundred sold to cover expense? If you're not at twelve hundred after a year of my help, you'd do well to get rid of me."

He made no sign of interest.

"You noticed the two in front?" I asked. "The men who just walked out? The boy was William Goddard, no relation to the joiners. He has 300 pounds family money to start a press and newspaper in Providence. He's not just a mechanic, but a writer and a fair wit, and he's of a mind to take the colony's government printing from you. He wants to show your *Mercury* to a disadvantage. And the gentleman he was talking to, the Reverend Stiles, is of a mind to help him."

"With us half a day, and already you know the town's mind?"

I explained some of my sour history with Stiles, apologizing for the pretension of the college year, thinking to soften any vanity on display with my particular knowledge of these people. "Stiles never liked me," I said.

"You'd have done better" Hall told me, "if you'd just come to me and said, I need a job."

Nothing had changed his mind. But before we parted, he asked if I knew why the same man who blacked my name that morning would have struggled to save my life on the ship the day before? I had no answer.

"Cat with mouse," he said. "If the mouse were dead, the cat would be off the chase, out of work, eh? Like you."

Hall's homely figure carried a heavy resonance, and for the rest of the morning I walked through Newport, up and down, between Thames Street at the bottom and Bellevue at the top of the hill. A little proud, a little worried, to think myself on the royals' list of suspects, too dangerous to be left unwatched. The surveillance might give me stature here. I might get used to this, maybe prosper as a figure of the Crown's interest? I turned around to see who might be following me.

<>

The town, viewed from within, surprised me again, so tightly packed with seaside enterprise along a half mile of wharves. The traffic of carting wagons, and carriages of gentlemen and ladies, the tradesmen, merchants, craftsmen and their young apprentices passed my open-faced appeal for conversation, scarcely noticing the new one among them. Why should they talk to a stranger in their cozy nest of privateering and slaving, six years into the French war and counting; where several hundred transients were always looking to sail after a French or Spanish prize, or carry rum to the Guinea Coast for slaves? They had no need of another opportunist in their streets.

The houses I passed on the hillside, uniformly tidy, whether small or spacious, were all faced in the same narrow clapboard, weathered to a rough gray, suggesting a life indifferent to storm and season. Wealth and modest income sat side by side. Most had a black at work in the yard or garden, or watching a child. They were wary; none had a word to throw at me, and none answered my gaze.

Set like a dozen wooden palaces, with steeples and without, all through the town were the meeting houses of the Quakers, The Anglicans, The Congregationalists (two), The Baptists, the Sabbatarian kind, Presbyterians and others. Scaffolding covered one wall of the Jews' synagogue in progress, being stuccoed by a crew of black masons whose hands flicked and smoothed the plaster so deftly I stopped to admire the rapid progress of the finished surface

At first glance through the synagogue's door I took the pillared interior for the pretension of a thriving merchant, but the Chazan came forward to ask my business. Isaac Touro, the very first to tell me there'd be a place for me in Newport, even for one still seeking the way. A Jew was the first to offer me kindness, and a hope that I'd prosper in his town.

Beyond the synagogue, on Barney Street, I caught sight again of Sally Warren off the Piety, hanging sheets to dry in a back yard. Remarkable to think she'd already found work. I called her name, presuming on our shared trip from New Haven. I could as well have been insulting her from the Piety's rigging. She turned away, clothespins in her mouth, hands busy, as prim and proper as a flat-bellied virgin, shaming my familiarity.

On Bellevue Street, I lost sight of the harbor, got turned around, and with the sun suddenly lost behind a low sky, had to ask my way of a carter. Which way was I heading?

"You're on Jew Street he said, "Past the Jews, there's nothing but summer places for the visitors, and the sea beyond. You want to turn back."

Head down for a time, keeping a pebble moving along a few paces ahead of my boot. Friendless, thinking one enemy would be enough to finish me here, I woke from my doldrums before reaching the waterfront, thinking of that proud beauty off the Piety. If a house maid, surely not for long.

On the waterfront again, with no more standing in the place than a ninepin, dodging a train of rum barrels rolling to the wharves, I turned in at the clock maker's door. The man, bent over his cunning little parts, wouldn't turn my way, but kept at his work.

"Do you know what makes time?" he said at last.

"Something moving," he answered himself. "

I was indulged that briefly, then dismissed by silence. Then at a cooper's, more working wisdom from a man too busy to raise his head. "Tight grain, fine tannin, French oak's the best, A stave's no use but it match the rest." Laconic tolerance, no welcome. It was as if they'd been to a town meeting about the arrival of a foreign agent. I walked out on a wharf toward the sea where I might relax and would not be judged by the ocean, where I could worry alone about another night here, and the honesty of the rooming house where I'd left my kit and the best part of my money.

A crowd was gathering at the foot of the pier, and I ambled back, curious at the commotion-an auction in progress. I could see no raised hands, just the side-to-side shift of the auctioneer's eyes. The *Mercury* publisher Samuel Hall stood at the front, and I pushed my way up to stand beside him.

"Unusual," he said, apologizing for the spectacle. There were eight slaves for the block that afternoon, six men and two women. It was chilly, and each had been given a covering sheet to be pulled aside as their naked bodies were examined. They were poked up into erect postures, probed, sniffed up and down, their arms raised, breasts lifted. Before they were done, each was made to bend and spread the buttock cheeks.

Among them, I recognized the two who'd come on the Piety, the ones who might have killed me, maybe saved here for last, to have the others bought and settled before these two could disrupt the sale. The boy was clinging to the man's arm, but was pushed backward. His eyes found my face, and he stared, motionless. The man was yanked forward by his ankle chain, and screamed something in his own language. He could not be made to obey, but was forcibly bent forward and beaten on the ankles until he pulled wide his buttocks. And the auctioneer announced with pride,

"No trouble there."

The black assistant, piqued by the slave's defiance, poked his stick at the vulnerable anus, and was met with a violent dysenteric explosion, a spray of excrement covering his pants, and dripping to his boots. The slave's body uncoiled, his arm whipped around and caught the startled assistant a crunching blow to the neck. The slave turned, picked up the iron ball he was chained to and brought it down full force on the fallen man's chest.

Several seamen jumped to the platform. The stick was picked up, and the shackled slave beaten left and right, until he fell to his knees. His head was soon laid open, and with a final blow, crushed. The sale of the wailing boy beside him was put off till later.

Pale next to me, Hall said he'd never seen anything like this. Slaves were not sold this way in Newport. Most everyone in the town had one, but usually they'd been raised here from childhood, in the family, and taught the family craft. These two had been offered on a weekday as a favor to agents of some Kingstown planters. Unreliable people," Hall told me, gaming degenerates, who raced horses over their bridge, and played at cards while slaves made their fortunes for them.

When the printer led me back to his office for a tipple of rum, I was sure the wind had changed. We had an awkward discussion about my peculiar, indefinite faith, which led me from one church door to another. I didn't tell him it was more out of curiosity than any notion to settle in a favored pew.

"If you can't find your church in Newport," he said, "You might as well give up and go to the devil."

Then he was telling me how amused his wife had been by the mock correspondence I'd written several years earlier when I worked at the

Boston *Gazette* - my supposed letters to the editor from Limpman Quill and his barren wife Patience debating infant baptism, yes or no. The dispute had led to a bundling board in the Quill marriage bed to prevent their childless misfortune from becoming the greater tragedy of conception and the divorce that must follow a forced resolution of the argument. A Baptist preacher from Worcester, in an open letter to the Governor, wrote the vile author of such filth should be dismissed from the paper and the Colony. And I was.

Hall's wife had told him as well that he'd be a fool to send me away without a test. He told me to write a short note for the *Mercury*, an account of the slave sale, and bring it in the next day. What he really wanted, but could not admit, was someone younger than himself to relieve the weekly strain of the paper's pressrun.

"A provisional week," he said, though only two days later he took me over to the town's oldest section, the Quaker enclave on the Point, and gave his word as my bond in leasing two rooms on Willow Street from Job Townsend, one of the favored in the tribe of joiners who'd been building boats, houses and cabinets in that neighborhood beside the Cove for the last fifty years.

TWO

A LITTLE KINDNESS

Swift Action Follows
Murder on Auction Bloc
Slave Desperado Dispatched

It was Hall's headline, and seeing it, I was glad I'd not written anything to mock the seaman who caned the slave to death at a safe distance from his whirling arms. Hall said my words "a black rain from Africa" were disgusting, unacceptable. He let stand: "The wailing boy left on the block would never forget that day, and had perhaps been ruined for any master."

My first week on the job I proved I could print the *Mercury's* run of eight hundred and fifty copies in two-and-a-half ten-hour sessions. The same work had taken Hall more than three, sometimes four days. If he used me this severely, he could wait an extra day before printing and still have the paper on the street and on the ferry to Providence by Friday afternoon. The second week, with the help of his apprentice Jacob, the press run took a day-and-half, and this was the weekly arrangement after that, no more heavy work for Hall.

He gave me Sundays off; the rest of the week I was to be in the office at seven, and not out before six, except Wednesdays when the three of us might stay till midnight, setting the final type, then pulling and proofing a first copy before the Thursday morning run.

The evidence of my arrival is on the page. Archived. You can see smudging, broken type, misaligned columns and irregular inking of the *Mercury* as it appeared in March 1762, and the improvement after April of that year. It was both barbed jest and compliment when Governor Ward told Hall:

"The colony's eyesight has improved since you hired Mr. Palmer."

To the printer's lesser credit there was no improvement in his dreary content. If theft of a pig from the Malbone estate, arrival of contraband stockings from the Netherlands, poesy relating a grindstone's hum to the taste of corn meal, a gathering at Mrs. Watson's dance studio, or the remarkable length of yarn produced at one of Reverend Hopkins' spinning socials, if these could sell the sheet, let the boring text continue.

But with William Goddard set to make trouble for us with his new press in Providence, I was biding my time. Hall's eye was always on my back. He knew a royal agent was watching for my shadow on every printed page. From one city to another my fictitious cranks and their twinned antagonists made a serial record of my employment. Before Limpman Quill and Patience published their strife in Boston, Les Pennymore and Worth Umbrage, imaginary merchants in Charleston wrote enough before exposed as my puppets to have the Royal Collector there fired for graft. One might have thought the King grateful for my help. But embarrassment of his agents was never in favor no matter how much was stolen.

I was young, foolhardy and still carefree, hardly sorry to be banished from the place, though I regret the trouble I caused the printer. It was my broadside "Our Charleston Planters," the last conversation between Pennymore and Umbrage, set and pulled surreptitiously while my boss visited in Georgetown.

Pennymore: These rice planters, don't they have the world figured to a leisured certainty? Six-month vacations on Pawley's Island, Murrell's Inlet, even Rhode Island. How do they manage?

Umbrage: The swarthy manage for them. The whole job. Plant and harvest in the muck with the snakes and gators. All under the whip, for a roof and a rice bowl. Two-thirds of South Carolina's population.

Pennymore: Where do they come from?

Umbrage: From cowrie shells, like shiny white vulva from the Indian Ocean. Black souls born from the cowrie's mystery crevice.

Pennymore: Leave off with your magic.

Umbrage: Black magic, white magicians. Sixty thousand cowrie shells, a barrel-full from the Seychelles good for one black from Africa. And there's inflation for you. Was a time you could get a good man for a hundred and sixty.

I hadn't been satisfied just writing that. I had to go on about the cowrie shell, a jewel in Africa, used as money that looked like pure fired porcelain. Porcine? A sow's vulva? "And so we have the porcine planters of the Carolina delta country," I wrote.

I was fired. I was young.

<>

My habit in Newport was to wake at five-thirty, walk off the Point and circle up through the town, turning down to the south end of the waterfront on Thames Street and back to Jameson's Coffee House on the Long Wharf Mall for my breakfast of a hard-boiled egg and a scone. And I became familiar to the morning crowd that gathered there, to the aging seamen looking for one more voyage, and the working-class of the town, the ones whose favor I sought.

But I was an interloper in their fraternity, perhaps too forward, too inquisitive, and maybe too eager to share their rationed wit. They called me Inkfinger and Blackhand; not behind my back, right to my face. Though I wasn't so despised as Walter Shiflett from the Alms House carrying another of his cryptic signs.

MEN USE THOUGHT TO JUSTFY THEIR WRONG DOING, AND WORDS TO CONCEAL THEIR THOUGHT.

<>

As a daily walker in Newport, I was bound to meet another regular stroller, Ezra Stiles, established there ten years as minister at Second Congregational. I saw him one morning at the top of the Jews' Street in a warm embrace with Chazan Touro. Crossing the road, hoping to pass unnoticed, I watched them shaking hands as if they might never let go. I'd almost got by when Stiles called out, "Hi there! Is that you, Cotton?"

He came hurrying across the street, the same slight, eager man I remembered from the semester at Yale, with a head too large for his shoulders, and the same voice, strong enough, but hesitant for a pulpit orator expected to echo God when scripture was colored red.

"You can't hide from me forever, he said. "I know you've been all around God's barnyard since New Haven. What do you have to say for yourself? No, that's rude of me. You needn't answer. Sam Hall says you're just the one he's been looking for at the *Mercury*."

Unprepared for a warm-hearted welcome I could only think of our last encounter, several years after my dismissal from Yale, where he'd continued teaching after his graduation. Still in New Haven, I'd found him surrounded by what I supposed were a little flock of admiring students, and asked before turning away, "Ezra, have you decided yet whether a man can sin while sleeping?" one of the puzzles Rector Clap used to tease our imaginations.

In front of his students Stiles' answer had been immediate, as if prepared. "I'd suppose *you* do so regularly, even sleeping with your hands above the sheets, if only in the impoverished brothel of your imagination."

Fifteen years since I'd seen him, and his swift, contemptuous answer came to the fore. I couldn't resist:

"No more trouble now, with the dreams, Reverend Stiles?"

"Oh, that," he said, as if we'd spoken only yesterday, "I recall that was your trouble. But let's bury the childishness, Cotton. I won't try to force you to the Lord's Table, if you'll grant me civil conversation now and then. No reason the hair should rise on your neck every time we pass in the street."

I was wary of easy reconciliation, imagining the conversation he must have had with Sam Hall. He'd want to be sure I was neutralized, prevented from gaining enough influence at the *Mercury* to cause him embarrassment. I thought he'd be a good choice for an editorial puppet in a new column I should write, turned loose against a preaching counterpart in Newport. The town was such a nest of religious quibble, with the way to heaven always in dispute. Whatever Stiles' pretense, I know he thought I was on my way to Hell. If I crossed him in public, he'd wish me there already.

Yes, Hall told me, Stiles wanted to know if I was going to let you use my paper for 'your gift of palaver to disturb the people's mood.' He said you take pleasure in religious confusion.

"That was all?"

"No, he asked if you were stable in the mind. He said you've knelt in five different churches here, and last Sunday you sat with the Quakers. You have him worried, Palmer. 'You're a tree grown from roots of religious doubt,' he said. And I should prune you before your shadow covers the town."

Hall wasn't pleased when I showed him Goddard's broadside from Providence, strewn in our streets like the confetti of our competitor's celebration.

MORRO CASTLE FALLS TO BRITISH FLEET

It was the decade's grandest bit of news, not delivered by us, but by this upstart Goddard while our *Mercury* slept. "*Havana falls, the French and their Spanish allies humbled. End of War?*"

"Where were you?" Hall wanted to know, as if I were responsible for his embarrassment.

"Anyway," he said "who do you think brought this in?" He gave me a nudge in the ribs, and let me read from a note written on a bit of pattern tissue in a clear hand:

"A woman with a good breast of milk. Well recommended. Inquire of the Printer."

I'd just seen Hall working at the case on our next issue, setting:

PROVIDENCE PAPER OFF TO FALSE START

INNUENDO AND BOMBAST FILL FIRST ISSUE

and following that with a report on the Goddard paper's recent insult.

"There is the sad case in Newport, of a still-born baby. To think there are some there who would insist with Wigglesworth that the un-baptized infant, a boy in this instance, cannot escape eternal torment, though perhaps he'll be allowed the easiest room in hell."

This news is laid on with relish in the new sheet of innuendo and bombast being published as The Providence Gazette. The report says the bereaved young mother, recently gone to Newport and employed in domestic service there, believes she was visited by the Devil, and that during this visit, she was delivered of her dead infant.

According to the Gazette, two sisters from a church in New Haven say her claim to have had a husband who died last year is a fiction, and that in her altered state she is of a substance that floated like a cork when she was dipped in a pond there. They say she had appeared mysteriously in one room and then another, perhaps passing through a keyhole.

The Gazette further alleges an argument between her and a man who made passage with her from New Haven. We cannot say whether the same man is the author of her family way.

A Citizen

"You're printing this?" I asked. "When she's in such a miserable way she'd custom her dead baby's milk? Suggesting I might be responsible for her trouble?'

"Indeed I am."

Hall never trusted me completely, but I'd taken the weekly burden off him, the physical strain of producing the *Mercury*.

<>

On Friday afternoons when the papers were on the street and on the ferries, we discussed the week's gains and mistakes over small beer in the tavern, to a mellow satisfaction. I believed I'd either serve and prosper here, or be lost forever to sour-hearted wandering with no purpose but bread and shelter, bound to a grudging shuffle in menial harness until I feebled up and died.

In Newport there was profit running downhill to hands as common as my own, but when had I ever been content as a hidden partner in any enterprise? I was under orders never to write without Hall's permission but after our late embarrassment he was pleased to have an extra set of eyes on the world, and at this watchful business I had more skill than he did.

On Mondays he sent me to the jail above the Parade for a weekly chat with Constable Withers. It was there I saw the black boy off the Piety again, lying on a straw tick, unmoving, his eyes vacant. For all the notice he took, I might have been another bar on his cell.

"Doesn't have a name," Withers said, Bannister had made provisional sales to two shop keepers who wanted something young and pliable to train up. Both had returned him. Not a Newport sort of slave, they said He was being kept temporarily in the jail, until passage south was found. A tag fixed to the string holding up his pants, "Charleston or Barbados."

I followed his story into the next week when his lading was fixed on a coasting ship, carrying furniture and candles off the Point to Carolina. The young slave was already chained on board, when my landlord Job Townsend bought him. Went on board himself with the bill of credit, took him out of chains, and by the hand. Plucked him right off the ship's deck. Townsend said he'd show the town what a little kindness could do to prepare any child for a useful life.

THREE

A WOMAN OF NO FIXED ADDRESS

From the Providence Gazette:

The traveling Quaker John Woolman, visiting with the Meeting in that be-Britished town of Newport this month, has convinced several families on Easton's Point there to make freemen of their servants. The Quaker Meeting is thrown into resentment and confusion. Will the new freemen remain for hire in their present situations, or leave that smug island of pas de soy and lace cuffs? Some of the Elders have urged the pious man to go home and practice his persuasion in his own city. This in a town where they allow a man to go about carrying blasphemy in the streets. The latest outrage is printed here.

MEN ARE SO FEEBLE IT'S BETTER THEY BE
SUBJECT TO SUPERSTITION THAN TO LIVE
WITHOUT RELIGION

"Be-Britished", he says. "Goddard's poaching over here."

Ignoring that, Hall asked me, "What's your part with that woman."

He couldn't get past my alleged involvement with Sally Warren. I didn't even raise my eyes from the *Gazette* and its attack on our homegrown Governor Ward and the *Mercury*, as "barely literate servants of the British and their church."

In the first year of our separate lives in Newport, Sally Warren's face and figure did make a regular appearance in my daydreams as an aggravating beauty, the same whose strolls along the Thames Street waterfront with uncovered raven hair to her shoulders were a provocation to the righteous. Some held a kinder opinion of her, gave her housework, and would not have an evil word spoken of her. She had a protector here, the unseen brother who stayed out of town, reputed in the tavern as a man of quick temper with a musket always close, guarding the privacy of his boatyard.

"So," Hall said. "You believe in him now, Thrip Warren?

"Her brother's name is Warren? There's no Mrs....?"

"Ah, your Dulcinea." Hall's sigh not as insulting as the assistant Jacob's snickering. A few weeks later Hall was setting Sally Warren and twenty-three other names, and Job's black boy came to my attention again

TWO DOZEN HOME FROM INOCULATION ISLAND
REVEREND BROWN SPONSORED TRIP FOR THE POOR
SABBATARIAN CHILD TOOK FULL DISEASE AND DIED
QUAKER'S SLAVE BOY AMONG THOSE TREATED
DID THEY RETURN TOO SOON?

Hall listed the names, giving the town fair warning of the disease that might be lurking next door, explaining the group's fortnight quarantine at the camp on Rose Island.

"Last month you promoted her witching," I reminded him. "Now you say she's taken a doctor's potion under the skin. Which is it?"

"You hold a brief for her, Cotton? You'd need a bit more Newport in you before she'd have you pleading her case."

"If she were a witch, wouldn't she know how to keep off the pox without inoculation? Anyway, she's moved down island on the cliffs, to one of the Lopez cottages. Keeping house for their cousins up from Jamaica."

"Does she like working for the Jews then, Cotton?"

"How would I know?"

"You know more than enough about her. How you know it is your own business. But I'd rather have you talking to the working trou' in the town, not the petticoats. What I pay you for, you know." But he didn't say what he paid me for was anything more than the strength of my back every Thursday, and Friday morning printing his paper.

What I actually worked for, more than his weekly 11 shillings, was the tempting proximity to the press itself, the town's wasted instrument of money and influence; a miserable waste under his management. With any editorial nerve, Hall's sheet might be read by every eye in the colony. With Newport's influence he could raise a howl all the way to Jerusalem.

Instead, he published drivel from this most favored harbor. And if I had command, wouldn't I run the paper crack on all sails into the Day of Judgment!

Instead, it was "Palmer, would you run down to Taylor's Wharf, and see if Thurston wants his woven stuff listed again?"

And how could he oblige the breeder George Irish, without offending the preachers or the ladies; deciding on:

"Brown Boy, whose name derives from his color will cover mares this season at his stable in Newport at one dollar a single leap, or dollar and a half for the season. Throws delicate-made foals of extraordinary courage."

I obeyed his petty commands, nursing my courage, and my seed as well, looking toward a more exciting season. To this time, my part with women made a sorry history. Those I might have favored in the past expected steady church attendance. I'd never stayed long enough in one steeple house to earn my moral marks. Years before there'd been a Baptist cousin with a long chin who'd taken an interest in the boy who'd been to Yale. I ran away from her company long before my indifference could be taken for betrayal.

My first year in Newport I visited a fancy lady twice, in a clandestine room out the North Road, clean and favored by a few ship masters and wealthy merchants. This was an extravagance I couldn't well afford, but at two times a year, hardly a ruinous habit; my indulgence there more a mark of virility, I thought, than a moral stain. But to me a poor substitute for Sally Warren, whose singularity and private wandering was as well guarded as my own.

<>

Over a year in Newport and still tolerated; I'd surprised even myself. Though suspected of a mischievous editorial ambition, I was Hall's steady journeyman, his useful right hand, a friend to some, though a threat to those who'd leave a thumb on the scale, or sell a lame nag as a sound pacer. The *Mercury*'s circulation had increased by two hundred and fifty copies since my arrival, no thanks given me.

"Nothing heard from Reverend Stiles?" Hall asked on a slow morning. I didn't know if he was just chafing, or looking for a counter-tug on the line that always hung in the air between us.

"Why would Stiles speak to me?"

I looked at Hall for some sign of play or irony. But saw none, and I suddenly felt pity for the age and worry that creased his brow and framed his eyes. Vertical channels ran down his upper lip, as if the skin had been crimped to fit the severe circle of his jaw.

"Does he read the *Gazette*?" he asked me. "I want you to go and talk to him. You should admire a man who's mastered Hebrew to better know his Bible." A man, he said, who knew the paths of the planets, plotted the course of comets, farmed silk worms, mapped our town-houses, wharves and warehouses, took our census, kept a check on the Anglicans' attempts to control us, knew every sect's rules for entry to heaven, and conversed in Hebrew with the Jews.

I hadn't known about the comets or the silk worms.

<>

I sat with the Quakers on the Sunday John Woolman first spoke in Newport against his slave-owning brethren. Hard for him at first, he said, wondering if he'd come on his mission here with God's approval, or been driven by vanity to meddle in other men's affairs. Job, among least of the offenders, was filled with guilt.

In the weeks that followed, when I went to kneel with a variety of Protestants, none turned me from the door, though they preferred I not share the Lord's blood and body at their rail. No danger of that. They too had their traveling scolds, and itinerant preachers making trouble in the pulpits of out-of-town ministers. Ezra Stiles was a favorite target.

On a Sunday when he was away on a restorative ride to Concord, I climbed with the Negroes to the balcony of his Second Congregational, and wasn't sure whether I was listening to a businessman who had found preaching to be a cracking good income, or a pure heart who thought all of us had a pathway to Heaven.

"I come here," this Reverend Murray began, "a sinner just like you."

Stiles, whose formula for election to salvation was generous, though never so forgiving as this, wouldn't be pleased with this retraining of his members by a man ordained by nothing but the laying on of his friends' hands. From the balcony I watched Stiles' elected saints in the front pews below me turn for a doubtful look at possible new brothers in eternity. Murray's preaching got louder. "Don't roll and scream," he advised, as if there were any chance of that in Stiles' flock of propertied convention. "Make your own sound of affirmation. Well. Let me hear you!"

This produced the oddest chorus, a restrained sort of grunting, sighing, and anxious ventilation that went on for most of a minute, and was fanned to greater volume by Murray's gathering arms, pulling the noise to him, like a conductor charmed by his own music.

<>

To please Hall, I put myself in Stiles' way, adjusting my morning stroll to pass his house and church.

"Hello, Cotton!"

Again he crossed the street to speak with me. He'd been told I'd visited his congregation, and wanted to apologize for my having to sit with African folk in the balcony.

"All human acts are voluntary. Yes?" I said. It was another of Rector Clap's old posits for expatiation. Stiles' jaw tightened, but he let it go, wanting to know how his congregation had behaved under the influence of another self-appointed apostle.

"Were they polite to him?"

"More than polite." I said, "They seemed hard-put not to applaud. Like a pond full of bull frogs who'd been told to keep the racket down."

Stiles wasn't amused. He said my newspaper did the community a disservice announcing the preaching schedules of men like Murray who invented their ordinations. The kind who encouraged people to go singing in the streets, raving their faith, with no study of the text all through the week, as if there were no work to be done in Christendom.

Piqued by my silence, he began to lecture.

"Are you here to spoil things, Palmer?" as if I'd come to Newport with a grievance to be avenged. "It's not like twenty-five years ago." he said, "when the men who denied the need for intellect in a conversion kept their preaching to the fields. Men like Whitefield. Now they sneak into empty pulpits, riling people and causing confusion. They steal from congregations to the advantage of their own pockets."

I wouldn't debate. He grew warmer.

"What good is a mindless conversion?" he demanded. "Are you proud of what you don't know? Of your ignorance? I suppose you know the talent of memory like yours is often paired with poor judgment."

"You'd want to talk to members of your own flock about these things."

Dozens of his members went the next weekend to what he called Murray's open-air entertainment, and still another of Murray's meetings was scheduled for the following Sunday. Stiles' problem wasn't irreligious people, but the tangle of texts he studied in support of revelation, all the mystery and contradiction they produced.

Whitefield? I didn't need a lecture about him. Several years before my Yale adventure, just twelve years old, Bible-taught, with the prospect of Hell in my path, I was taken for a walk in the countryside by my father. My life would never be the same he said, but his zeal and haste were a caution. We'd gone perhaps a mile north out of New Haven to a junction with the pike that ran east and west.

I was afraid of the look my father got when religion overtook his senses. I had a presentiment that he had the mission of Abraham in mind, and I was Isaac. It was way out of ordinary that he was leading me away from civilization on a Lord's Day.

Beyond the crossroads a platform was raised. It was a relief to see too many people there for my father to act on a murderous intention. Great clouds of dust swirled over the pike on either side. On the road from New Haven a procession of horses, carts and wagons had followed us, a huge audience flowing toward us on every side, a sea of Sunday suits and bonnets. My fear then was of being crushed by the crowd.

We were sweating in the crush when a plump man with a round head climbed to the stage. "That's him," my father said, "that's Whitefield." Hard to believe his voice would reach to the rear of the throng. The words poured from his mouth, and even at twelve I sensed his real achievement was a masterful ventriloquism, as if his message might be coming from the distant clouds.

I *was* changed that day, not so that I believed in religion's magic but in one of its magicians, amazed by one who could draw forth the sound of hundreds simultaneously moaning, and later make the same number fall to their knees. They moaned and he turned his back on their despair, waiting for silence, and began again.

"You dead Christ-less, sinners, stinking in your cave like Lazarus, bound in grave-clothes, a corruption of stinking pus. You're crushed by the stone of unbelief on your stupid hearts. You leak corruption into your coffins. For years, stinking in God's nostrils! Go on, boast of free-will and rational argument, but don't pray with me if your heart is not filled with Him. Unconverted piety is an abomination. Go home. You put us all in danger!"

My father was weeping. On either side people beat their chests, while waiting for more of this abuse.

"If he makes you cry," I asked, "why stay.

My father shook his head in sorrow, maybe resigned to my damnation.

"There!" Whitefield said. "Do you see him? He's coming! You think he needs a human path. Here he is, right beside me. If you don't see him, the stone still sits on your rotten heart."

Our view was blocked by the shifting crowd. "To come all this way, and miss the sighting," I said. My father slapped me, and began to cry again. Long before my arrival in Newport my parents, with George Whitefield's assistance, had left that permanent stone of doubt on my stubborn heart.

<>

While dozens of Stiles congregation were drawn to "Murray's entertainments," the Quakers were in their shops and counting houses on the Point, reconciling piety with their silver and decorated side-boards and their ownership of blacks; the Anglicans of Trinity were paying a pastor to make venial their mercantile theft from Africa and the Crown; and the Jews at the top of the hill,-fifty or more families-must have been looking down on that turmoil of conscience in wondering gratitude for their freedom in one religious hodgepodge of a splendid world.

<>

Stiles, ever mindful of my menacing proximity to the *Mercury's* fonts, challenged me in the print shop right in front of Hall. "Is it true? What they say about you and the Warren woman. If you conceive an affection for the woman, if you have to do with her at all, bring your suit into the Church before the two of you fall completely from its protection."

"Which church would that be?"

"What would you say," Palmer, "if I told you not one of my three-hundred hearers is under scandal?

"I'd say your church was in need of a confessional."

Hall laughed in his sleeve.

We have a fine thing here," Stiles said. "Don't make one of your messes on our cobble. And one more thing. About you and Colonel Malbone."

If there was a high lord of the wealthy in Newport it was Godfrey Malbone, Sr., retired to his counting house and simple pleasures, a hero to Stiles, though Anglican. Colonel Malbone was a friend to all, living at ease among his servants in his red stone mansion above the Point, looking over terraced gardens to the town and harbor, and he sat on a prime plank of walnut in Trinity Church. My friendship with him was nothing particular to my credit, Stiles told me.

The Reverend and the rest of Newport, were obliged by the modest way Malbone wore his wealth when mixing with the public-fifty thousand pounds Sterling and more-mostly gathered in the years at sea before he was forty. Now in his late sixties his pleasure was his pipe, sea stories in the tavern, midnight meat suppers, gaming and fellowship in the coffee house. Without guile or resentment, he lost cheerfully at cards. His nature was all for peace and tranquility.

"The Colonel doesn't care for political noise," Stiles went on. "It's all one to him whether Pompey or Caesar rules the world."

He didn't have to tell me these things, which were all leading him to, "Leave the man alone. He's nice to everyone, no matter what he thinks of them." Colonel Malbone, he said, was too polite to tell me my evening attentions, the way I plied him with questions and turns at the tavern pump were a nuisance to him.

Actually the Colonel had recently asked for my company, calling me to join him in Pitts Head, probing around my reputation as a traveling rascal. He'd asked more than once if I'd tamed the lass I brought from New Haven.

"Malbone's in the tavern long after I'm asleep," I reminded Stiles. "If he's bothered he's got his man Augustus to carry his lantern and chase away a nuisance."

Neither apologetic nor proud of the cruelties behind his fortune, Malbone nightly offered anyone, rough-tongued sailor or the librarian of Newport's celebrated Redwood collection of philosophy and literature, his perspective on what had been in Newport and what was to come. In retirement he could afford a calm approach to the commercial war in progress, now that the British Navy had control of the ocean road, and the new battle was between colonial smugglers and the Crown. Smuggler, patriot, traitor, loyalist, were all rhetoric to him, vain labeling that left an impolite stain on a conversation.

"Forget all that," Malbone said. "Sit down, Palmer, and let me explain it to you. The Quakers and Jews got things started here. You'd ask the Quakers to build your boat, and ask the Jews where to sail it."

He could cede all this because he'd been the sea-going real thing in Newport, untitled admiral in a free American merchant marine. He'd gone to sea himself, put his life in the gale, and his hands into the black decks of his ships, unlike the newer merchants, who seldom sailed out of Newport unless it was on the Providence or Tiverton ferries, but depended on the nerve of their storm-forged, Indies-bronzed, Guinea-hardened slave-ship captains.

He helped make the rules of the game and played it himself, educating others to the sport that paid so well unless it killed them. A note written in the Malbone office to London creditors in 1730, its ink turned brown, almost yellow, was pinned to a wall at the *Mercury* above Hall's desk, a testament to the town's genius, an early tutorial on how to become a rich merchant on this island of plenty.

In respect to the debt,
we propose to make the next importation
of molasses into a cargo of rum
which we will sail to the coast of Guinea

for the purchase of slaves,
which we will transport to the West Indies,
and sell there for bills of exchange
for remittance to you

It was a lingering sorrow for me that my life in Newport had not caught up with my romantic reputation, that the fact of my thorough innocence in Sally Warren's life also meant she'd never allowed me a conversation. My mother always said men make free to admire, but are quick to despise what they cannot have. Mother, it is not so. Never mind the whistling sailors in the Piety's rigging, or the insinuations of Samuel Hall, or the "Citizen" who condemned Sally in the *Mercury*, even the crafty probing of the least judgmental, Colonel Malbone, all of whom realized she was out of reach, either beyond decorum or her interest. Pregnant when she arrived and, for all they knew, coming their way from the streets of New Haven to throw herself on Newport's mercy. Want? Fancy? Yearn? Need? It was a notion whose fulfillment would have frightened off most of her Newport dreamers before consummation could damage their chance of celestial election.

My mother's little conceit hardly applied to me. "Conceive an affection for." That was Stiles' way of saying it. Prissy but accurate, to his pious credit. A conception created in my own head without encouragement, but embellished by another sighting as I was coming out of the *Mercury*'s privy in the alley behind the school house, hitching up my trousers as I stepped out the door, thinking how having sheets of the *Gazette* beside the bench hole was an appropriate use of our competitor's columns. I think she was hoping not to be seen by anyone, coming to our back door to ask for a notice of another trip to the inoculation island.

Maybe she thought I'd timed my exit to force her delay in the smelly passage. I could only say, "Mrs. Warren" before she ducked away and down the steps to our basement door.

It would diminish her fetching eccentricity, and be a lie to say she was the ideal of beautiful. There was some imbalance in her face. Her eyes were deep set and not easily read. The flesh at the corners of her mouth gave her lips an artist's exaggeration. Still flouting convention, she wore no bonnet over her shiny black hair

I wouldn't say she was imperious, though quick of step, purposeful, and dismissive as she passed me. I went around the schoolhouse, and down the Parade for a stroll, not to embarrass her again while she did her business with Hall. I knew she had just taken work with a Sabbatarian family, the Woodrows, who'd recently freed their houseboy. They lived beside the Quaker enclave.

I thought of following to her new church, but what if she then grew restless with the Sabbatarians, and moved again? Would I follow to the next steeple house that I might glimpse the back of her head once a week? So fickle in faith? I thought of the Quaker Captain Wanton who'd married a Presbyterian deacon's daughter, and told her, "I'll give up my religion, thou give up thine, and we'll go to the Church of England and the devil together." Which is why Wanton's pompous son Joseph sat with the other King's men at Trinity, his head under so much tumbling wool his face looked more like a sheep's ass than anything human.

I'd seen the painting of Newport's slave captains carousing in Surinam, the older Wanton among them, so far gone in his cups he didn't notice the man vomiting into his coat pocket, or another lighting a candle under his bum. If these masters of land and ocean walked so shamelessly through life, how badly off could I be? And was it a sin to think of Sally in the attic bed where she slept, now that much closer to the house on the Point where I paid rent to Job Townsend.

<>

As I strolled up-island on a Lord's Day in mid-May my heart would have jumped to know she was following me. It was foggy as I went past the burying ground and the town's gun-powder magazine, beyond the Malbone orchards, into a countryside of sheep meadows; the stone-walled fields so neatly drawn on the landscape they seemed a challenge to creation, a quilted improvement on the land.

I turned and made out a dim figure in the mist, perhaps a quarter mile behind me. Not caring to explain a Lord's Day delinquency, I stepped faster, gained a knoll and took cover on the far side behind a wall. Peeking over the stones as the stranger came on I saw it was no stranger all, but Sally Warren. In a dark cape, her raised hands held a shawl behind her head, as if pulling herself along the empty road.

I stood, giving her a start. She came toward me, scolding. "Why would you frighten a body? What were you hiding from? Anyone would think you're for the gallows. Look at you, all aquiver!" Closer, I was struck again by the shifting planes of her beguiling face, and the way she set her head at an angle, giving one eye the main work of a closer look.

Ambushed by truth, I said "I'm ignoring the Sabbath.

"Your newspaper should be so honest. Why do you let them tie me to you? Your eyes follow me everywhere

"My eyes seek their solace," I said softly.

"On my bosom?"

"I've never had a chance to say I mourned the child you lost. You never allowed me a word. Anyway, it's Sam Hall's newspaper, not mine."

"Your word counts for nothing there?"

"A voice is not the same as influence. You were following me?"

She sighed, the sound of resignation to the chore of explaining a bit of herself. Orphaned as a child, she told me, when her parents had both died of a summer fever in Connecticut. She and her brother Thrip, three years older, were taken into the home of a failed school master outside New Haven. "

"Thrip doesn't care for company," she said. "Maybe you'll meet him if you can pull yourself away from the South end. But that's where the money flows, isn't it? Out of the slave pen."

"Have you noticed a change at the *Mercury*?"

"What's it to me whose Navy you'd scuttle? My people sail for freedom."

I'd expected the voice of a housemaid; what I heard was the clarity of a schoolmarm.

"You favor the Sabbatarians now?"

"No more than you, the Quakers, I suppose. I could admire the Quakers, but the self-denial is such a pose, the thees and thous."

I knew what she meant - the distance between the piety of address and what they actually said to each other, as when I heard Job disputing with his brother in law, 'what the hell is thee talking about. Those ball-and-claw feet were carved by Pompey in my father's shop.' And 'go shit thyself' was the reply, 'anyway, thy family never had balls so large a sparrow couldn't clutch them.'

“They do make their own furniture.” I reminded her.

“Yes, with many a flourish and turning,” she said. "Do you know their founder’s journals?"

I didn’t.

“George Fox. There was a man you could admire, but not want for a friend. He'd have you in jail with him, marching into one church and another, calling out the hypocrites. I suppose no religion should know too much about its founder."

Her easy familiarity with these things diminished me by comparison.

"Who are the ones you admire,” I asked, “the ones who sail for freedom?”

She didn’t say, but went on about the other faiths in town - the Congregationalists, the Sabbatarians, the Baptists, and the Catholics. “They’re all worse,” she said, “clawing their way to heaven as if God was the enemy."

She was sizing me up, I think, waiting for me to declare an opinion of my own, but I was dumbstruck beside her confidence.

"I think I could turn and live with the Jews,” she said. “They don't pretend to false charity. They offer support outright, or back away without dithering." It was clear the appraisals came from her own observation. She didn’t quite trust me yet, though she could have whistled me to duty if it pleased her. I stood there in admiring confusion as she turned back toward town.

<>

It was only a week later that my confounding idol let me know with a little signal of her hand that she had softened further in my direction. She was touching my belt when she said, “I’m going to take that moony mask off your face.” She’d intercepted me at the top of the Parade as I took my noon lunch. We were looking over the harbor at the British ship St. John laying with its guns broadside to the town, a dozen Newport sailors aboard, newly pressed into royal service. The colony’s cannons on Goat Island had fired into the water around the royal ship two nights running.

“A menace to all of us,” I said.

She rolled her eyes to heaven, impatient with patriotic whining. In this she stood with a wide Newport sisterhood, which could imagine the futility of insurrection against an overwhelming British force of bombarding ships and invading marines. But she took my hand, and pulled me away, out of town on the North Road, past the powder stores and burying ground. How could I know she'd come fully prepared to lift my gloom, as she promised, with a vinegar-soaked sea sponge secreted inside her. The shifting pressure of her fingers on my hand made her intention clear. Again I was tongue-tied. She squeezed my hand harder, and teased my wandering faith.

"Will you sit next with the Jews?"

"It wouldn't embarrass me."

There was a little tic in my cheek, informed by a waking conscience. She touched my face, asking "Do you have a favorite place?"

"Place?"

Losing patience, she said, "Maybe I should leave Newport. Stow away on the Tristram. Sail to England, and tell them what's really happening here."

The Tristram. The brig lying at Long Wharf, already cleared for London with another bag of letters from Tory informers naming tariff-cheats, news intended to keep Parliament riled and insurgents at bay.

"You wouldn't leave," I said.

She crossed her lips with a finger, as if hushing a secret, and pushed against me, guiding me off the road.

All this happening so quickly, though maybe not quickly enough for her, as if she were getting something out of the way before the useful part of the day could begin, behaving with no more restraint than a night-walker on the waterfront. Close against a stone wall, sheltered on the lee by a sumac copse, Sally pulled me down as if we were out of sight of man *and* God.

She was standing directly over me, then bending forward to lift her skirts, sliding a mystery of white linen down her legs, slowing for a moment, watching me watching her as she stepped out of her lace-fringed hobble. Straddling my amazement, she raised all her curtain and scrim for my inspection of her underworld, falling forward, offering her breast to my face with lifting hands.

If enflamed by the sudden reward, I was wise enough to know this was as well a path to guilt and obligation. No gentle embellishment, no endearments, only her bald advance, and my urgent part in this delayed transport. I was too stricken in the moment to think this might be her way of breaking the nagging purity of my interest in her. Her busy hands dropping to my buckle and buttons reminded me of urgency in a privy.

"Couldn't you help?" she complained.

Soon she had us topsy-turvy, other way up, perhaps with me a bit more in charge, but only because she'd engineered it. Then, "Couldn't you say a bold word?" and "Couldn't you move a little faster?" So familiar with the mechanics. A little disappointing to be taught in the flesh that she knew a good deal more about these things than I'd hoped. The vinegar-soaked sponge? I could tell there was something there, but had no idea what it was until she told me.

She was speaking a little verse in my ear. Maybe of a piece with the sponge, that is, prepared ahead of time.

Inkfinger went a sporting
With Sally on the lea,
Stone wall for a head-board,
With Sally he made free.

We both knew it was the other way around. And wasn't I astonished as her backside kept accented rhythm with the words that pleased her so well that she repeated them several times? She showed a canny knowledge of when to pull free, before the brief bliss that turned me from a happy child of Eros into a shamed son of Onan, my stain on the ground met with some remorse. She gave my shoulder a little push. To lift the new gloom, or lift my weight off her? I wasn't sure which.

Odd, the very next day I was ready to suffer the same humiliation, in fact longing for license to repeat my part in the same embrace, no care the consequence, too vain to recognize that her shameless behavior, which could have had her in the stocks or banished, was performed with a particular obligation in mind. But how unkind that again Sally would have so little time for me, still not ready to enlist me in her scheming.

FOUR

THEY PROSPER AND YET THEY RUN

Not long after I'd become Job Townsend's tenant, the Quaker Meeting brought a Negro up from the Carolinas, Cuff Charleston, who knew five West African languages. He'd worked in the city that named him as healer to the slave market's problems of anger and confusion among arrivals from the Guinea coast. He was employed by a little consortium of merchants' factors as their translator.

As his English improved, Cuff had become too black-fancy for Charleston taste, and a coasting captain favored by the Townsend family in their southern trade had bought him with no great difficulty. He was brought up to Newport, and made a quick success as a freedman, explaining slaves to masters and masters to slaves. And teaching in the slave school run by the Quaker Meeting.

His first service in Newport was as translator and confidant to the slave boy off the Piety, whose name was at last known-Castle Quant. At least that's what he'd been called as a child playing in the sand under the walls of Cape Coast Castle. No sooner had Charleston disclosed his name than the boy ran. The *Mercury* carried the usual note and drawing of a black runaway with stick and satchel.

It was a particular embarrassment for a Quaker to report an escape, with all that might imply about the fugitive's treatment. But Job Townsend's two-hearted ownership of his slave was already known throughout the town, and without a published promise of reward, a capture and return from the hinterland might take a while.

Cuff Charleston came to the *Mercury* office, and agreed to tell me as much of Castle's history as he knew if I'd do what I could to make the slave's life easier when he was found. I explained that Job Townsend needed no encouragement in that direction. He'd only want to know what hardships Castle had suffered in his flight and capture.

Cuff explained the boy's name, "Castle," had no more significance than the stable name of a pacer, but was given to all the children who played on the beach at Cape Coast. His mates began calling him Quant when he arrived there, perhaps no more than three years old. Castle told Cuff he'd never answer to any name in this place, and why should he. The man he was chained to on the boat, the one beaten to death at market, had told Castle they were being taken across the water to be eaten. Why else would they be carried all that distance over the vomiting surface of the world? The same man, his protector on the ocean, he'd seen beaten to death and carried away in a cart. To the white man's meat market, for all he knew.

Castle's skin had never been scarred before the Piety voyage, but his back was figured with cross-hatched welts over the right shoulder, marks left by Captain Clarke's mate Crawford. Cuff believed the boy's rigid posture, and uncommon awareness for one so young meant he'd come from an inland tribe. He spoke a confusion of several languages, along with some Portuguese words taught by the mother-in-charge at Cape Coast, who kept the little ones until, one by one, they reached a slave age and would "go for a travel."

If we were lucky, Cuff said, this one had Angolan blood and was born to passivity, but Townsend should hope the boy was not of the Igbu, inclined to suicide before submission, nor of the Coromantees, whose instinct for rebellion would not be surrendered in captivity, no matter what face they showed their masters.

It wasn't rare for some Indian from the woods beyond the Providence Plantations to bring in Newport runaways for reward. It was a tall Pequod who led Castle back on the ferry held by a leather collar with rope attached, and leather hobbles. Townsend went under cover of night to claim his property at the jail, too late for the town to see him walking Castle back to the Point.

<>

Through the following winter Castle was kept at night in the locked counting room of a lumber warehouse shared by the Townsend family joiners. By day Job tried to train him again. The boy walked out in the mornings in new leather britches and a green woolen jacket.

Rewarded with new clothes for bad behavior, for running away? It couldn't have been on the ferries; there must have been some interfering tender-heart. A night-launch in a small sailboat was all Cuff could discover. Had the boy been given a running start into a wilderness of wolves and Indians?

<>

Soon Castle was walking by himself in the morning to Cuff's class for slave children behind the Quaker Meeting House. In the afternoons Cuff gave him informal extra lessons, starting with the alphabet and simple ciphering and an introduction to the Quakers' inner light. Cuff, only recently instructed in these matters himself, liked the notion of a bit of God inside him, and didn't mind passing the notion on to the boy.

Castle, who'd been told he was crossing the ocean to be eaten, was especially wary of me, shying away with baleful glances. “He remembers you from the ship,” Cuff said, “always showing him your teeth.”

“Smiling,” I said.

“Yes, like the big cat.”

Castle's voyage, as he explained it to Cuff, was “sick to vomit every day.” The metal throat was forced in his mouth, and a mush of beans poured in, until the beans ran out, and the horses on board had to share their oats.

“When I do nothing the man whips me until his arm is tired. Then the other arm. See this?” He was showing Cuff the cross-hatched welts. “When I knock over the man with the always teeth, there is no whip. The woman brings the water at night. Washes us with her blood rag.”

Hard to believe Sally could have snuck below the Piety's deck when backs were turned, gone under there in the worst kind of air. But why would the boy lie about that?

Hearing all this, Hall thought an account of the slave-child's passage from the Guinea coast worthy of a column. “Something of a positive slant. Have a go, Palmer.”

Excited to hear the starter's pistol at last, I began setting a column without a second thought. Hall had never seen anything like this, the way the type was jumping out of the case, into my fingers and onto the stick. Composing as I set, I was laying out the story as quickly as the words came to mind. No pause. Humming as I worked, my back to the editor, who was reading over my shoulder.

The Mate's signature tattoo was preparing the young black shoulder for a game of naughts and crosses. Twice a day the captain forced the slave's mouth with the speculum oris, the metal throat, at once an instrument of nutrition and torture, which kept the child from starving himself.

I was forcing Hall to see that he'd hired an editorial curiosity, something like a machine with a good memory and the gift of composition. Stiles had warned Hall: "Palmer has the Pentateuch by heart, but don't let that fool you." If you turn your back, this same man whose talent could make you rich, might just as quickly destroy you.

I could see the possibilities were churning - circulation, fame, and success, or notoriety, sedition, calumny and ruin - as, letter by letter, word by word, he removed every piece of type I'd set, and returned it to the case.

"All your experience," he said, "and still no sense of proportion."

<>

Job Townsend was out to prove something when he bought Castle. He explained his plan to give the boy his freedom by degrees, so that when he was ready for independence at eighteen perhaps he'd have an education, a religion, and a skill to make him the equal of other craftsman in Newport. A step in this transition came that Spring when Job gave Castle his own quarters, installing him in the attic above my rooms on Willow Street He asked that I keep an eye out for his slave's welfare, and that I encourage him in his studies.

I had no warning. One evening there was commotion in the stairwell, my door opened, and there was my landlord with Castle, who shrank back on the landing. Townsend had his arms filled with bedding and another suit of clothes. The boy had a block of wood in one hand and two chisels in the other, which he raised over his head behind Townsend's back, baring his teeth. Fool that I was, I smiled back at him.

Job gave me a little money for taking Castle to breakfast with me in the mornings. After breakfast I was to allow him to make his own way to the school cabin behind the Meeting House, where Cuff would take custody for the rest of the morning, then walk with him back to the Point to do his afternoon chores and be introduced to his craft.

"I want you to see something," Townsend said, after leaving Castle to settle above me. He led me off to his Cousin John's shop, where he showed me a block of poplar carved into an African's head. No mistake, the slant of the forehead and round cheeks made an adequate likeness of the man Castle had been chained to on the Piety. I wondered at the boy's visual memory and sculpting talent of his untrained hand.

Job showed me as well a piece of mahogany Castle had shaped into a shell whose crenellations were perfectly symmetrical, identical to the model beside it. The same design the Townsends were applying to the fronts of their elaborate desks and bureaus.

"I don't decorate much," Job said, "but John, or my brother-in-law, could train him up to a master's hand if he's a mind to it. He's half way there, and I doubt if he's thirteen yet."

In truth Castle's gift was astonishing, but I didn't sleep easily one floor below him and his chisels.

<>

I'd heard the traveling Quaker Woolman in the Meeting House, modest to a fault, mistrusting his own motivation in traveling the country to preach against his brothers, doubting the purity of his intention, then doubting the sincerity of that doubt, tortured in his modesty, and so on, such that his mouth might have been stopped completely by this circle of self-examination if, as he said, "the way had not opened." But it had opened, and he'd come north to condemn all who held slaves or traded for them.

"You tell me they prosper here, and yet they run," he told the Meeting. He was right about that.

Job Townsend, who listened to the same sermon, was a lukewarm likeness of Woolman, occasionally apologizing for speaking against the worldly pretension of his kin's cabinetry while taking ownership of a slave. If he couldn't stop slavery, he said, yet he might improve on it.

I shouldn't criticize the Quakers. They were my keepers in Newport. The ones who risked censure taking in a man with an out-of-town reputation for verbal brawling, and no particular church, allowing that I, too, might have an inner lamp worth lighting. These, my keepers, the sly Quakers as they were known, fairly or unfairly, the flourishing tribe of furniture makers on Easton's Point, the intermarried Townsend and Goddard families. No kin, at least none they cared to claim, with the printer Goddard in Providence.

As Job would admit, and Sally had reminded me, his kin's competitive excellence, the detail of their craft gave an awkward lie to the vaunted simplicity of their faith. "In this world but not of it?" At one time, he said, the vanity they disdained had been as hidden as the closely cut dovetailing behind their cabinets' plane facades. But straight-faced pine bureaus of his joiner forebears had become the shiny, smooth amber-hued mahogany secretaries decorated with finials of miniature pineapple, elegantly sawn curves in their block fronts carved with the matching shells, and filigreed brass escutcheons under their drawer-pulls. Only the merchant princes of the colony or the governor himself could afford them. Job forgot family modesty, showing me one of John's masterpieces, just finished, ready for Governor Hopkins in Providence.

<>

As requested, I took Castle to his breakfasts. Or he followed at what he thought was a safe distance behind me. He was sitting one morning with his face turned away nibbling at a piece of pork and some toast. I was speaking very slowly for his benefit. When he heard the word "school," he made straight for the door. By Cuff's account he never arrived at his class. If he'd escaped off-island again, no one was willing or able to say how.

The silhouette of a runaway appeared in the *Mercury* sixty-seven times while I worked there, but this was only the second time I'd locked the lead boy in place. I took care not to give him so much ink that his head became a featureless balloon, or so little that his staff shrank to a fishing pole.

<>

Job knew Castle was getting help from someone, and asked Hall if anyone in the print shop knew something about it. That would be me, so why didn't he just ask me. Cuff, whose allegiance must have been confused, told Job this much; that Castle had it from Kalika, his shackle-mate on the Piety, to remember that in the journey from where he was stolen to Cape Coast, he had been moving to the left of the sun's rising. But this partial clue to his origin, moving to the left of the sun's rising was, practically speaking, useless, a fix that had no reference point.

<>

Sally, known in Newport as the woman who'd offered "a good breast of milk" to several infants, one of them black, during her first year here, all thanks to her notices in the *Mercury*, was still with the Sabbatarian family Woodrow. Her name, too, was connected with Job's missing slave boy, whom she had succored on the Piety, if the boy could be believed, and who had certainly taken him to the inoculation island. Assuming Castle was off-island, Job was waiting for another Indian to claim a reward.

Cuff, the first suspect questioned by Constable Withers, admitted he knew that the slave was good odds to run, but impractical. The boy talked all the time about the other children on the beach at Cape Castle. Under a coming moon he hoped to leave Newport, and one morning arrive across the ocean to tell his friends what could happen to them.

<>

A messenger off the ferry brought the *Mercury* another "Citizen" letter from Providence, tying me again to Sally Warren:

From friends in Newport we learn that a wet-nurse who gives suckle to black infants or white without discrimination may have conspired with a journeyman printer there to arrange the escape of the slave boy Castle Quant from the home of Job Townsend. The woman is of no fixed address, but her part has been taken up by several notable women in that licentious town. The journeyman occupies rooms let by Mr. Townsend below the slave's attic quarters. The runaway has tribal scarring in a box pattern on his right shoulder, and will pretend innocence when spoken to.

This time Hall had better sense than to print such a jumble of fact and fiction. Job had told him how the boy feared me. The Warren woman was a different matter, though like me, without allegiance to any one meeting-house. If the rumors of her tender care under the Piety's deck seemed beyond belief, our readers knew she'd been the black boy's chaperone on the inoculation island. Not hard to imagine her holding his hand while the touch of poison was served up against the full disease, and cradling his following fever in her lap.

<>

Hall was away in Providence, looking for hogs in their streets and mud on Governor Hopkins' boots, anything to answer the *Gazette*'s attack on Newport and our sometime Governor Ward. John Robinson, the Crown's new collector found me alone in the *Mercury* office. Fresh from England, he came through the door, cocky in brass-studded trousers and a billowing blouse, more like a tavern dandy than the Royals' new head-man-with-portfolio. He had one crossed eye in a solemn face, clean-shaven.

Robinson took the pose of a long-lost friend and informer, a man the colonies could depend on for a fair report. "Aren't you the one who really runs this ship?"

I raised a hand of protest.

He sat on Hall's stool, took out his pipe, and scraped the bowl. Settling in for a chat, fingering in his pouch for more tobacco.

"Mr. Palmer, do you know what it cost to keep the Indians out of Rhode Island last year?

I didn't know, but the Indians were no bother here, unless it was in haggling over a reward for returning a slave.

"Two hundred and twenty thousand pound Sterling."

"More than obliging," I agreed.

"Exactly," Robinson said. Before he got around to Britain's generous reduction in the sugar tax from 6 to 3 pence a gallon, he asked me to concede that without the ten thousand British troops in the colonies, chief Pontiac might have pushed us off our privy seats into the sea.

"What have the colonies been paying for this protection?" he asked.

"From Rhode Island? A bit of graft to the customs officer, but how would I know how much. You'd have a better idea of what it would take to corrupt him."

He flinched. "You're a man of influence here."

"None at all."

He winked as if he were on to a bit of modesty, leaning forward, ready to share information with a local wise-man.

"Do you know your merchants' books as well as you know ours?"

"I know the size of their houses. Any more would be invasion of their privacy."

Though that very week I'd read four years of disgruntled correspondence from Aaron Lopez's factor in Bristol, the history of a credit nightmare for the middleman. For pennies, a carter brings me such paper, anything that might interest the *Mercury* that could be rescued from a merchant's dustbin.

Robinson was tamping more tobacco in his pipe, as if he and I had all the time in the world to sort things out between the Crown and the *Mercury*. Then he attacked.

"Your merchants' fingers are all sticky with French molasses," he said.

"And aren't the hands of Parliament tarnished with Barbados Sterling, before they're raised "aye" for another tax on us.

"You've got a lot of nerve, Palmer. You'd dare not print that."

He'd been hoping for a *Mercury* endorsement of England's new demand for its stamp on every piece of commercial paper changing hands in the colonies. Onerous and greedy I told him. "You'll have the mob on you."

"Are you threatening me? Do you know who I am?"

"Robinson, you said."

"The apprentice Jacob was making himself busy with a broom, pretending to pay no attention.

"You stay right here," Robinson said, as if he might be off to fetch a redcoat who'd arrest me, actually just stepping out to find a live coal for his pipe. When he came back, I'd left for the tavern down the Parade to tell evening ale mates about the new Collector's bent eyesight, how he'd be looking at molasses casks, but counting flour barrels.

Colonel Malbone, from his card game across the room, said I was making too much noise. What he meant was too much sport at royal expense. He called me over to ask if Hall was sending someone to Point Judith to watch his horse run against the Providence mare.

"Pay attention to the start," he said. "Don't let them cheat me again. Take this."

<>

Sally Warren appeared again in the Mercury office, her face hidden in a shawl. Finding me there with Jacob, she sat on Mr. Hall's stool, swiveled, and asked the wall "What's been heard of Mr. Job's runaway?"

I should have let the wall answer, but told her. "Nothing. As far as I know, nothing." I reached for her hand, but she slid off the stool, and was on her way. I called after her, but she was already through the door, slipping away in the fog.

<>

That season the British ship Maidstone intercepted a Bannister home-bound slave ship, seizing half the crew for Royal duty. While Hall wrote a column calling for colonial restraint I followed a mob of several hundred who had got an axle on two wagon wheels under the Maidstone's longboat, and were pulling it to the top of the Parade where they burned it to ashes. I gave Hall a full report. He was in a sweat, ready to condemn the mob, but afraid to name a single member of it.

He was fuming. "How can a man think? You write it, you saw the whole thing. No, I'll do it." His editorial might as well have been a plea to save the cherry trees and love our fellow men.

After that The *Mercury* and Goddard's *Gazette* began to feud in earnest, and the exchange turned venomous.

"Liars"
"Gutter dwellers," they called us.
"Scarce literate," we answered.
"Crown pimps."

The more shameful to the *Mercury* because we were the pimps. Hall had us bending to Mr. Robinson's will, giving space to the letters of Newport's most vocal loyalists, though too timid to print their own names under their argument, signing themselves with mystery initials, O.Z. The less zealous sort like Colonel Malbone, sat in the pews of Trinity, and held their noses while dock-side mobs pummeled a British impressment gang or took back confiscated cargo from the customs-house. In fact, Tory ships were as slippery as any. Our Anglicans, still favoring private persuasion of the collector, were the last ones to see that Mr. Robinson would not be bought.

Ever cautious, the same Trinity merchants loathed our "disreputable" contests for governor; Newport's favorite son Ward and Providence's Hopkins, battled for the office, year after year, with cash and rum. The Tories feared for their fortunes already in hand, and called for revocation of our charter so that a royal governor could be seated. Hall gave their argument space in the *Mercury*:

Rhode Island is a burlesque upon good order. The colonies have been wrong-founded. They ought to have been regal governments with every executive appointed by the King.
"O.Z."

The Gazette made merry fun of our collaboration with this O.Z. bunch, called them "nameless cowards and a dirty drinking, drabbing, contaminated knot of thieves, beggars and transports from the four winds, bringing libel on all good colonists, with the aid of the *Newport Mercury* and a wandering Jew reporter and his whore from New Haven.

Jew again?

Tory Anglicans were the plurality here; Hall couldn't ignore them. But when he set lines for O.Z., he couldn't look me in the eye. Instead, he found petty fault with me. He enjoyed having the apprentice there to witness his control – Jacob, who hopped around the shop at his command, always with a jealous eye on me. The boy had put his own twist on Collector Robinson's visit, telling Hall, "He thought Palmer was governor of the shop, and Palmer never denied it. You'd think he ran the town. And your paper."

"Gamble with your own life Palmer," Hall told me, "not mine. You want a night-gang off the Maidstone knocking on your midnight door?"

I should have taken more care with Jacob, though he was the kind to make more trouble for himself than for me. I learned more about him in the tavern than I ever heard from him; that his ambition was to rise above his father, an ordinary seaman, always in debt to one ship's master or another, thus always at sea, which had made Jacob a mother's boy, in fear of his father's beastly shore visits. Perfectly literate though, trained up by the generosity of his church. Always servile to Mr. Hall, and a more spiteful enemy of mine than I realized.

After Jacob's report, Hall was ready to have me walk through the town with the shop's boards draped over my shoulder. I'd sooner put my head and arms through the stocks than wear the *Mercury*'s plea on my back:

Kind friend when they old shirt is rent
To paper mill let it be sent.
Rags for the Newport Mercury. Please!

"Up Jew Street and down Thames," Hall said. "And everything between."

"Wear them yourself," I told him. He might have fired me on the spot. He stared a dagger, but changed his mind.

"Let the boy carry the sign," he said.

I supposed that was the end of it because moments after shaming me in front of Jacob, Hall rewarded me with an assignment to Point Judith on the mainland to cover the race between Malbone's black gelding Sambo and the Kingstown mare Pocahontas, making me a writer once more.

The Point Judith Ferry the next day was crowded with people going to the same event - merchants and their ladies, Africans loose on their word, a rail full of midshipmen on shore leave, handymen who worked the Newport wharves, even children with black tenders, sent off for the race day sport. I saw Bannister's valet Christopher with a leather purse pressed so hard to his side I pitied his anxiety, and feared for the target he made of himself and the notes he carried, all of it to be laid on Malbone's Newport gelding.

On the short voyage there was bad blood between a young stableman from Newport, and a Kingstown planter's agent battling over the favor of a Newport freed girl on board, ripe to be carried away they supposed, though she paid no mind to either of them. My notes said:

"You've got a mongrel lot of blood in your Newport corrals."

"Don't you Kingstown boys breed the mares with your own sausage, and your foals look to stagger on two legs."

As if we couldn't find one to lap your black at a slow trot."

"Keep away from the girl, you selfish rot. Wouldn't share a turd."

"No. Why improve the odor on you?"

Fists flew, and the older one was knocked back, his head slamming against the rail. He was still lying motionless when the boat reached the Point Judith pier, no doctor aboard, and the winner in a sweat for a witness to his self-defense.

I had it all in my notebook. At the race-ground several hundred were already there, men calling challenges, flashing bills and betting slips. Mingling, I followed behind a Baptist preacher who blessed strangers as he wandered along the track, a wide path cut through the woods.

An African boy with a bush of wild hair, and his Indian master came leading a bay horse right over the ground where I stood, pushing me aside. The African, in stable boy's leather, struck my eye as the very image of the missing Castle, but taller and with hair to shock the timid. He stared into my face with brazen defiance. The Indian smacked his arm, and looked to me for pardon. They led the horse away, and I followed their progress until they disappeared into the woods at the far end of the track.

By then I was certain it had been Castle Quant. But I gave no alarm, not as much for his sake as mine, against a return of that accusing eye. Of course he'd be taller now. I hadn't seen him in nearly two years. It was a full freedman's tangle of hair he'd grown. The hateful look he gave me, nothing different from his past scorn. I was as pleased to lose him in the crowd as he must have been to lose me.

I knew Hall wouldn't print all this, but kept scribbling away: "A bitch in heat lost her trailing suitors to a roiling battle for a bit of tossed fat. The snarling pack was scattered with a limber branch of sumac before chasing into the forest, on the main scent again." Walking back and forth in the crowd, I listened to the wagering, the Kingstown sorrel Pocahontas heavily favored over Colonel Malbone's Sambo. At race time a web of promissory notes ran the length of the track, a string of commitments whose tidy discharge might obey no rule but fist and pistol.

Spirits were still high where no one had lost a farthing. The crowd began to swell with the arrival of chaises and flys of the Kingstown planters and their women. Touts were still making book on a race that was only minutes from starting. The Baptist preacher was offering the sanction of his collar to the sporting crowd in return for a tipple of rum here and there; betting on his own account as well, he accepted the one-pound Sterling wager I placed for Colonel Malbone.

The starter from Kingstown, pistol in hand, called the horses to the line, the people surged forward, and the two mounted jockeys emerged from their lairs in the woods. The black jockey on Malbone's Sambo warned people back with his crop as his mount advanced calmly through the throng. Not so the sorrel Pocahontas, coming forward at a nervous, prancing oblique. As she went past I saw her hind quarters already in a lather. A man beside me called her a loon. "She'd rear up at the sound of her own snort." Before either horse had time to gain advantage the starter fired them off to an even start, and I moved back, onto a rise where the whole track would be visible.

The horses reached the quarter post with the Kingstown mare a length in front. Something, perhaps a thrown stick, flew out in front of her. She shied and stumbled, but recovered, and half-way home she'd put another length between her and Sambo. By then some were yelling false start, and foul, and interference.

Pushed to a longer stride, Sambo made up ground. I judged him even with the mare at the three-quarter post when more debris flew out in front of them. Something hit Sambo's foot, but it was Pocahontas who lurched sideways. She careened off the track, scattering the crowd, before her jockey could steer her back between the course poles.

At the finish, with Malbone's Sambo in front, it took only a moment for a part of the crowd to vanish. Some were taking to the lane toward town or disappearing into the woods. I looked for the sporting preacher who'd taken my bet; nowhere to be found. Men holding wagered money were surrounded by gun-waving disputants. There was rifle fire all the way back to the ferry; no deaths reported.

FIVE

THE TRAVELING QUAKER

The morning I returned from Point Judith Ezra Stiles was in the *Mercury* office reminding Hall, “Your Palmer’s not just a danger to himself, he’s trouble for you too, a scribbling fraud wherever he’s been. He’s an embarrassment to every church he sits in. And there’s something else...”

My appearance in the doorway cut the conversation short.

“Yes? Go on,” I said.

“I was just leaving. But tell us about Point Judith, Cotton. The Colonel's horse ran well?" he asked, with no real interest in my answer.

"Neither horse ran well," I said. "But you already knew that. Why would you ask, Ezra? You heard the news last night. Or you're the only man in Newport who didn't."

"But Sam says you'll write about it. Colonel Malbone scored a pretty purse?”

“You’d have to ask him about that.”

Stiles flinched. “We heard Job’s runaway was at the race ground. You’d know his face better than most.”

“Why? Is your African getting restless?”

The Reverend had put a hogshead of rum on a ship eight years earlier, trading for a ten-year-old boy brought back from the Guinea coast. His experiment in slave education and religious training had gone better than Townsend's, and Stiles’ wife, whom he'd gotten with six children in seven years of marriage, had someone to help with chores, the back-cabin-dwelling boy they called Newport.

"No one raised a cry?" Hall asked me, and Stiles said, “William Ellery from my congregation saw you there."

"Ellery, at the race-track? Not one of your visible saints, then?"

"I suppose you couldn't be certain whether you'd seen him, but never mind that." He had another question to be asked in front of Hall. "This man who stands outside the tavern door carrying sacrilege. I think you give him money for his rum? Do you provide the blasphemy as well?

"Enough," Hall said, turning to me, "Where's your story?"

"Done," I said. It was in my smallest hand on the back of a *Gazette* broadside picked off the deck of the Point Judith ferry, written on the short passage home. Maybe a thousand words; five-hundred more than he had room for, seven hundred more than he wanted, and eight-hundred more than he used, after his revision under his own headlines:

Runaway Boy Seen At Race Ground
Constable Investigating New Escapes.

He finished editing the piece before asking me again. "Was the boy there?

"I believe he was," I said. "He was taller with a black haystack of hair."

"I'm not running an anti-slavery sheet, he told me," in a mood to be rid of me again, but he couldn't bring himself to fire me. Not because his circulation was up another hundred; he'd never admit I had a hand in that, but because I still did the heavy work of producing the paper each week.

He was nettled that Newport's most troublesome beggar, the pathetic Walter Shifflett with his weekly message carried on a pole in the street, had become a curiosity beyond Rhode Island, and with no help from the *Mercury*. His satire and sacrilege had been reported in papers as far as New York. Not in affirmation but to embarrass the town; so widespread was the jealousy of Newport's wealth.

Shifflett was in more danger than the sting of spittle sent his way from men entering the tavern. I made a regular Friday afternoon walk to Pitts Head not to miss his latest bulletin, and on occasion gave him a few coppers. His signs skirted the edge of tolerance, but like bawdy stories they were scorned more on the lip than in the conscience. I asked him if he knew what his signs said.

"Wouldn't you have a penny?" was as much as he could manage.

<>

Unable to get me fired at the *Mercury*, Ezra Stiles turned his criticism of me on my landlord. When Job asked me one Sunday to sit with him in his Meeting House I was ready for trouble. As we walked up the hill he was introducing me to his wider family, and surprised to find me already on easy terms with his cousin Prescience, a widow and versifier who usually had a smile and bit of news when she saw me on the Point. She was lively and a humorous gossip on the tics and jealousies, of the inter-married Townsend and Goddard clans. A forward hussy by their standards, and just as troubling, a would-be poetess.

"Cotton," Job said, "do you sleep well on Willow Street? Have you found your way to comfort in Newport? So's you'd know whose kin you're talking to and not get yourself caught in a tangle?" He meant the over-confidence one could feel in a place where others had lived all their lives. Especially a too-wise journeyman printer and provocateur like me.

It wasn't just the family lines branching in all directions, but the business ties, or ruptures, resented but no longer mentioned; an awkward flirtation, or maybe the unforgotten lust of an otherwise visible saint for his slave; or a minister's appointment that split a congregation along a line so deep that the next generation still practiced its prejudice; a riddle in full that a relative newcomer couldn't hope to solve. Which is why he felt free to say,

"Cotton, you may hear all the rumor in the tavern, and gab with the Colonel over his rum, but you've got a long mile to run before you catch the actual Newport scent."

What could I do but agree and ask for his help in the hunt?

"From where I sleep in your rooms, I smell the salt, I smell the mahogany, I smell the whiskey, I smell the tar, God knows I smell the tannery, and I hear the cannon at the harbor point. Who could I trust for a better scent of here than yourself?"

"Yes," he said, "a challenge is well met by flattery. But, Cotton, remember the things you aren't close enough to smell. Things that may reek. But don't let that newspaper of yours guess at a man's motives. When Castle comes back, just state the case you know, not your opinions about how he left or returned."

"They would be Mr. Hall's opinions, not mine."

Job led me into the Meeting House, and I sat beside him for the best part of an hour in complete silence, nudging him when his eyelids fell and his head tended toward my shoulder. I was startled by someone behind me.

"Ride? Let him ride home! He has no business here!"

All heads turned to the querulous voice. I shrank down, wondering if he meant me.

"Riding Quaker?" he said, "or riding fool? We have the orders of our faith. They'll be obeyed in good time. Not when Mr. Woolman declares his conscience must be ours. Will he take my Susan off the street if I release her? I think not. I know he will not."

As he sat down, an elder on the facing bench rose and waved an admonishing finger over the meeting. "Arguments made in heat," he said, "lack the force of moderate speech. And they're seldom informed by the inner light; more often by a sore conscience." He sat, and the man beside him, maybe too lame to rise, in a voice yet more gentle, inquired, "If an argument be whispered, is it then to be more admired than one spoken with a warm conviction?"

A whisper moved across the room, then silence. The commotion was put down. All was well again. The elders turned to each other; the whole company reached to shake hands forward, behind and beside them. There was a man in back of me who looked away when I offered my hand.

On the walk back down the hill to the Point, Prescience gave her cousin a defiant eye. She took my arm, and held me back behind the rest of Job's family, his wife Rebecca and the quiver full of children she'd given him – thirteen all together, eleven of them in that Sunday's church party - including nineteen year old Job Jr., who was about to inherit his father's shop and business, and whose favor I'd need to continue in my rented rooms. The blood of embarrassment rushed to my face, but Prescience held fast, and began to whisper, as if we shared a romantic secret. No good trying to pull free, she wouldn't let go. Her disapproving clan went walking past us. There was more I should know, she said.

A decade earlier, she told me, Job had taken on young John Goddard as apprentice, and this John had soon put Job Jr. far behind him in woodcraft. He'd married one of Job Jr.'s sisters, and with the rest of his family, had taken to calling the Junior, "Bed Post Job" because he spent most of a day turning bed posts and table legs on the shop lathe, going into a kind of trance at the treadle, with chisel in hand and a rooster tail of chips flying at his apron.

And why was this my business? You should know it isn't fair, she said. Not just one, but two of his sisters married Goddards, and the lot of them tease the life out of young Job. He's a passable hand at the work, but his father and brother-in-law are always over his shoulder, looking for daylight between his joints, and no wonder he'd rather spend the day turning wood than sawing it, ignoring the talk behind his back.

I thought what Prescience really wanted was my confidence and a path through me into the columns of the *Mercury* for her verse. But she turned on me and asked, "Aren't you ashamed?" The *Mercury*, she said, was being left behind by the scribbled lines of the derelict Shifflett standing all day outside the tavern, carrying more wit over his head than the newspaper printed in a month.

IF ADAM HADN'T SINNED
THERE'D BE NO SMALLPOX
NOR THE ITCH, NOR THEOLOGY
NOR THE FAITH WHICH SAVES US

"When Castle comes back," Townsend had said. He seemed sure of it. He said I'd soon be hearing footsteps in the room above me again, but not to worry. This time there'd be no need to keep any sort of guard or watch on the boy from Cape Castle. He'd go to school on his own, and walk to the Point afterward for his training in woodwork. He could decide himself if he'd build houses, ships or furniture.

By then, even his own family were taking Job for the Quaker Quixote.

"You had nothing to do with his escape."

Job's assertion was actually more like a question. If he knew it, and I knew it, what need to reassure me?

One morning in January of 1765 Job took to his bed, "a little fatigued." The week before, he'd resigned the offices of town treasurer and surveyor of lumber. He suspected his heart's new syncopation was the rhythm of his coda under God's baton. On the eighteenth of that month he died and Hall wrote in the *Mercury*,

"Aged sixty-six, Mr. Job Townsend, remarkable for Honesty and Integrity. A Revered leader in his community. His Death deemed a public loss."

His renown the more daunting for the surviving junior, my new landlord, "bed post Job," who assured me on several occasions my lodging was safe into the future. If it were so, why the need to repeat it so frequently?

Young as he was, Job Jr. was as driven to do the right thing as his father had been, but far less confident. If his face was a florid likeness of his father's, his stride was shorter. He was more apt to stumble over something in the shop. Still a day dreamer at the lathe, he'd mumble 'Look where you're going. See where you've been.' Considering the path of the chisel or the course of his life? At the funeral I observed his worried trance. He hadn't the nerve to tell his clan that if his tenant Palmer walked out the North Road on a Sunday with the lady from New Haven it was none of his business, or theirs

And Sally's candle was briefly lit for me again. It was on a stroll out the North Road that she led me into the field once more, behind the familiar stone wall where we could lie on orchard grass and ivy. I raised my hand against it, and a new estimation of me took hold of her. She turned that curious eye on me, took my arm and we turned back to town, talking openly at last.

"Do you want to be ignorant all your life?" she asked me.

I wasn't so much insulted as eager to hear where improvements could be made that might please her. For all my reporter's curiosity, she said, I took precious little interest in the chronic miseries of the world. "And your interest in me is superficial. You stare at my face and figure." It was true, whoever she was, still mostly rumor to me, though I knew she thought a good deal about religion and her soul regardless of her behavior.

I stopped, palms up, waiting for her story.

Too much of it would make you uneasy, she said. Better I should know a little of her childhood and a fraudulent miser's scheme. There was no self-pity here, rather the implication that I might be part of a complacent world that favored the decorum of silence in the face of shameful injustice.

She had been eleven and her brother Thrip fourteen living in New London when both their parents were taken by the trembling fever in the same season. The town offering no aid, their care was taken over by a Reverend Jameson, an abusive school master who had turned his failed academy into an asylum for orphans and the occasional turned out Negro. Jameson took charity for his good-works from several churches, then turned a profit, hiring out his orphans and aging Negroes for work on neighboring farms.

He made Thrip and Sally study their letters by candlelight with Bible as text. A poor recitation was an affront to Jameson, God, and his hazel switch. After a whipping, the brother and sister were often put out of the house to sit on the stoop at night where wild dogs bayed in the surrounding woods. "God asks less of you than your iniquity owes Him," he'd say.

While the two were in Jameson's care, indigent Negroes were directed to his home by Philadelphia Quakers, who trusted his pledge of a caring hand for the duration. Julian, an older black, almost blind, whose freedom had been bought by the Philadelphia Meeting became a shy ally of the siblings in the Jameson home. He was alert to the repeated episodes of punishment in the house.

If Sally was put outside, Julian might sneak to unlock the door for her before slipping away to his bunk. If her brother was denied supper Julian would leave his own crust at Thrip's door. These small acts of charity, easily detected by Jameson, were added to his ledger of the Negro's deceit. Julian had carved a piece of wood and hung it on a string around Sally's neck. An angel for a child of the woods, he said. It looked more like a squirrel with wings, a reminder of his weak eyesight and devotion; she meant never to remove it.

One day Julian was gone. Thrip was away at the time, rented out in a neighboring hayfield. Sally begged to know more about their black friend's disappearance, and for her impertinence, was put outside the house again. When Thrip came home, they made plans for an escape, first writing a note addressed to the Philadelphia Quaker Meeting.

Walter Jameson is not the kind heart you think. Do not send more freed men to Walter Jameson. When the Negroes are no more use to him he burns their free papers. He takes money for them, and they are put with others in a carriage for Carolina.

They had nothing to offer the postal rider, Sally said. They got the letter into his hand, but he dismounted and took it directly back into the house to Jameson.

<>

In the alehouse that season, before the geese flew again, I heard cocky talk about how little our colony risked in sneering at the Crown with the armada that might damage us an ocean away. How could the several British ships in the harbor remain much longer before they became our humbled prizes? But by late summer it was hard to sleep at night, even in my rooms on the Point, with so much turmoil on the wharves. The British Schooner St. John began chasing and boarding incoming ships. Cargoes of sugar were impounded and the St. John sent press gangs ashore to seize likely men on the wharves for royal duty.

One night there were footsteps on my stairs, my door was thrown open. I had no chance to light a candle before a bag was thrown over my head. I was shoved to the floor. My hands were tied behind my back, and I was led out of the house in my nightshirt.

“Bootless, pushed to the wharf..."already composing the story of my theft from Rhode Island but who'd know if I was to be turned that night into a Royal marine with the only escape, a leap into the sea.

Prodded along to the end of a pier, I could hear a wharf-mob screaming. When the sack was pulled from my head I saw the man pushing me was no royal marine, but a Newport sea dog in sailor’s rags, telling me. “Move your sorry ass, Inkfinger.

The mob was pouring foul language on the Customs House, which sat dumb as its doors and windows, and was soon smashed for its mute insolence. The torch-waving crowd was led by the Stiles congregant William Vernon, a slaver, recently stung by Collector Robinson’s seizure of molasses from his ship’s late three-corner reach. His casks were being rolled out of the customs house onto the wharf where a barge waited to float them back to his own warehouse.

Two men held me over the water as Vernon came up behind me. “Take him up the hill,” he said. My hands still tied, I was pulled up the Parade where a gibbet and noose were waiting. The rope was rubbed against my neck. Vernon laughed as he untied my hands. I was only there to watch the hanging in effigy of Collector Robinson, a straw dummy doused with Guinea proof rum and set aflame.

"No more O.Z., eh?"

With the mob behind him, Vernon played the bully with me. He wouldn't go directly to Hall with a complaint about the *Mercury*. People still liked Sam Hall and wanted his favor. Though I'd been several years with him, I was being treated as the author of the *Mercury*'s errors; so men like Vernon wouldn't have to confront the editor himself.

<>

Later that season I was in the tavern when hammering was heard at the top of the Parade. "Stay away from it," Colonel Malbone warned me. "Your name's on the Royal list too," all the encouragement I needed to explore the commotion. Another gibbet was being knocked together up the street, this one strong enough for more than a straw-filled dummy. From a distance I could hear men and women jeering the carpenters who were not Newport men, but navy boys off the St. John.

"Night rats!"

"It won't be straw hanging from this one," came the royal reply.

"And who'll be judge? One of you scurvy grog sots? Pig-thieving bastards!"

"Won't matter, will it, when your Johnny stiffs and you're dancing the blue-foot."

If this was just a threatening stunt, it was working on several women who were pulling their husbands away. The navy finished their work, and walked their lamp-lit shadows down the Parade and out Long Wharf to the St. John's longboat, humming the King's health all the way, but in the mournful way of a dirge for America.

I stayed to see the gallows chopped down and turned into a bonfire. This brought drunken companies of men out of the taverns, and as the flames rose, more residents of the hillside. A cheer rose as the pole and cross-tree fell into the flames. I stayed until these were only pulsing embers, and wished I'd left sooner when Prescience Townsend tugged on my sleeve, and asked if I had looked at her verse yet. Her poetry was still sitting unpublished in a notebook that had moved from Hall's desk to mine, and back to his, without comment.

"We've been busy," I said.

"Look there," she said, pointing to a couple standing beside the dying fire. Cuff Charleston in conversation with Sally Warren, so animated they might have been arguing, but Sally was smiling, pushing at the Negro's shoulder. She saw me watching and, true to habit, turned away. A few minutes later they were walking up the hill, with him a respectable distance behind her. I assumed he was walking her back to Clarke Street, where the never-settled Sally had recently been taken up by the widow Chambers as cook and keeper in another slave-free household. Under Mrs. Chambers' protection she'd been sitting in First Congregational.

"Don't worry," Prescience said, reading my mind. "It's not Cuff she's on about. It's Townsend's missing boy. He's coming back. Listen. If you won't put my poems in your paper, I'd like them back

<>

The Quaker school, with the Townsend family's approval, sent Cuff Charleston onto the mainland to follow backward along a trail of messengers, the chain of people who had passed the story of the slave boy's abuse by Indians in western Connecticut to young Job in Newport. Two weeks later Cuff walked in with his prize.

Again, Castle was put in the room above me, ready to study with the other slave pupils under Cuff's instruction. He was treated gently again, this time in Job Jr.'s shop. I supposed he'd given up the vain hope of finding his way back to Cape Castle, tired of being whipped this way and that by the band of horse-trading Pequods who held him, maybe convinced by Cuff that, after all, his best prospects were right here.

<>

When Colonel Malbone died the *Mercury* asked

WAS HE THE RICHEST MAN IN NEWPORT?

The obituary noted his seventeen slaves, a remarkable number for a Newport household, even for a mansion like Malbone's, an unmanageable number for the surviving son. He couldn't keep order in the house, or keep his men from running. “Too soft,” the same criticism thrown Job Townsend's way. “Soft as his father, the way he treats his boy Castle, spoiling every African on the island.”

I was there at the slave market on Spring Street, watching a scramble sale, reporting for the *Mercury*. Again, not the usual thing at all, this kind of sale in Newport. The Guinea cargo off the Charlotte Brown brought buyers shoving through the cordon at the sound of a horn, swarming over seventy Africans. It happened so quickly with such a moil of bodies, and thwarted men cursing, there was no way to record every detail. A price per slave was set, the horn was blown, and the free-for-all began.

Each buyer with a rope in hand. Some grabbed single slaves and pulled them out of the competition, pushing off any unwanted body that might be clinging. I saw one man throw his rope over four men, cinch his quarry and lead the eight-footed package out of play. Another used a serial wrist knot, gathering three women and a man without a struggle... But a near riot began when a slave, yanked backward by the neck, threw an elbow into the face of a buyer, who doubled over as blood poured from his nose. A slave was caned to his knees for the offense, but not the one responsible.

I missed much of the proceeding, but saw a buyer making half-hitches around each neck of choice, until contented with seven. Options dwindled, there were fingering inspections. A reduced price was called for the few left. In the end one boy with a badly swollen knee, sat on the ground, one of his eyes draining a milky fluid. No one touched him. He was pulled off to the slave pen at the south end of Thames, Cuff Charleston following, translating his misery.

I gave Hall my report. "You're exaggerating, he said, then used the account of Reverend Hopkins of First Congregational, hardly different from my own.

A farmer wouldn't treat his stock that way, not even on the way to slaughter. Such a miserable circus belongs in Surinam or Jamaica. This shaming disgrace should never happen again in Newport.

One of my scouting carters brought me a letter from the Colonel's son John Malbone to a creditor on our South End, found in his trash collection.

I paid six pence for it, though I knew Hall wouldn't print anything that suggested Newport Africans might one day be ungovernable:

Friend,

I've not been master of a dollar since I saw you. We suffer repeated theft by my father's Negroes Joseph, Jack, James and Master Primus. These boys have broken open the Mills near the farm three times, stolen forty odd bushels of corn and meal; broken into Downers shop where they took eleven pair of shoes (three recovered). Our locked cellar was burgled; they say they only stole one long bottle of rum. This confession induced by stripes in the prison yard. They disposed of the goods through Naphs the Crimp. Primus confessed the whole thing.

Each night there was a tramping on the floor above me as if Castle were contemplating something deep and dire, back and forth with an about-face shuffle at each end of the attic room. When we passed, or followed one another down our narrow stairway I always offered greeting.

"Good morning," or "Good night," and was answered only with a wide show of teeth and a softly spoken, "Newphart Rigeing" as if Cuff had taught him nothing since the day of his arrival, and which I understood connected me once and forever with his passage here. I knew in fact that he was learning English. I'd heard him tell Townsend:

"Yes, my room I don't like. The man below makes rattle breath at night."

I returned to Willow Street one evening after a circle through the town, hoping to inspect Castle's room, to see for myself if those chisels were still kept at his bedside. Knocking with no response, I entered. He was there, working by candle-light, carving another figure, the torso of a woman, awaiting legs. He turned to me,

"I did not speak yes."

The tramp, tramp, tramp in the attic above me continued for a few days, until Castle was gone again, disappearing in the night. Job Jr. put no notice in the paper; he was offering no reward. As if the news could be kept from the town. I heard our Quakers scorned as dangerous fools who were letting their guilt overcome common sense

The scolding Quaker Woolman came back to salt the conscience of the Newport Meeting again: "Slaves are the moral superiors of their masters. They know it and keep it to themselves. You know it, too, as you wait for your retribution. Where is the self-respect when the slave's hand outperforms your own?"

I thought of the deft-fingered Custis in Thompson's Costumes, the whole trade resting on his skill as he cut, pieced and sewed while Thompson, whose fingers never touched a needle, sat in his loft with the accounts.

Prescience, who'd heard it from a cousin, told me Job knew where Castle had gone, but wouldn't force him back, satisfied that the boy would prosper or fail in the way of his own choosing. "You're quite content these days, aren't you?" she said, as if she knew my mind, my contemplation of another meeting with Sally behind the stone wall on the North Road.

SIX

HIS BOATS DON'T HAVE A NAME

Of all the Newport holy houses I sat in the most unnerving was the Synagogue. There was raillery among the men going in but once inside I saw brows lowered into stoic resignation to an unnamed but inescapable fate. I understood not a word of Hebrew. It was the early summer of 1767. Two more Newport ships had been seized by Navy schooners, and there was talk in the taverns against the Jew Lopez who would not sacrifice his candle trade to the non-importation agreement. Though neither would some who sat in Trinity, Tory merchants in the rum-for-slave business.

I'd walked into the synagogue a week earlier. "I wouldn't know when to move my lips," I told the Chazan, "but may I attend your next Sabbath meeting?"

"You want to write about us?" He showed me around the building, and noticed my eyes were not following his. They were stuck on the dais we circled.

"Oh, the bimah," he said. "You want to know if it's true about a tunnel under there. Wouldn't I be stupid to tell you? If you look at the architect's plans, it isn't there." Seeing me relax my suspicion, he explained the bitter history of centuries, and perhaps a thousand synagogues across Europe, and all the way to Jerusalem. "Wait for the Sabbath," was the rule. "When the Jews are inside, lock the doors, and throw the torch. Are we safe in Newport? I think so. Today."

He was staring at the bimah's floor.

A few days later, with a black skull-cap balanced on my head, I heard him come briefly out of his Hebrew chant into English for my benefit. Newport, he said, was the fresh continent's heart, moral and immoral, a commercial engine, courageous, greedy, but suffering all persuasions, sinning and repenting in all directions, the more to prosper.

<>

Curious about complaints in Ezra Stiles' church, the next Sunday I sat again among the blacks in the balcony of Second Congregational and heard him preach to a sullen flock about rendering in turn to God and to Caesar. I watched William Vernon stand ramrod straight, turn to kick open his pew-box door, and walk out of the church.

"You can't walk away from the word." Stiles said.

Another stood and followed Vernon. Then two more.

"If we're afflicted," Stiles called out to their retreating backs, "he will deliver us. In the meantime it's our duty to obey. Anyway, what kind of coward comes with blackened face in the night to chop down your house?"

Yes, I'd watched it. Four men with broadaxes at the corners of Collector Robinson's house brought the building to its knees in a few minutes. Robinson, under arrest, called out to me, "I see you, Inkfinger" as the Sheriff marched him down to the waterfront. He was put on the Tiverton ferry, and told, "Don't come back." But he did come back a few days later, an angry man, under protection of a British squad off the St. John, and took up residence in the Customs House on Conanicut.

After Stiles' service I avoided the line waiting to shake his hand. People were avoiding me too, heads down or turned to the side. A caution, I was on the Red Beard's Newport list for hanging. Collector Robinson, as well, wanted me sent to England for trial. Meanwhile those with freedom on their minds would have me in the stocks on the Parade for the *Mercury*'s royal slant. If that wasn't enough to frighten me, I had it from Sally that a doctor with an interest in her had suggested my permanent removal, and that one of his patients might oblige him in this, in return for a discreet treatment of his "unmentionable" disease.

I should have had a plan ready for escape from Newport, though I was a small marker in the game being played with England all along the Atlantic coast. Dare and double dare. I burn your brig to the water-line, and scuttle your schooner; you turn your swivel guns on my warehouse, splinter my docks, and steal my pigs and chickens for your ship's larder. I throw your thieving sailors in the Marlborough Street jail, you tell your King and Parliament what I've done; I run your Collector out of town and throw your crimps in jail. Then back to trade as usual with sufficient coin to the Customs House to keep your armada at home.

<>

Those who thought Hall cared that much about tea mixed with harbor water didn't know much about newspapering. Yes, he covered news of the saltwater tea party in Boston, but his mind was on the cost of paper, and when word came in 1766 that the Stamp Act was repealed, it was tax-free paper that wore the headline of British concession. Cannons were fired from the Point, the balls splashing around the Collector's schooners like rocks thrown back at a bully. The town's windows were lit with spermaceti, and the *Mercury* went on printing without portion to the King for paper.

Even Tory homes showed all-night flame, the churches too, though not Trinity's menacing steeple. Walking out at night under its domineering shadow, I could already hear retribution ringing from the pulpit: You ill-tempered, ungrateful pups. You've never seen such a navy as will soon be lying broadside to this impudent shore, never seen so much tramping red under arms as those ships carry.

<>

One of Prescience Townsend's strange verses had stuck in my mind. Walking away from town I recited as I stepped along:

While ocean is a daunting place for ships,
Where but water were they made to sail?
Though land's ill-made for wagons where it ruts
Where but earthen path would carriage roll?
Though Noah landed on a mountain top,
What captain through what storm,
Has nerve enough and God's authority
To trade off Guinea in the sun,
And carry such a cargo home to we?

One step, one syllable, I made my way along the shore north of the Point over land I hadn't walked before. No wharves here, but occasional paths back through the sea-grass covered here and there with drying nets draped in front of fishermen's shacks. I was sorry I'd quibbled with her, suggesting: 'Home to thee,' her own clan's diction.

Prescience repaid my help with pity for my soft head.

"If I meant thee, I'd have written 'thee'."

"But 'we' is incorrect," I insisted.

"Yes," she said. "You're beginning to understand."

I could admit she'd made her point - that colonists had been stealing African souls for years, and not least of the thieves were her nervous Quaker tribe.

If the *Mercury* wanted to run such anti-slavery verse, it no longer had to worry about criticism from our nemesis Goddard. He couldn't pry the colony's printing work away from Hall. His *Gazette* had gone under the waves. But when I proposed accepting one or two of the Quaker widow's poems Hall stiffened. "You favor her now, Palmer? Your New Haven hussy wouldn't hold still for you?"

I went walking maybe two miles beyond the Point to a little cove where the water lapped against a rough pier. A small craft was moored alongside with a single mast, the narrowest beamed sailboat I'd ever seen. On its raked stern I read TALL SALLY. Above the shore two buildings were tucked into the woods, a modest shore-house and long barn whose double doors opened onto wooden tracks leading down to the water.

From inside the barn the clip of an axe kept pace with the back-and-forth of a saw. I was about to look inside when all noise stopped, save the squawking gulls over the water. A round iron rod rose slowly against the edge of the doorway, gradually shrinking to a coin-size circle topped by a bead drawn directly at my forehead. Behind the bead, trigger and stock of the fowling piece, a gray eye squinted in an angry red face. The gun remained raised and used as a pointer guiding me to the side of the building. The doors were pulled closed by someone inside.

"Just exploring," I said. "I'll turn away and be no trouble."

"The *Mercury* man? Expert on this and that? And you'd have to do with my sister."

Before I could say anything he told me to shut up, and leave his place unmentioned in my newspaper. It was Sally's brother Thrip, large, powerful, and caught off guard by my intrusion. He seemed unsure how to deal with me.

"Where were you going?" he asked.

"I've come far enough."

He set down his gun, and came down the bank.

"You couldn't write an honest letter with boatful of type, could you?" he asked.

I hesitated for a moment. In Newport since 1762, and tired of my sticky reputation, I told him no one trusts a writer unless his story's seventeen hundred years old. "Anyway, I haven't published a letter in that paper since I've been here."

"No? Then who's 'A Citizen'? Who's 'A Friend'? Who is 'A Farmer'? Who is the 'Repentant Lady'? Like no lady I ever spoke to," with you hiding behind her skirts."

I began to wander, garrulous, all over Newport's charms, omitting the black-skinned heart and muscle at the root of trade. He went for his gun again.

"Your tongue's run out of your head," he said. "What would you know about boats anyway?"

"Very little."

"Nothing?"

"Nothing."

Looking back as I walked away, I saw two men coming out of the barn watching my retreat. There was still the noise coming from inside. I had no chance to see who swung the axe.

In Pitts Head that night, I stood alone until the late Malbone's son John rescued me from melancholy, calling me to his table by the fireplace. The usual company of his dependent topers were tempting a mouse onto the hearth with bread crumbs. A cat crouched behind the fender. Malbone himself put an end to the blood sport with a well-aimed spoon, sending Stripey back through a crack in the mortar.

"You met Thrip Warren," he said, "and look, you're still with us. Don't worry; he won't shoot you. He just doesn't want anyone stealing his lines before his boats are in the water."

To keep Malbone going, I went for two rums, and he obliged me with the whole shape and cunning of Warren's boat-craft and reputation. Far faster than I could take it all in.

Oak, white not red, for frame and planking, white pine for mast, locust for trunnels; iron bolts for keel to rib, and keelson to keel; oakum in every seam and around every peg. All covered with fir, tar and hair if you're sailing to warm water. Warren's boats don't need it; coasters and river runners. Blocks, cordage, suits of sails, all available in town. His credit is good as Bannister's. Builds to his own satisfaction. The next one's always his last, and always faster than the one before. Someone has to have it. A couple of weeks after a launch, and there's another keel laid.

“He has help?”

“Two sawyers. You didn’t see them? Neither one talks so you could understand. Tongues cut out by Indians on the Chesapeake for interfering with one of their women. Sunrise to sunset, they’re in the pit, one up, one down. And he's got young Job’s African as well. But you’d know all about that. You and his sister, eh?”

"But what are they, what do you call his boats."

"They don't have any name but fast and dangerous. The design came up from Baltimore-small clippers. Two raked masts. And hardly stiff enough not to tumble in a breeze, far too much sail in a squall. They're made to carry secrets, when deviltry and speed run together. For people who don't want to get broadside, just want to get away. Phantom coasting and river running. Spies, messages, rum,” he was winking as if we shared a secret.

“Or a slave’s ferry out of chains?"

<>

After that, how could I stay away? I walked out again to Thrip Warren's retreat and found the shop door locked, and no one about. Out in the bay the narrow craft that had been tied at his pier the week before; one mast, two sails, was flitting back and forth, making swooping turns, heeling over to her low rail till her strange boom swung, her mainsail flopped, then filled again as the boat bounced up on a new heeling tack Moments later, "ready about!" rang across the water.

"Listen to me, damn your stubborn black ass...”

Thrip Warren’s voice carried over the low chop on an incoming breeze. He was making a sailor of his gift apprentice.

I sat down on the rocks to watch them. The kind of little clipper Malbone had described was modified here to the banana curve of a river shallop, but with far more cloth than other craft of its narrow beam. Quite suddenly my newly informed naval eye proved prescient as a gust put the little ship on its side. All the way over it went till only the keel was breathing. I jumped to my feet, and like a fool, waved at the swamped sailors.

Loping up the shore, looking for any dinghy, I found one with oars shipped in the locks, and pushed off into the bay, setting a slip course, rowing against the breeze and running tide. Right away, I saw the futility of my effort, coming closer to the overturned boat, but drifting far off a line to reach it. Sliding past, perhaps no closer than several hundred feet, the stranded pair sat on their upturned keel; Warren with one arm around his rudder, the other holding on to his pupil, Castle Quant. I went floating past toward the far shore. A river coaster sailing up the bay swung around on a course to save them.

SEVEN

ALIAS PROSPER EVERWOOD

Things were about to change at the *Mercury* as Colonel Malbone had predicted. In the spring of 1768 the ever suspicious Sam Hall was replaced by Solomon Southwick. No more biting my tongue as my words are taken off the press. No more snickering between Hall and the scheming Jacob who suffers a little demotion in the shuffle. Southwick seems strong for independence, and not one to temporize. Hall walked out and Southwick walked in. Six foot tall, straw haired, a blue-eyed Saxon by contrast to my black locks and dark eye. Not without his prejudices.

"Hall says you've got some Jew in you. I don't care what you come from, or who you'll want to sit with, I want you at the *Mercury*. If you stay I'll raise you to fifteen shillings. No more press work. Two monkeys can do that. Or young Jacob with a little help off the street. "No," he went on, "I want you around the wharves and warehouses, up the collector's nose, in the Quaker lockers, over the clerk's shoulder in the State House, carding with John Malbone, and in the Jews' business too. Keep friends with the Chazan."

Southwick moved our shop to Queen Street in the middle of the Parade. He was a sometime scholar, whose political fire maybe burned too hot for his own good, an attitude after my own heart. In our new quarters, he posted his honorary degree from the College of Philadelphia. Unframed, and a document of most modest distinction.

"Without the usual foundation of critical learning and language, he discovered an aptness worthy of encouragement in mathematics and branches of philosophy..."

If flattered, I was apprehensive about performing each week for a mathematician-philosopher, but excited beyond poise when he said, "you'll be my pen." Aware of past aliases, he asked me to become a fictitious scold to lash a Tory's conscience once a week in a full column. This in addition to filling our several columns each week with the town's news.

When he enlarged our Kings Arms symbol it was only a diversion. Pretending to a quiet purpose he added

"Containing the freshest advices,"

As if he were content to be an event calendar and commercial bulletin, but soon enough our masthead read

"Undaunted by Tyrants - We'll Die or Be Free."

In that week of transition I received the word from Cuff Charleston, that Sally was anxious to see me. Not by the stone wall on the North Road, but in Mrs. Watson's tea room, a respectable house, not the place you'd expect to see "the woman with no fixed address" or a man with ink-stained hands.

Sally was there as promised with a gathering of wives from the Jews' Street. Why these wealthy matrons would sit to the counsel of a housekeeper was beyond me. I overheard.... your husbands courted in business ... abused in the ale house .... Rivera ... a price pact with Providence...Lopez ... wharf and warehouse ... arson ...Hays...all the Collector's pet dogs ... ignoring non-importation....

Sally was lecturing them! Telling them their refuge in Newport should instill a duty to the stolen people. When she was finished with the Jewish ladies, she came to my table, sat, and cocked her head in that shameless way, staring at my confusion.

“So Hall's gone,” she said. “I don't trust Southwick. But there's you.”

<>

Ezra Stiles‘ seven-week-old daughter died and I wrote the *Mercury*'s brief obituary without speaking to the preacher, not wanting to intrude on his grief. Stiles came to our office to complain of a cold-hearted indifference in the notice. He gave Southwick an earful of my shifty reputation, asking the new editor, “Does he believe in anything?” though his own faith was in confusion that week.

He told Southwick his wife had been seized with a fit soon after he'd observed the comet then south of Pleiades, and that three days later with the same comet joined in Bellatrix in Orion's shoulder, his little daughter had died. Was it coincidence, he wondered, which suggested he'd rather believe his misfortune was linked to astrology than the will of God.

It was only another day before he came back to assure us he'd not meant to imply a belief in astrology. He said Newport, by God's grace, was free of the superstition confounding so much of New England. While he was still grieving, it would have been cruel of me to remind him of families who asked Henry Stafford for help when the Lord didn't respond; Stafford who told them where lost things might be found, and the propitious day and hour for their ships to sail. Or of Stiles' own congregant, Granny Morgan, who stuck pins in cakes of flour and urine for divination when prayer brought no answer.

He might have been composing a sermon when he said "The vessel of sorcery is shipwrecked in the colonies; only a few scattered planks float on the wide ocean of humanity." He wanted us to know his little girl had been baptized and that he'd seen her smile.

<>

In my new guise at the *Mercury* I was the scolding suitor Prosper Everwood, the correspondent of an aggravating vamp, the two-hearted beauty Instance Newport. Instance was the town of Newport herself, dressed to dismay, flirting to prosper, with cane in her tea, rum on her breath, and her heart filled with innocence on the Sabbath, one eye on salvation, the other on England. If it was her duty to civilize, first she must plunder the Guinea Coast for black heathens. I wrote:

Dear Instance,

I missed your theatrics in the Cock and Bull last night. If you insist on walking out unassisted by a patriotic arm, you should expect that sort of pawing by a Royal Navy grog mutt. When we last met you looked over my shoulder at every passing boy in red. Maybe I should have left you long ago to the protection of the Anglicans of Trinity. Little hope for you there.

Your reputation is not improved by parading at dusk on the waterfront. Why don't you take your evening stroll in the upper town where there are no brawlers, and no rummy lizards prowling? On High Street perhaps, where men don't blow their noses on their sleeves.

The pump boy in the Cock and Bull says you worry for my neck. I suppose you trust the Tories' promise of safety in their good report of us across the water.

Then some odds and ends I overheard in the tavern:

'If he sheared the wool off his wife he might love her better. He can't bring her inside. She frightens the children.'

'Can't be too careful. Ask Townsend. That's his tenant Palmer there, in his small beer.(looking at me) The Mercury's man. Was after saving Thrip Warren from drowning. Tell my misses don't send him after any splash of mine. You, Palmer, come and have a drink. Trained to the oar in your kitchen tub, were you?'

Never too old to be taken in measles. The whole town knows Bannister's apple sack is swollen.

'Barrels of gunpowder floating in the bay?'

With men so far gone in their cups, there was nothing they said safe from repetition by Prosper Everwood in the *Mercury*. And sometimes Prosper showed me as a fool too. Self-parody might pay a nice return in fellowship.

EIGHT

YOU HAVE TO BE BORN ON AN ISLAND

I've seen John Townsend's finest mahogany highboys with their ornamented block fronts and the Goddards' elegant cabinets. I've seen Admiral Pocock's grand painting of a ship of the line laid over in a gale, and Greenwood's new-style portrait of "The Jockeys at Kingstown," and his shimmering blue-black likeness of the champion Ravenwood. None of them, joined cabinet, or painted life, came as close to moving my heart as the frame and fairing lines, the shifting double curve of a boat shaped for speed on the cradle in Thrip Warren's barn. The thing coming to life with Castle leaning over a mold station amidships as Warren bent a strip to the line of his new hull.

It was a remarked marvel that Warren didn't need the sweep of a compass to mark his lumber, but took pride in the compass in his head. I could see Castle's fascination with the thing taking shape under their hands before he looked up and stiffened at the sight of me. Who would suspect he was contemplating the shape of deliverance, a ship that might sail over the earth's turning to the coast where he was stolen, then home, to the east of the sun's rising?

Warren made no effort to disguise his work this time, or hide the boy.

"Job sent him," he said. "He lives with me."

Warren took a long sip of water and handed the same cup to Castle for his own lips. If the boy no longer thought he was in a land of cannibals, he still bristled at the sight of me. He moved to the other side of the boat, and as Warren began to explain the work, leading me around the shop, the boy moved too, always keeping the same distance between us, on the opposite side of the hull.

So long busy with words, envious of practical talent, I asked,

"How do you learn to build a boat?"

You have to be born on an island, better a small one."

No use explaining the process to me, who barely understood the riddle which made ships so useful, their trick of reaching Providence from Newport even when the wind was mostly out of the north.

When Thrip moved to the door he didn't have to tell me it was time for me to leave. I slid my hand along the hull's curve appreciatively, bow to stern as if I were estimating the sail to be carried, a fraudulent posing. He said nothing of the mess I'd made of his rescue, or having to be saved myself by two apprentices from a boatyard on Conanicut, before I'd drift and be smashed on the mainland rocks.

<>

Sally came looking for me in the new printing office on a Friday afternoon, the week's issue already out the door and off the pier.

"Your Mr. Everwood," she told Southwick, "I'd like to speak to him."

"There is no Everwood," he told her.

"Yes," she said, "that's him, the one sucking on his quill."

Oh God, were my lips black? I followed her into the street where she suggested another sit-down at Mrs. Watson's. On the way, she kept a step or two behind. I slowed so that she might come alongside, but she was determined to lag, and we didn't speak until we were sitting in Mrs. Watson's front room.

I reached across the table. She pulled her hands quickly into her lap, and launched into an examination, turning that busy eye of hers onto my lips' hesitation. She was probing for my politics, my world-view. Had I ever had a transforming experience?. I thought of the day I was taken to hear Whitefield; my father so far gone in religious enchantment that I thought he was looking for the hill-side altar where he'd sacrifice me. "But you see I was delivered."

Sally was disappointed in my answer.

"You mean a sign of grace, a miracle?" I asked

"More like you were in a rowboat in the bay, about to swamp and drown when two black angels came off Goat Island and pulled you to safety. Something more contrite, more generous to the black men who saved you."

With Hall gone and Southwick in charge, Sally needed a new agent at the *Mercury*. If I hesitated it was only that I wanted an explanation. She said she knew something about men who would be writers. Her sometime guardian Jameson had aspired to sermon writing, pretending to a wisdom beyond normal human ken, she said. And he might have held her in his fraudulent sway if he hadn't made a habit of using the hazel switch on her and her brother.

"Your letters from Everwood," she said, "they're heartless."

I flinched.

"The *Mercury* could help me again," she said. "The way Mr. Hall did."

If Hall had been her ally, he'd done a good job of hiding it from me.

Better for now that I didn't know more, she said

Why didn't she just ask Southwick for help?

Better, as well, that the new editor be left out of this, she said. She told me again she didn't really trust him. When she gave the signal, I was to change one letter, a new Caslon v, to the badly worn piece of type passed on to us by the Franklins - the v in the *Mercury*'s new masthead slogan, "Containing the freshest advices."

<>

Cuff Charleston had come to Newport a free man of thirty-five, already with white hair around his ears. Without having read a single volume in the Redwood Library, no knowledge of Latin, Greek or Hebrew, he was yet revered as linguist and practical mind of last resort where the blacks were concerned, maybe the most valuable intelligence in Newport with his five African languages. There wasn't a slave in the town whose tongue he couldn't translate directly or through the agency of another African. He was pampered and paid beyond what the Townsends gave him, when called to interpret between a new slave and his master, or mediate disputes in the black community.

At the same time, Cuff was not completely trusted by the people who paid for and admired his talents, not certain of what passed between him and their servants, though he was often called for consultation when a slave ran for freedom. He lived in a small house on Bridge Street provided at no cost by his dozen Quaker sponsors.

Cuff had proved himself an effective teacher of the several-dozen children in the Quaker's slave school. He spoke to them only in English. As a visitor, I watched the younger ones giggle and cling to him with affection as he walked between their chairs. The older pupils responded to him with a deep respect.

This work gave Cuff privileges. His Quaker sponsors had sent him on an unusual ride-away after a year in Newport. His mount, Townsend's sorrel, was loaded in September on the Providence ferry. It took some nerve for a lone black to ride off like that into the Massachusetts wilderness among wolves, Indians, trappers - vagabonds of all stripes - with nothing but freedman's papers to protect him.

"Do you know how your newspaper gets to Northampton?" Sally asked me. I didn't know it went that far, or just what she was getting at, but she gave a precise answer to her own question: "Three hundred copies to Providence by ferry; sixty of those by Colony Post to Woonsocket; twenty of that number to East Village, twelve of them to Sturbridge; of those, six to Amherst, then five to Northampton.

On his ride-away Cuff had been told to follow this diminishing westward circulation of our coastal news, riding alongside the colony post carriers as far as Sturbridge and then beside the mounts of two citizen postmen to Palmer and Northampton. The trip out had taken six days. Backtracking home through these outposts, Cuff took longer, passing nights in homes in those same villages. His Newport sponsors thought he might have ridden away for good.

Sally Warren said they should be happy if he came home at all, though she knew he would, and exactly where he'd been. I thought she spent an unconscionable amount of time with him, strolling Thames Street and watching the slave market.

<>

Sally must have known Prosper Everwood's letters to Instance Newport were more than the plaints of a man spurned by his town.

Dear Instance,

When I see you set your bonnet for the regard of that caddish British Parliament without care to modesty, I wonder that you ever achieved the wealth, talent, and repute which brings the world to worship at your feet. Among American coastal ports, none wear the jewelry of commerce with the same fascination or success. And yet...

Your ministers, all champions of that freedom of conscience you admire, while they maneuver for your favor, now fret as I do to see your virtue bent so easily by this cajoling fellow, Parliament. This freedom of conscience, which even allows a synagogue, and has brought so many suitors your way, and made you a wealthy woman, though kept by none, stings the English sense of primacy. I warn you, Instance, this Parliament has a Tory pulse and an Anglican heart. He'd bring you under the control of an American bishop if he dared.

And what of ***his*** *morals? Parliament is no porch-sofa man, but a frustrated bundler. While your head's been turned his agents have taken an auger to your bundling board. What is your protection from his rapacity now except the family fowling piece? You have no voice in his mischievous fees. What are you then, but his dandled lady?*

He claims this tribute as your legal duty. You have virtual representation, he says, since his voice speaks for all Englishmen and their common interest. Absurd. A pound removed from your pocket is a pound put in his, and at the cost of your virtue. What common interest is that?

Did you know he has friends here who would see your comely figure swollen till your sash circles Massachusetts and Connecticut as well? And once he has you girdled in a single frock, it will be that much easier for him to pick your pocket. What will you be? Less than a vassal, a slave.

Your servant if you'd whistle,
Prosper Everwood

<>

There was a man in Newport whose attention was a nuisance, a would-be friend at the start, then more like a plague of burrs on my stocking, first attached in Pitts Head, and clinging afterward at any sighting - Ramsey Cormichael, "the Ram." He had no trade, but lived on inheritance from his sea-widowed mother. When not in the tavern, he loitered by day near the *Mercury* office to be close to the town's press and a would-be influence on the news. Hall used to chase him out of our doorway with a broom; now he pestered Southwick.

I'd answered the Ram's first approach with the gift of a pint in the tavern, a gesture whose reward was a pestilence. He combined a noisy insecurity with political ignorance and a foul tongue learned alongside the town's slave ships and distilleries. The Second Baptists gave him moral cover, tolerating his attendance in a rear pew when he was able to rise on a Sunday.

If I turned my back on him in the tavern, he'd tap my shoulder to let me know he wasn't finished with me. After Hall sold up, the Ram came into the *Mercury* to tell Southwick he knew where a stolen dory was hidden, asking a reward for the information. "I've got a bit of news for you, too," he said, "about your woman from New Haven. The one so generous with her milk," nudging me as if he'd said something clever.

<>

Ezra Stiles rode off on another restorative journey, this time a fortnight's travel in Connecticut. Poor timing for him. I went to sit with the Second Congregationalists the following Sunday, and was surprised to see Stiles' old nemesis, John Murray in the pulpit again. He was still busy clearing a path to heaven for everyone. Stiles would have another re-education job when he came back.

"I don't care what you've been told," Murray preached. "No one is going to be damned. Not the guiltiest among you. Why would God cast such a cunning thing, a human being, a piece of his own handiwork, into hell? The only thing that makes sense is universal salvation. You people in the balcony, you'll be there too."

So, black accommodations as well as white.

On his return Stiles came first thing to the *Mercury* office.

"You only attend my church when I'm gone," he said.

"Your people are easily swayed," I told him. "Will you preach against Murray?"

"No," he said. He wouldn't condemn the man. A congregation could swarm if it was not given room to find its way, but a few years later there would still be unreformed Murray men sitting in Stiles' church. By then the community mind had turned its first study from eternal to temporal concern. To leave Newport or to remain under threat of invasion by the homeland, and with what political allegiance?

A fear was settling over the town, former neighbors and ale-mates suspicious of one another's loyalties. When Stiles asked me again, "Won't you please settle into one pew?" he could as well have been asking which way I'd turn if the British actually landed here. But he dared not ask.

NINE

A PATH INTO THE WOODS

A rap on my door after dark usually meant a visit from Job Jr., ostensibly to ask if everything was going well in the house, more likely to see if I was available for a chat about my soul. It wasn't Job this time. The knock, soft and slow, wasn't meant to be heard in the rooms upstairs or down. I put down *The Female Quixote*, the same romance that led me into mischief years earlier at Yale, and opened the door to Sally Warren.

I touched her arm. She moved backward, raised her hand, and said, "Tomorrow." It was time to switch the v in the masthead.

"You're risking your reputation coming here."

"As if I have anything left to fear from rumor," she said, already easing her way back down the stairs.

The next evening, with all type set for the new issue, Southwick was off for the tavern, leaving me at the press to wait for Jacob and the two young men, who by our new routine would help pull the paper's sheets through the night. I removed some lines about the poaching preacher and the heading:

Murray Remains In Newport
Says Heaven's Gate Open To All

Making room for some of Prescience Townsend's verse, concluding,

If in his image, God would be
As handicapped as we.

Then worked on the masthead slogan, "Containing the Freshest Advices", inserting the damaged v. Jacob came through the door as I was locking it all down. Southwick returned unexpectedly, and Jacob asked him outside for a chat. They came back winking at each other, having a little giggle over my imagined new fancy, my Quaker poetess, nothing more. Next morning the week's copies of the *Mercury* left the pier for Providence to be winnowed step by step on their way into the hinterland, waking outposts on the backwoods trail, all the way to Northampton.

No surprise to me that the Malbones' James, a husky fellow of many talents, disappeared that week. I set the runaway figure and our report:

ESCAPED. GONE IN THE MIDDLE OF THE NIGHT

From the Malbones, their man James, age twenty-five, five feet nine inches. Scar above his left eye. Missing the first joint of little finger on his left hand. Face almost fine, light brown. James may be carrying a violin which he plays well. Adept at masonry, house carpentry and stone work. Recently whipped in the prison yard where he confessed to thieving from his master's grain stores. Seen entering the Synagogue? Too well known to use the ferry. Reward: Seven Pounds and expenses.

First fingers pointed not at the Chazan but at guilty hearts in the Quaker community. Sally, so frequently seen with Cuff Charleston, was always under suspicion. You could count on Ramsey Cormichael to fly to Southwick with an accusation. "It's your Ink Finger's nigger-lover behind it, the New Haven hussy. Wasn't she talking with him in the jail yard?" As usual the Ram was looking for a reward. Southwick hustled him outside.

<>

Ezra Stiles, gradually winning back his congregation from a too easy path to salvation, came by the *Mercury*, not to thank Sol Southwick for not mentioning his nemesis Murray, but to deliver a thorough scolding for another notice in the paper, an advertisement paid forward for three months.

"You're promoting fornication," he said, holding the offending lines under Southwick's nose.

Kegner's Pills: Effectual cure of the secret disease. Every person may become their own doctor in the most private way. So secret as to be concealed from a bedfellow in any season or climate. Cured 37,000 soldiers and poor persons of both sexes.

"Hall would never have accepted this," he said, waving the paper, "human suffering is not the Lord's pleasure, but has its divine purpose."

"For all I know, Hall used the pills himself," Solomon told him.

We looked at each other with long noses, as if the wind had just been broken, and all of us fell to laughter.

"No," Stiles said, "actually I came to see your journeyman." He asked me aside to say a Quaker from the Point had seen Sally Warren coming from my rooms at night, and that our names were linked again in scandal.

"Show yourselves to the town in an honest way. You're in more danger than you know, and not just from Divine observation. If you won't declare an honest intention, please don't sit with us on the Lord's Day."

I ignored Stiles' advice, and sat to his sermon the very next Sunday. He must have thought better of his ban, smiling on my attendance, and preaching on the Lord's preference for closet prayer over public displays of piety. He was looking my way when he said "If there are collaborators in schemes of freedom worshipping with us today, let their actions be guided by the laws of the colony. If the laws be wrong, righteousness will wear them away in good time."

<>

Two days after the Malbones' James ran, I met with Sally again in the tea shop. Her door was being watched every night, she said. One of Malbone's agents had followed her to the tea room and was waiting outside to see if she returned to her own lodging. She was whispering instructions.

'Wait until midnight. Go to the cabin on Barney Street behind the synagogue. The door will be unlocked. When the man appears take him out the North Road to the path through the burying ground, down to the shore and out to Thrip's pier.

I was surprised and flattered by her new trust and expectation, but slow to respond.

"All right," she said. "You want to know more?"

"Not about James. About you."

She'd never finished the story of her childhood. She sighed, looked around the room, buttered a muffin, and began where she'd left off.

Maybe she was only Thrip's half-sister, she explained. At least that's what she'd been told by their shifty tutor Jameson, who trained them with threats and frequent use of the switch. Though they despised and feared the man, they credited him with their early education. With no wife to temper his moods, Jameson's color ranged from a choleric red to a pale swoon, with tears of piety when he read a pious sonnet. She'd seen him chop off the fingers of two chicken thieves, then beg God's pardon for his own blinding temper.

When Jameson saw the children's damning note to the Philadelphia Quakers he came after Sally with the switch, trying to lift her skirts to a bare ass - "is this the way you use the letters I teach you?"

Thrip, standing behind him, swung a poker that might have broken Jameson's leg. He was lying on the floor screaming at them to get out. With just a sack of clothes they made their way to New London.

Sally was ready to tell more, but Malbone's agent came inside and sat at the next table. Our conversation was over.

<>

It was dark in the cabin on Barney Street, but I saw him rising slowly through the floor, apparition into flesh. His voice sent me back against the wall.

"Who are you?"

"James," he said.

We walked out in the moon's shadows, meeting no one on the road or path but two snarling dogs. I threw a rock in their direction, and they cowered around to growl behind us all the way to the waterfront. It was a mile more over stones and roots to Thrip's pier. He was already in the Tall Sally, bow into the wind, his sails raised and flapping.

"Get aboard!" Thrip was casting off the lines.

"I don't go on the water," James said, leaning back against me.

Thrip reached over and pulled him onto the deck, then ran amid-ship to push away from the pier. The bow cleared, the sail filled, and they were on their way as lights approached along the shoreline, the swinging lanterns of two loping deputies.

"There he is!"

<>

Thrip Warren was accused of transporting James. I told the constable I'd been on a customary night walk past the burying ground, when I heard dogs barking and a call for help. Later, Warren testified to ferrying a friend back to Providence. There were lies told under oath. No formal charges brought, but with pressure from John Malbone, Sally lost her job at Mrs. Chambers.

Malbone took me by the arm in Pitts Head.

"If the Quakers want to let their boys go free, that's their business."

He made no accusation. I felt shabby in my dishonesty, pretending ignorance, unwilling to lose the good will and tavern-chat of a man who had his shipping news from a dozen counting-house clerks, knew the history of the lash told in his father's Guinea logs, knew how Lopez cornered the spermaceti trade, the size of the last under-table payment to the Collector, all the base secrets of the town's wealth, all tempered by the purifying light that shone through Newport's plentiful stained glass on a Sunday.

<>

Against her brother Thrip's advice, Sally took a job at Chalmers' Ropewalk - the only woman under that long roof, where orders and insults were called back and forth some six-hundred feet as the hemp strands were laid and gathered. A twister's arms hung exhausted at the end of a shift. Sally spent most of her day in the shop's counting house, but sometimes took a shift on the line, laboring along with men who ogled her.

"She's got a cow's gift and wouldn't I be her dairyman."

Soon afterward, the man who said that got himself in the way of Thrip's thrashing arms in the tavern, and was carried home for repairs. After that, any familiars directed Sally's way were under the breath. And she proved herself worthy of the hire and the men's respect, having to do with none of them; no trouble or jealousies there. She moved out to Thrip's small boatyard, sharing quarters with him and Castle and the two sawyers.

By then the young African's skills as a shipwright had advanced to marking and cutting. Thrip, proud of the boy's progress, pretended it was nothing out of the ordinary. Castle might have found work in any of Newport's boatyards, but seemed devoted to Thrip and Sally, showing no interest in moving on.

"He wants to know how a man sails to a place he can't see." Sally told me. Thrip was starting him off with a navigation primer whose diagrams were incomprehensible without text. Castle agreed to return to Cuff Charleston's classes twice a week, with the sailing manual as his reading goal. A month later Thrip sent him up the bay alone in the Tall Sally to Providence flying a single reefed sail, and Castle returned a different kind of man, as if free to go anywhere in the world, superior to those stuck on shore, though Thrip had yet to teach him sea faring under stars, or how to take a fix on the sun's angle.

<>

A late bit of advice to Instance Newport:

My Dear Instance,

For several years past in this fitful courtship (your dalliance with my heart), the annual celebration of Repeal, with candles, cannons and public inebriation, made this chap Parliament, think you might yield to his new demands. I told you then and remind you that before he revoked his Stamp action, Mr. Parliament claimed your duty of submission to his whim. With one hand at your pleasure, his other was in your pocket. To your shame you enjoyed the moment with no thought of tomorrow. His so-called Declaratory Act, was all his declaration, none of your own: 'I have full power to make laws binding the colonies of America in all cases,' he said.

Now forced into the streets again, you cry for protection. I am at your service.

As ever your fool?

Prosper Everwood.

You'd think after years of off-again-on-again with Sally I'd no longer suffer a fool's pain, forlorn and elated by turns, silly or serious to distraction; if on a country walk, sometimes suddenly striding along in admiration of the body and soul I found desirable beyond all others-Sally Warren whose uncovered arms, under labor at the ropewalk, became muscled in a way that only made them more appealing.

I don't follow Sally, but somehow find her here and there in my path. Of course she'd be at the ropewalk where I was sent to report on the misadventure of a British boy off the Rose. Always short for pleasure on the naval allowance, his kind sometimes looked for a day's work in the town. He asked one of the Chalmers men for a job, and was told,

"You can shovel out our shit house."

The fight that followed wasn't fair, the King's boy outnumbered and beaten to the ground. It was when he came back with a dozen mates that I was sent up to report on a battle-royal that never happened, their officer arriving in time to order them back to the Rose's deck. Sally turned away from the fuss like a disgusted mother from squabbling children, and went back to her work in the office. The English officer brushed aside my questions. "We know you," he said. "You'll get the rope, and I'll be watching when your Johnny stiffs and your feet hop the jig." Always the Navy's favorite figure, a colonist in the noose.

<>

"She's been warned out," Cuff told me. As if Sally would ever stoop to asking Newport's charity. She makes as much as the constable who served her papers. It was just the counsel's way of saying the town didn't want her here. Cuff had really come to let me know that James, the same who'd risen through the floor of the Barney Street cabin was safe in Northampton, delivered along that chain through the woods from Providence to Woonsocket, East Village and Sturbridge, hidden by day and accompanied at night to that pocket of safety in western Massachusetts. Sally, he said, was looking for another man to deliver into the woods.

<>

Newport, prospering far beyond any place of its size on the Atlantic shore, was still balancing its dual allegiance to the colonial government and the Crown; obeying each so far as convenient. The town was inured to mortal combat on a small scale. The loss of a man pressed on a royal frigate, a royal marine missing morning roll, a dock smashed by one of the Rose cannons, a British longboat scuttled. I woke up one morning and it was 1772. Ten years in Newport, I was stretching tolerance on all sides; neither hanged nor run out of town, or even fired. Not yet.

TEN

SARAH BELONGS TO THE RAM

Solomon sent me down to the slave market to report on the sale of three Africans sent down from Providence on the Wednesday packet - fellows advertised as likely yard men and gardeners. It was the warming time in the spring of 1772, the right moment to catch the attention of one of the estate managers on Aquidneck. The three for sale all had a wandering habit, men who might be better controlled on our island.

It was dishonest, like selling drugged, hot mares for saddle horses, but nothing you could go to law about. These three were to be sold by the same auctioneer being trusted to find a buyer for a black girl of becoming features, the cause of trouble between an overseer and his wife on a Kingstown plantation.

The auction failed; the reputations of the men too well known. They were chained in the slave pen for return to Providence. Then there was the coal-black girl named Sarah. Coal black or a stunning blue iridescence in a certain light, as stunning to me as she must have been to Ramsey Cormichael. She was maybe fourteen years old; there was plenty of interest in her, though no decent Newport citizen could be seen bidding for a teenaged bit of house trouble like this. Cuff thought she'd come from North Africa, with Arabian blood. She wore a shift not quite loose enough to disguise the nubile truth of her. Her eyes were wide with fear.

A half-dozen men hung back in feigned disinterest, making gestures of assent as the price of Sarah rose. Some were factors for hidden buyers, some bidding on their own account, maybe gambling on a premium if they could take her back to the mainland for resale among less constrained consciences. Cormichael, unsteady on his feet, had begun to bid for her with a foolhardy enthusiasm.

The Ram, loathed and loathing, still in it at thirty-five pounds Sterling, bidding without common sense or scruple. He was still calling out in reckless increments when the only man left bidding against him was the auctioneer's own agent, so eager for this girl of unproven usefulness, who might know nothing but the fact of her stolen life, and how to set her Kingstown master's table.

At forty pounds, pushing on. His inheritance leaking away as his eyes moved from his prize, left and right, around the astonished crowd to let us know this sudden interest in a house girl was his business and none of ours. Sold at forty-three pounds Sterling. Sarah belonged to the Ram. With nothing to guide her but the warnings of mentoring black mothers on the Kingston plantation she came from, and now the calming voice of Cuff Charleston. He was saying something in her ear in a language no one else could understand. She grabbed his arm, but the Ram pushed him away. "Don't I have a place to keep, as well?" he said, leading Sarah off to his little house on the west-side cliffs.

<>

Captain Peck, just off Aaron Lopez's candle ship from London under ballast and carrying a dozen passengers came in to tell Sol Southwick he ought to keep an eye on the Jews.

"What Jews?

"All of them."

But every religion here has another looking over its shoulder. So many meeting houses, so many suspicions. Jews, Anglicans, Baptists. Congregationalists, Sabbatarians, Presbyterians, poaching preachers, each with his own way to heaven. The variety in our town unequalled anyplace else in America, and I still wander from one steeple house to another without fear. Ezra Stiles can't pin me down. Nowhere else has my conscience been quite so easy.

Peck's gossip was laughable: "....men on the Jew's boat discussing an intelligence office.....on some Jew street in London.... thirty clerks working under cover of a Jew counting-house,....gathering reports on every event in America....sounded to me like a Jew affair." The number and street he'd scribbled while eavesdropping on his conspirators, and given to us in strictest confidence, turned out to be the address of the English Ministry.

And who would not marvel at the whispered news of the Jewish ladies; the candle merchant Aaron Lopez has been circumcised - wondering at the religious devotion of a man driven with his tribe out of Lisbon where his faith had been practiced three hundred years in secret, to this unique safe harbor, only now in middle age, to suffer the pain of the moil's knife.

<>

There came a week when trouble with Quakers was put directly in my face, maybe because I lived among them on the Point. Ezra Stiles caught me up on my evening stroll up Clarke Street, asked if he could join me, falling in step, regardless of my answer. Unable to have me fired at the *Mercury* he was suing for peace.

“Instinct tells me you'd be a righteous man if you allowed yourself."

With no response from me, he began again. “I'll describe someone and I want you to tell me if he resembles anyone you know."

A cunning way to lay a trap, but I let him go on.

"He's learned enough, skilled at his work, sure of himself. He'll adjust himself to new possibilities, but never studies deeply in a subject, preferring to find his news of the world in the tavern. So he only has a surface knowledge of things, satisfied by the generalities of experts. His language is crude or refined depending on his company. Men may enjoy his palaver, but sometimes discount his argument for its bawdy tendency."

“You mean Prosper Everwood. You mean me."

"You might think so, but no. This is a Quaker from Philadelphia," he said, "used to be all for the Sons of Liberty. His name is Pemberton, a friend of Woolman. Now he's gathering Quakers against independence." So Stiles too, was switching sides, and right in front of me. Now he wants the *Mercury* to know he's all for American freedom.

"Never mind what I've said before about obedience." England had lost his allegiance; viscerally with the killings on Boston Common, he said, intellectually with its declaration of our subservience.

As we passed the slave pen on the south end, and began to inhale the fumes of the distilleries along Thames Street, he wanted to be sure the

Mercury recognized the "dangers within." Not just a small knot of Tory Anglicans; he was upset with the Quakers for bargaining with the Crown on their own behalf. The colonial congress had acted, he told me, with a unity close to sacred, precisely because it set doctrinal and local interest aside in its quest for freedom.

This was all new for Ezra. Suddenly I was his brother in patriotism, his face gathering blood as he told me “Pemberton pretends piety though he'd sell the colony’s freedom for his own faith's protection. If he had a true religion, he wouldn't bargain with it. This Quaker criticizes *me* for keeping a slave in the house. He charged me with that! Now they’ve got this woman writing poetry.”

Stiles flew off in another direction as if he'd lost his place: “Don’t the Townsends sign their cabinets as if they were books or paintings made for the ages. What kind of modesty is that? Quakers? Meetings to vote on principles? And all those airy proclamations with nothing solid to hold on to. Of course 'the way opens,' as they say. It closes, too."

But wasn't it the Quaker Redwood's library that gathered and housed all the texts he admired, and made a cozy place for his philosophical discussions?

"Yes," Stiles admitted, "but Redwood says he'd give up his faith before he’d give up his slaves.

“What if your church asked the same of you?” I asked him.

"It doesn’t," he said. "Besides, our boy Newport is like family. I'd guess he knows more Latin than you do."

The boast seemed to exhaust his spirit.

I didn't know how sick Stiles' wife was, how troubled he was for the half-dozen children she'd got him, a man with a “full quiver” as favored by the Lord, wondering how they might be spared the threat of siege, or war. "Open, open, open!" he carped. “The rest of us make do with a few moments of enlightenment.”

The next minute he admitted it was hard to condemn a man like Woolman, who'd ridden two-thousand miles through the wilderness, shivered in wet clothes and blankets while quibbling with himself over the purity of his conscience. A man who asked brotherhood of Indians where only a few miles away the scalps of Englishmen were being taken. “In another faith he'd be a saint.”

Stiles confusion sent me back to the Meeting House the next Sunday where another traveling scold was condemning the Newport Quakers more bitterly than Woolman had. This man said he'd come home here thinking to retire in the cradle of his faith but had changed his mind.

When he joined the community sixty years earlier, he said, the Friends were a plain people and contrite. Twenty years later they had taken up the fashions of the world. Where had the humility gone? After forty years some were so rich they made "a specious appearance in the world." Costly garments, silver on their sideboards. Now, going on sixty years, he said, there was no room left for the Holy Ghost to make an entrance. He couldn't stay here, he said

<>

Prescience Townsend came to the *Mercury* to ask if we'd print something against the people harassing Walter Shifflett, who still kept his daily post outside Pitts Head, despite the scorn and occasional stone thrown his way. Prescience admired the way his messages pricked the town's conscience, but was concerned for Shifflett's safety. She coaxed me down to the tavern to read his latest bulletin, a clear echo of her late versifying.

IF GOD MADE US IN HIS IMAGE,
THEN WE'VE RETURNED THE COMPLIMENT

Prescience was disgusted with her Meeting and her family, which offered no support when an elder on the facing bench stood to censure "the lady among us who takes pride in her pretty writing. Vanity is the devil's pleasure," he'd said, "and sometimes his messenger."

Prescience wanted the rest of her poems back. I couldn't tell her Southwick had thrown them into the carter's bin, and that they'd gone to the incinerator. She left me standing beside the spider-legged Shifflett, who swayed under his sign.

"Do you know what it says?" I asked him.

"Penny for the pub?"

I gave him three. Shifflett dropped the sign in the gutter and went inside.

No church in Newport could have a quarrel with the message he carried the following week.

IF THERE WERE ONLY ONE RELIGION
THERE'D BE DESPOTISM.
IF TWO, THEY'D CUT EACH OTHER'S THROATS.
SINCE THERE ARE THIRTY, THEY LIVE IN PEACE.

ELEVEN

A BALL IN THE THIGH

One summer the vilest name on the Rhode Island tongue was William Dudingston. No one so despised since the British lizard George Rome collected his debt from the spermaceti merchant Flagg, putting him, Flagg, out of business and his partner out of his home, taking the house for his own.

Dudingston was only a Lieutenant, but commander of the Gaspee, a swift eight-gun schooner. A brash King's peacock, he'd ordered Southwick to appear on his deck to receive formal complaint of the paper's description of him as *a martinet, a popinjay, a thieving pirate, and royal pest of no legal standing in the colony.*

Southwick ignored the summons, and Dudingston's rancor grew. He ran his ship up and down the bay, boarding any entering or leaving the harbor, demanding duty, and seizing cargoes. I suggested luring the Lieutenant ashore, even set the trap of a supposed social in our paper:

Evening of Reconciliation
Admiralty Ball at Abigail Stoneman's

Southwick took it off the stick. "We don't print lies," he told me.

Late in April of 1772, I was at Warren's boatyard when he and his young black mate Castle raised sail on a slim new craft. In an offshore breeze, I watched them glide north, south, and north again on close hauls, Thrip at the tiller, Castle on the sheets, for a trial run. As they maneuvered, a chase blew up behind them in the bay.

Dudingston's revenue schooner Gaspee, was closing on the Newport packet Soberman. I saw a warning shot splash in front of the packet, then the report as smoke rose off the Gaspee's swivel gun. Thrip and Castle turned away from the confrontation, and back to the pier. The Soberman was run down and boarded.

I knew Sally was living here with Thrip and Castle, but it was still a surprise to see her come out of the house at the sound of the British gun. How many rooms in there, I wondered. Which was hers? We watched together from the dock, as Warren's boat docked, while the Soberman, to the crew's shame, was taken back to the custom house on Conanicut in command of a Navy boy off the Gaspee. Sally, untroubled by the humiliation on the bay, was more concerned that the *Mercury*'s defective v should be at hand, ready for service again.

<>

There was town-wide perception of an immoral emanation from the Ram's cliff-side cottage, where he'd lived a bachelor twenty years before bringing home the untrained black child Sarah to ease a life already indolent. More traffic than usual was passing his way, matrons of the upper town at daily constitutionals, then weekend strollers, with that whiff of something unwholesome. Carters, too, slowed as they passed on their way to the summer houses at the south end, listening for a howl, or a clay something smashed against a wall. I passed there myself to see what sign of trouble might be leaking from the house.

<>

Sally wasted no time giving me new instructions. By then I knew all the steps on her path to freedom, beginning with the damaged v, the signal passed in our masthead, delivered by packet boat to Providence, then rider-by-unwitting postal rider, to outland friends, town by town, alerting the freedom chain to a fugitive coming their way. This time Sally wanted a good deal more from me, and it took no special pleading on her part.

In the smallest hour of a Friday morning in the Ram's empty yard, I was waiting under a tamarack's cover for the girl to come from the house. It was her second Friday under his roof, and she emerged, ready for a sprint, without a clue which way to run. It was a warm night, but I folded her trembling body, under my cloak, and we went in a stumbling, awkward way, back along the cliff road. We were already at the synagogue door when the alarm sounded in the upper town. The Ram, awake to his loss, was beating a wash-tub, calling the town to rise and give chase. Sarah was pulled quickly inside, and the door of the synagogue closed in my face.

Cormichael's posse of several malcontents, looking for excitement, made straight for Thrip Warren's boat yard. I must have been back in bed when Thrip fired from his window, unloading two barrels on the vigilantes, sending them away with some small lead stinging their backsides. Sally exulting in the story, gave me still more orders.

<>

Cormichael was on the rampage at the *Mercury*, and in the Constable's office, threatening trouble for the paper, and violence for the criminals who robbed him. I had set the damaged v, and now I was setting the runaway icon over the notice of Sarah's escape.

Two days later I was waiting for the young slave girl when she rose through the hatch of the Barney Street cabin just as James had. In candle light, she came up head first, like a coal-black Egyptian queen rising from her tomb. Someone in the synagogue had given her a small man's outfit of stockings, britches, a pleated shirt and a felt hat to dress her like a well-turned-out carriage boy, though she was going to ride from Barney Street under a wagon load of straw until we reached the woods beyond the burying ground.

It was after midday on the ninth of June, 1772 when I delivered Sarah, undetected into the care of Thrip Warren. The day and hour recorded as the same at which another chase-for-keeps was blowing up the bay. Thrip pulled Sarah onto the Tall Sally, got her out of sight in the half-cabin on the foredeck, and yelled at me to jump aboard.

Where was Sally?

In the house, Thrip said, looking after Castle who'd taken the flux and a fever. "Move!" he said.

I leapt off the pier, reaching for a web of lines amidships as the boat slid clear of the pier. I landed on the rope webbing, and crabbed sideways onto the little ship's rail before jumping to the deck where Thrip was already giving me orders, and we sailed into the bay on a course to meet the chase in progress.

This time it was the Gaspee running down the packet Hannah on her way up from Newport to Providence. Again the navy schooner fired shots. The Hannah ignored the warning. Her Captain Lindsay was too well schooled in the local shoals for Dudingston.

All three of us were gaining on Namquid Point, which ran off farmland into shallows, some seven miles below Providence. The tide was on ebb about two hours with Lindsey standing easterly, Dudingston on the same tack close behind when the Hannah hove about at the end of Namquid. The Gaspee took the challenge, coming about a moment too late. I saw the British boat shudder to a halt on the bar, going full aground, and a navy boy flying over her sprit into the bay.

Moments later we were passing the foundered ship, and I was staring across a hundred feet of water into the face of the Red Beard who raised a musket on the Gaspee deck but never fired. He'd not been seen in Rhode Island for several years. We watched another ball from the Gaspee fall harmless into the water, and began a merry run up the bay, our swifter Tall Sally, running back and forth across Lindsey's bow, not so much a taunting as a demonstration of the craft's speed, more fame for the Warren boatyard.

Thrip slid into a berth at the Providence town pier, while the packet was forced to anchor out. Lindsay was being rowed ashore, his men going double time at the oars, a sign something more was hatching. It was hours before the tide could float that piece of royal trouble seven miles behind us on Namquid Point.

We were still lingering on our deck, whispering patience to the frightened and uncomprehending Sarah in the cabin, when Lindsey called down from the dock,

"What's inside?"

"Now't but ballast and the printer's man."

Lindsay told him to hop off his empty ship, and come with him if he wanted a bit of the evening's business to his credit. "Don't bring that one with you."

Thrip took an acrobatic leap from our rail onto the pier and disappeared with Lindsey at a lope into town, as if there was no time to waste. Sarah was suddenly my problem.

I could hear the drum; Captain Lindsey gathering Providence to his cause, not mine to know. The last thing they wanted was a newspaper man as witness. The wharf cleared. Called from their evening tables, merchants and sailors fell into the ranks without hesitation. Four dozen of them, enough to fill eight longboats, five oarsmen each, and men at the tillers, all with muskets and a common grievance against the roving Gaspee.

There was no one left dockside to see a gentleman's chaise pull alongside the Tall Sally, or hear the driver call down to me,

"Where's the boy? Get his sorry ass up here!"

Good theatre, no audience. I pulled the hesitant Sarah from the cabin, and pushed her up the ladder, watching as the frightened child climbed unsteadily onto the carriage's groom-step. She held tight as the rig spun sharply, and was drawn away at a swift trot. No one but me to witness Sarah performing her livery charade, on her way to Woonsocket, second station on her freedom journey to Northampton.

I was off the boat and sitting at the bar in the seaside tavern as a posse formed, my head down and mouth to mug, still hoping someone might say, you come too, be our writing witness. As if Providence didn't share the same mistrust as Newport for any man who hovered over words. These men were as cautious as they were vengeful. One took notice of me and called "Get him out of here!"

I was hustled out the door and told to flush my memory of the faces I'd seen; the merchant John Brown, most prominent among them, giving orders to the rest. The tide wouldn't lift the Gaspee off Namquid till near three a.m. Oarlocks of the attacking longboats would be muffled.

I was marched rudely back to the Tall Sally. A church bell rang ten when the longboats pulled away from the wharf; midnight when I saw the sky begin to glow in the south, and seconds later heard the explosion that sent a shiver through the rising tide into the harbor. It would have meant your life to name a player in that attack. Before it was over Dudingston had taken a musket ball in the thigh. And his Gaspee was burned to the waterline, nothing to salvage but the iron fittings of his ship settling in the shallows.

<>

I watched the southern sky turn orange that summer night, and half a year later in the warmest January anyone in Newport could remember I was barred with the rest of the public from our Court House where Crown-appointed commissioners took evidence in the Gaspee affair. *A court of inquisition,* I wrote; *good men asked to make scapegoats of their neighbors.* The Admiralty, trying to put more backbone into informers, anchored two more men of war in our harbor. They were that ignorant about where the longboats had come from.

Barred from the proceeding I flew at the type case with no thought of a pause to pretty my argument

Ten thousand deaths by the noose or the ax are preferable to a life in chains, under a pack of tyrants, whose avarice nothing less than our whole substance and income will satisfy; and who, if they can't extort that, will glory in sacrificing you and your posterity to gratify themselves.

Reading over the published words, I didn't mind that Southwick had taken credit for them if it meant he was becoming bolder. The next week we ran a Tory's account of the Commission's work. A royal embarrassment, he despaired; unproven assertions, and muddled witnesses. The Admiralty had called for six-month postponement, which meant that was the end of it.

"Take a hatchet to it wherever you like," Solomon said. I wasted no time deleting a mention of a related person of crown interest whose detention and removal to England for trial had been proposed by Collector Robinson, who said the troublemaker could be seen at any mob action, a man of aliases, who lately signs himself, Everwood. His seditious writing has even called for armed insurrection.

That would have been my advice to get down the family fowling piece when Mr. Parliament violated his bundling board. I was well warned that I might be snatched from my bed on any night, or off the street, bound and thrown into the hold of a frigate for England, with few who'd come looking for me.

I thought of the list who might miss me; it wasn't very long. Southwick? Not much. Prescience Townsend, still smarting from our careless treatment of her poetry? No, nor young Malbone, though he still accepted my company in Pitts Head. Sally? I wasn't sure. She came into the *Mercury* shop again, going after Southwick.

"I suppose you're finished with the Gaspee story now that your boys dodged the rope, now that Providence has done the work for you, and a black man took a whipping for it." She meant Briggs, the black who named John Brown as leader of the Gaspee attack, his testimony thrown out when another swore that Briggs' statement was coerced with the whip. In fact, the Commissioners had made no special effort in their royal duty, more worried for their own safety in Newport than in a search for the truth.

Sally was interrupted by Cuff Charleston's alarm. "Quick! Up the Parade!"

I followed the two of them out the door and up the hill to the jail. Inside was the Ram's slave girl Sarah, a half year older, in tattered remains of the ridiculous groom's livery, on display behind wooden bars. It was winter, only a week after the Gaspee Commission's harmless finding. Cormichael himself passed a blanket to her to be sure his dearly-purchased girl didn't freeze before he got her home.

Sarah rolled herself into a cocoon, her head disappearing, tucked back in a woolen tunnel. She made no sound, or movement, not even responding to what Cormichael dismissed as Cuff Charleston's "African gibberish."

"Shut that darkie up," he said." A paper was signed, and Sarah released to him. If I could describe the Ram's demeanor at that moment, I might give up a printer's life, and take up biography. So easy to say 'words won't do,' and there pretend a deeper understanding or that curiosity has been satisfied.

But imagine a man whose celebrated loss has brought him more censure than sympathy. A man pointed at, whispered about as he enters and leaves the tavern, a man shunned as he stands over his ale by all but the barman. A fellow so wronged in his guilt-ridden conscience that a sudden reversal of fortune - the return of his still-alive, black child-woman, now moon-bleeding (Cuff's information) house-maid - has left his face a shifting mirror; glee, suspicion, scorn, and fear taking turns on his curling lip so that a sneer becomes a shy turning-up at the mouth's corner before he raises a hand to hide a silly grin from his gawking audience, maybe disgusted by his own confusion, or a little afraid of what's in store for him.

<>

It's said Newport breeds alertness and industry, rather than that lazy receptivity which I found and fled so many years earlier in South Carolina. Of Newport, the bracing climate and fresh air are the first things mentioned. Agreed, if you mean not just the air that fills the lungs, but the same that fills the sails and drives a free commercial armada around the wet earth. Believe me, the place is alert now. And not just church watching church, but member watching member, preachers, too, all being marked as Patriot or Tory for a coming retribution, the winner to be in charge of the word "traitor." The day of reckoning is a certainty, Patriots betting life and livelihood on slim odds, according to Tories, who beseech their neighbors in our pages: "*Be sensible. Don't risk it all on a toss of the dice. Don't ruin it for everyone.*

<>

Another dangerous King's man is one people chat with in the street as he charts the town by royal order, the British cartographer Blaskowitz. Busy this season as no Newport mapmaker has ever been before. Yes, Ezra Stiles mapped the streets and houses, wharves and warehouses, but this Blaskowitz is different, with his two-hundred-foot tape, accurate to the inch, a surveyor's glass and level, and pens of the finest line. He's turning us into a thousand targets on a single sheet, and whistling as he goes about his business.

Still we let this designing spider sit with us in the ale-house. He's made a friend of Malbone Junior, who says the man does us all a favor, this man whose stock in trade is the measured foot from pier to windmills, and back to First Congregational, a target-plotting draftsman.

Second Congregational, too, has been marked for early destruction. Wallace on the Rose has told Ezra Stiles so. It will be retribution for what is considered his turn to full sedition in the pulpit. A badge Stiles has begun to wear with a pride tinged with fear for his church and family. If Blaskowitz's real business is relative distances and bullseyes, why do we let him go to and fro, down Thames, up High Street, around the powder stores, as if he were no more than an artist making a likeness of the world we inhabit for our admiration? Prosper Everwood wrote:

Stop him! Break his glass. Shred the notebooks full of elevations, house numbers, churches, ship yards, wharves and your seaside homes.

<>

For a month the Ram never left his house by day without Sarah on a leash behind him; to market or the bakery, perhaps the occasional grog shop. He doesn't trust the girl with the briefest moment of freedom. Neither does anyone see him touch her. She has to be tugged this way and that. He seems confused by her diffidence.

The Ram's fear of Cuff Charleston's tampering with the girl's mind was eventually outweighed by his dismay at her intractable manner. He had to learn how this worked, how others' servants were kept compliant and useful. He wanted the girl explained to him, to know what had happened to her among the Indians in Massachusetts, and finally he let Charleston speak to her. The Ram learned nothing, but we did.

Now, thanks to Charleston, the Ram had a morbid fear of her. Sarah's escape had been interrupted just before she reached Northampton. Two men posing as deputies had a warrant for her. What they had was the *Mercury*'s notice of the Ram's five-pound reward for her return, her identity fixed by a scythe-shaped scar on her forearm. They sold her to a Nauset Indian trader for five pelts, saving themselves a trek to Rhode Island for the reward.

Cuff said Sarah had no night-trouble with the Nauset tribe's men who had no taste for a black woman on their blankets, but was pestered by the head woman who tried to teach her naked pleasures. Unrequited, angry, this boss woman used the girl hard at washing and scraping the blood and tissue from fresh skins of the hide-trading band. It was when they traveled close to Rhode Island that one of them saw an advantage in returning her to Newport for the five pounds. And this man had forced her legs before pulling her on a rope into the Newport jail.

<>

Thrip Warren, who built the fastest and most dangerous boats on the bay, gained further notoriety for speed unmatched on Narragansett after the Gaspee chase and arson. A Providence merchant, hoping to steal a look at the latest hull on Thrip's cradle came uninvited, by ferry and foot, to the little boatyard. He took Thrip and Castle by surprise and a week later Southwick published the man's scolding letter to the *Mercury*.

To the proper folk of Newport (Quakers and Jews as well)

For a decade and more a man of your port has earned a reputation as the region's master engineer of water speed, river coursing and narrow-passage agility, building boats of a Chesapeake figure, with raked masts, fore and aft rigged for ready reefing, low freeboard craft. These ships defy an ordinary branding. Not just a shipwright, this man sails these craft to the disadvantage of all who challenge him on Narragansett. In a celebrated display of this bold superiority he tacked under the spirit of the Hannah up from Baltimore, even as the speedy packet left the lamented schooner Gaspee - no longer sailing with us-in her wake.

I came to your shore this month in admiration and good faith hoping to visit this master builder, and perhaps learn a trick at his side, unaware of the secrecy he practices. I hardly expected to be driven away with an oath, and in the sights of his musket. Though not before I witnessed a bit of presumption that any property-respecting citizen and advocate of civil order must find disturbing in these troublesome times.

Your feisty genius of the waves had a sextant in hand, demonstrating its use to the young black apprentice at his side. I'm told this Negro has been given command of his master's boat on errands running all the way to Providence, in his own charge. You may ask, and I'd ask with you, of what use is a sextant, or a reading of the sun's slant in the confines of Narragansett Bay.

If you value your property - rum, cordage, candle, cabinets, or your Africans themselves - turn your attention from his Majesty's ship Rose for a moment, and consider the tutoring of home-grown insurrection and flight on your banks.

A Citizen of Providence

When I asked Southwick why we'd publish such a thing, he hid behind our masthead's latest boast.

Open To All Parties, Controlled By None

More likely controlled by his desire to increase circulation by promoting any controversy if it didn't upset too many readers. As if this prying man's injured pride and fear of black revolt deserved attention in this season of our threatened destruction.

<>

It's warm again, and my confounding idol Sally, so confident in her rebellion, holds me in her sway. I think, she was born complete, like a cat, as they say, knowing who she is and what she wants. I can only admire that. She indulges me in the occasional tryst between the same stone wall and sumac copse which shelter our naked truth from all but the eyes of God. Then straight back to her first concern, her freedom schemes.

This season she is mother, cook and queen of the Warren boatyard, attending to every need of Thrip, Castle and the mute sawyers. Our latest intimacy is followed by a querulous challenge. We've walked back into town and are standing at the top of the Parade when she asks, "Don't you have any influence there?" Why had I let Southwick publish that letter?

Again, from the top of the Parade we were looking over the harbor at the town's real threat, three men-of-war broadside to Newport, their cannons pointing at every significant building in town. Not even the high Redwood Library beyond their destructive impulse or range.

"Those British ships are a threat to you as well" I told her. Again she rolled eyes. Like most Newport women, she hoped for a bloodless British victory, though their husbands were hurrying to arms, ready to march off in their ragtag companies. Playing at soldiering, the women thought, in a fair way to getting themselves killed by an overwhelming Royal force that could bombard and burn every Atlantic port to the ground before landing the first marine of their armed horde.

"It's mostly the Quakers leaving so far" she said. "Even your little poetess."

It was the first I'd heard of it, though Prescience had told me how disgusted she was with her clan's pose as political ciphers, not of this world, and speechless against the people calling the affect cowardice. There had been a flurry of announcements in the *Mercury* of houses to let and houses for sale, most of them on the Quakers' Point. They weren't afraid of the British, they were afraid of their neighbors; safe enough if the boys in red came ashore. But every day you could see carts carrying beds, rolling pins, and wardrobes to the ferries.

<>

I wrote:

Dear Instance Newport,

You've never acted with a consistent will, unless it was in your determination to practice this very inconsistency. I doubt I'll ever find a way into your soul, but I believe a duplicity informs your wandering. It amounts to the declaration of your continuing freedom to choose. Instance, there's a price to pay for a heart that beats to both drums, the Patriots' snare and the King's kettle. I watch your nimble feet, shift in mid-step from one rhythm to another, roused by the patriotic rat-a-tat, then following the royal boom-boom. I wonder whose step you'll keep on the day of victory, which will be the same as the day of defeat.

At least you've finally called Parliament's behavior, its latest acts, "Intolerable. I'm told Trinity's Reverend Bisset turned the pages of the Bible last week to "fast not as the Hypocrites," while I sat again with the Second Congregationalists, and heard Reverend Stiles tell us again of the murderous work of British heathens at Lexington and Concord, those "who shed the blood of God's servants like water. "So, you are not of one mind, Instance.

Confess what you're really afraid of - the mob. The rabble has been incited before and can be turned loose again. They could burn down your stores, or your house. They laid the Collector's house flat, and that was before Dudingston began to chase and plunder anything that moved on the bay. They fired on the Saint John, they burned the Maidstone's longboat, tore apart the Liberty's cabin, drove customs officers from the wharves, watched the Gaspee burn to the water line. And now you worry the mob could fire on a brig, and bring the reign of terror in full on our heads.

Let your heart beat with a patriot pulse. After all, a loyal pose can be a marvel of hypocrisy. Think of the way your Tory gallants get clearance in Jamaica for duty-free molasses, only to have their captains fill their casks with water and speed off to French Hispaniola to spill the water and fill the barrels with the cheaper French product. They hide their deception under your skirt; their lading books show but a fraction of their trade. And only a fraction of the swarthy men they carry, who never reach your port, traded for wonderful bills of exchange in the islands and Carolina.

Now, with their coffers full, the Tories beg you not let your gamesters risk all on a single cast.

TWELVE

THE RAM GOES MISSING

I'd become so dependent on Cuff Charleston for town news I no longer resented the time he spent as Sally's confidant on Newport Africans. He told us it was one of the servants from the Lopez house on the cliffs who noticed no light in the Ram's cottage for several nights running; a boy who had taken a fascination with the slave girl Sarah when he saw her being led by the Ram on a rope down the Cliff Road. After a third day of mysterious silence, and no one coming or going, he rapped on the Ram's door, entered the house and found Sarah, locked in her attic room, semi-conscious on a straw tick, with Cormichael nowhere in sight.

The girl, revived from a famished state with water and a crust, seemed to have gone mad. Coming to, she yelled at the boy, pushing him away from her, and when he went for help in his master's home, she ran off down the road, screaming at each house she passed in a bit of English, "Did not, did not..." though most of her ranting was in her native tongue. I followed the small crowd leaving their tables at Pitts Head, drawn to her commotion in the street.

She was possessed, her arms like windmills, her eyes rolling in her dark black head, which bobbed left, right, up, down. Fit to be tied, as a doctor said. And that's what finally happened. She wouldn't be held, pulling free of anyone who tried to stay her swinging arms. I saw Sally Warren coming off Long Wharf to stand in the girl's path but she, too, was pushed aside.

Sally went up the Parade and was back a few minutes later with Cuff Charleston, who was able to slow the girl's babble, but could not make her stand still. Constable Withers, roused from his bed, was there with a rope to bind the mad child's arms to her sides, and lead her up the Parade to the jail.

"Let me have her," Sally said, and Cuff took her part, trying to explain it to Sarah, who went limp in the rope, exhausted, her mind gone missing for a time. Sally got herself in front of Withers, walking backward up the Parade, trying to convince him that in her care, with Cuff's assistance the girl might be returned to usefulness.

"You're mad as she is," Withers said. "You've been warned out. What could you do for her? She belongs to Cormichael."

"Not anymore."

"Who said that?" Withers searched the faces around him, but no one owned the words. The Ram, on his normal schedule in the tavern, should have been there with the rest of us on the scene, taking custody of his slave.

"Where is he?"

Nobody knew, or would say, so the sheriff pulled the girl into the jail, locked her behind the wooden bars, and sent a deputy to the Ram's cliff house to bring him into town. Cuff and Sally sat on the floor outside Sarah's cell, waiting for the girl to revive. I was shamed out of the building as a prying newspaper's voyeur.

But they were ordered out of the jail as well-Cuff and Sally. They came back together the next morning. Between them they'd raised eight pounds colonial for bond. Withers accepted their money on the promise they'd return the girl when the Ram was found.

Southwick accepted my account for the *Mercury*.

We have the unusual case here of a young slave girl whose master has gone missing, or should we say run away. He may answer to "Ram," unless the caller be after recovering an overdue account, in which case the fugitive may answer to nothing at all. He is a stout man of no great height, is apt to blow his nose on his sleeve, and is likely in a green vest with torn pocket from which spills the occasional shred of pipe tobacco. His fingers are shorter than common. Long a stranger to labor, he has spent the best part of an inheritance in the tavern.

This runaway is not swift; being afflicted with gout he favors his left foot. Lacking equilibrium, he cannot keep a seat in the saddle, but may be seen going along a road at a slight list to starboard.

His left-behind chattel, a black child of no means, and off in the head from her various colonial misadventures, wishes it known that she offers no reward for his return. For that matter, she cares not if he ever comes home. If you must capture and bring him to Newport, expect neither cash nor night's lodging, nor even the cost of passage, as the black child has no house or property of her own. She pleads, that if he be secured in one of his Majesty's jails, you leave him there where the food may suit him better than her own.

When I saw it in print, I regretted every word of the conceit, a jest at the black child's expense, and not just because it led to another season of Sally's indifference. I'd never told her the last thing the Ram had said to me.

"Your milkmaid sweeps the Doctor's office too, eh Palmer?"

The Ram was full in my face with the vile insinuation. I'd been in the *Mercury* office watching Southwick remove something "too strong for our readers" from another Everwood letter. With rum on his breath and spittle jumping from a thrust lip, the Ram backed away from my fending arm. As Southwick pushed him out the door, the Ram had the last word: " She isn't just a nigger-lover, she's a nigger thief!"

<>

A body floated to the surface of the harbor beside Taylor's wharf and was gaffed to the deck of a coasting schooner. I ran down to the pier at the first commotion. The corpse, a swollen pasty thing, maybe the Ram, but too mutilated to tell for certain. About the same height and girth. A boot was missing, the bare foot eaten by crabs. They'd eaten a good deal of the face as well. Women and children were turned away as the men fed their own eyes on the horror of decomposition.

I heard one of them say it was Cormichael, and another say it was not, "he never had so much hair." Most thought this a just reward for a despised citizen. Not much was really known about his treatment of the slave girl, so the town passed around a story that suited its prurient suspicion.

Malbone, Jr. carrying on in the ale house what Malbone Senior had practiced in the coffee house as an advocate of passivity, asked

"Why did he own a slave?" answering the question for himself.

"People like me, people like Reverend Stiles, even people like Ramsey Cormichael. "It's a simple right by history and practice." We'd been born to this immutable reality, chained to it by providence and holy writ, and if we drank with him, he said, we admitted our part in his world.

<>

I pressed Cuff Charleston for more of Sarah's story, and Southwick, pleased to think the Ram might be out of his hair forever, was happy to print Cuff's retelling of the slave child's experience in the *Mercury* if he, Southwick, were allowed to edit or revise it.

The story of the slave girl Sarah of Newport as told to Cuff Charleston and related by him to the *Mercury* that we might advise our readers, of her short time in service to a man whose soul, some believe, must have passed on to judgment, having drowned in our harbor.

The child Sarah never really lived with us, sequestered as she was in a cottage on the cliffs. Her brief time in Newport was an imagined hell of ropes and forced duties in the locked rooms of a man, no longer drinking with us. No one in Newport, or all of Rhode Island, claims kin to this unlikely owner of a single slave.

Ramsey Cormichael was consigned to eternal flame by his embarrassed townsmen long before he disappeared. Now with no family or advocate to dispute it we have this account of his behavior as owner of the black child. It's her word as told to the free African Cuff Charleston, and we have no reason to doubt the worthy freedman who speaks five African languages and Portuguese, though you might wonder about the girl's reliability in her present confused condition.

First, it isn't true that the missing Cormichael never worked a day in his life. As a young man, he was ten years before the mast of a coasting sloop, carrying prime timber and mast pine from Portsmouth to Chesapeake Bay shipyards. We have this from the master of a small boatyard here, who remembers the Ram's noisy arrivals in Baltimore, his feats of strength on the receiving piers. That alone, he carried a ten-foot oak beam six-inches square on his shoulder, and once, the raw pine log measured for a clipper's mainmast. This was before an early inheritance turned him to idle dissipation. He was always ready to dispute with anyone in the tavern, though seldom assisted by logic.

More than a year ago he took a notion to buy a slave. When he arrived at the auction corner on Spring Street, and saw the face of a half-clad girl child in the pen, he was determined to have her, no matter the cost, which was 43 pounds Sterling, certainly a record for a black child here in Newport. During her first week in our town the girl said her master did not want her anywhere close to him, afraid of some disease or infection she might carry. He took her off island to a place where they stuck a tiny metal arrow into her shoulder. This contained a poison, she said, which left her with a burning sickness, but did not kill her.

When her master brought her back from the inoculation island, she was very weak, and he suspected she might have some other disease, something an African could survive, but which might kill a white man, this belief encouraged by the interpreter Charleston. Cormichael had bought the girl to do his daily chores, he claimed, but when she went to the cooking corner of his home he would not let her touch anything.

Several weeks later, still shunned by the Ram in his own house, she supposed she was to be sold again. Even when unnamed friends enticed her to run away. She supposed she was to be taken by people who would use her as they pleased. She was taken to the waterside, and carried in the front of a sailing boat to a landing where she was put on a carriage, and then carried on horseback by one stranger after another.

Four days deep into the forest, her journey was stopped by two men with a piece of paper which made her theirs. Her guardian of the moment did not believe it, but a pistol was fired to prove it, and she was given over to them. These men sold her into a hard life with a pelt-trading Indian band, which eventually brought her back to Newport for a five-pound reward.

Again, we're told, the Ram was ruled by fear. Hoping the girl might become useful to him, he brought her into town to buy her a presentable shift, and ease her into compliance. Also to be interviewed by our interpreter Charleston. The session did nothing to relieve his anxiety. Charleston told him that her earlier master on the Providence plantation had infected her with the unmentionable disease. If the Ram forced her impurely he might rot his member, and eventually lose his mind. And the only cure would be a liquid metal, which could turn hard inside him, blocking his daily duty.

There was a second session with Charleston who told Cormichael the girl had a dangerous knowledge of foods, and that mixing the ordinary staples of a kitchen, though harmless on their own, she might concoct a dish that could kill him over time. It could take several months, and the food seem harmless when eaten. She asked Charleston to tell her master this would certainly happen if he misused her. He advised Cormichael to sell the girl rather than risk her presence in his home any longer. It was after that meeting Cormichael locked her in the attic.

She was watching through a slit in the loft's casement panel when a carter drove his wagon to the front of the house and called for the Ram to come to the door with his discards. But it wasn't a carter. There was some shouting, and a struggle. Cormichael was subdued, tied, and carried off in the wagon under a canvas.

Locked in the attic, the slave girl languished, and fell into a faint of unknown length before she was revived by a boy from the Lopez summer cottage.

(Constable Withers asks assistance in identification of the carter, a description of his wagon, and the horse that pulled it. No reward. Ed.)

THIRTEEN

A MENAGERIE

A menagerie is what Southwick had been calling the Warren compound. The word carried a hint of licentious behavior and his disapproval. Sally was out there, and Thrip, plus Castle, and the two mute sawyers. And now young Sarah. Southwick had never been there so his comment could only be based on my loose description of the little boat-yard community. That, and the Ram's earlier insinuations, the last, his mention of the town's milkmaid and her extra duty in the doctor's office. And then words that cut deeper, another sot reminding everyone in the taproom how she used to twist and pull at Chalmer's rope walk. Which is when the Ram had said:

"From the looks of her, she twisted when she should have pulled." The silence in the barroom sent him shamefaced into the street, but calling back over his shoulder, "bad cess to all of you, and Palmer, I hope you fall through the hole in your shit house." He was too drunk for anyone to take a bully's pleasure and further flatten the nose on his face. But was Sally pregnant again, and did the rest of the town know it before me? Was I to be a father despite her precautions? I was eager to congratulate myself.

<>

Thrip had built a connecting room onto the house for the sawyers, supposing the two grunting oafs, his tireless rip and cross-cut engines, would never leave him. The two of them could slice an eight-foot board within a quarter-inch tolerance, end to end. But how did they all manage in such small quarters? I'd never been invited into the house. Two rooms? One upstairs, one down? Three? None of my business Sally made clear, as if I'd asked her 'Does anyone watch you prepare for bed?'

<>

"Have you been out to the Warren menagerie again?" Solomon asked me, just a provocation to spice another day of quiet humiliation under the sights of British cannon in the harbor. General Wallace is demanding a dozen more sheep slaughtered and butchered, two cattle as well, and five hogs, plus two-hundred weight of potatoes at the town wharf for loading on his tender by week's end. Comply, or we'll begin to see the destruction of our town; wharves and warehouses first, then our churches, he says.

A Tory sheep farmer on the North Road, pleased to provision the Royal Navy had his barns burned. With all this going on Southwick had time to bait me with "the Warren menagerie," and "I wouldn't care to live in that jumble."

<>

It was out of the way for young Job to put a hand on my shoulder and ask for a word. There was something to be paid for the gentle touch.

"It's the sense of our Meeting," he said, "that a Friend's business should conform with his principles." He'd put off this moment, he said, longer than was convenient to him, considering one article and another assumed to be the work of my pen. "As well," he said, "thee's been seen at the tavern giving coins to Walter Shifflett."

Hectoring elders in his Meeting had been working on Job's tender conscience. Locked over his lathe, spinning away the hours, forced to work on his Quaker tribe's riddle - how to practice a masterful craft without shame for its ornament. If the turning made a pretty spindle, it must be the product of a force above him. The act could even be purification if it kept his eyes off the accounts. But his trance at the lathe invited other voices warning against sheltering his unchurched tenant who wrote in such a bawdy style.

"Speak plainly, Job," I said. "You're evicting me."

I could have made it harder for him. Hadn't his family sold their finest chests to the perennial governors Ward and Hopkins, and hadn't they both been chosen as patriots to the first Colonial Congress? Instead I shook his hand, and thanked him for his long forbearance.

"Could I have two weeks, I asked. In the meantime, he could tell the Meeting his troubling tenant would be finding other lodging here.

"Oh!" he said. "You'll be staying in Newport? You have other prospects?'

Which brought Southwick's 'living in that jumble' to mind. He must have known what was happening to me, and he too would be wanting a word with me. No hypocrisy there. He'd already told me things would have to change. "Dwindling population and all." And he'd been after me for still reporting the Ram's disappearance "a mystery."

"The whole waterfront must know what happened, and you're in the dark?"

I walked out of the office for a late afternoon inspection of the Thames Street taverns, where the drinking at that hour was more melancholy addiction than pleasure, and any information gathered would be one part reliable and two parts informed by spirits.

The town's philosopher-in-rags Walter Shifflett lay on the ground a few feet from the Pitts Head door, no one to protect him from the constable's boot. His sign lay on the ground beside him.

IF ST. MARK AND ST LUKE CONTRADICT EACH OTHER IT'S ONLY ANOTHER PROOF OF RELIGIOUS TRUTH TO THOSE WHO UNDERSTAND SUCH THINGS.

I leaned over him and asked "where do you live?"

"Two B"

"No, where do you live?"

"Two B," he blurted in my face, annoyed at having to repeat himself. Only later, I learned that Two B was his room number in the Alms House.

"Where do you get these signs?"

"Is it worth a penny?"

"Who writes on them?"

He fell back in a stupor.

Inside the tavern no one had a word to say about Cormichael. All I gathered was: "The Quakers are sending their smart African onto the Rose."

Back at the *Mercury* Southwick was standing in the shop door. "Don't come in here," he said. "You're finished," his mouth twitching, his hand shaking, holding a letter just off the Providence mail packet. It was from a farmer on the Connecticut River who wrote that a cousin in Worcester said the *Newport Mercury* was using a signal in its masthead to help running slaves. Southwick was holding his evidence under my nose.

"God damn you," he said, "go start your own freedom sheet!"

I made no excuse or apology. Cast off, and soon to be forced from my rooms, I was off as I'd arrived, kicking a pebble down the street, on my way to brood in the tavern.

<>

Cuff Charleston was petrified to think of facing the scourge Wallace and his lieutenants, though the Quakers were promising him he'd be safe.

"You're free," Sally told him. "You don't have to go."

She was for him taking refuge in the town jail overnight, then disappearing.

"You don't know free," he said. "Where am I to live? How do I eat if the Quakers don't want me?" Two of the Meeting elders were on the pier, promising he'd be on the Rose for only an hour or less, translating for a raving African pressed on board. The wild man would admit to no English comprehension.

Cuff wanted me there on the wharf as witness when the two marines rowed in to pick him up. I promised to wait for his return. Of course, Sally was there as well. She might have been Cuff's shadow if he'd allowed it.

Yes, she was swollen. I could see that, pushing the bread cart. Cuff's lips were tightened, against her argument. He was about to give himself into the hands of the most powerful tribe of sailors on earth, whose unknown war plan was making a flexible thing of the colonial mind, and whose whimsical anger was an observed truth. Just that week, another splintered dock.

It was only a day after one of Thrip's mute sawyers, the one called Orkum, had gone missing on Goat Island. He'd taken a day away from the boatyard, nursing a petty resentment against his mate, Gummee. From the ferry landing Orkum was seen walking up-island into the trees. He never came back.

"But are you....?"

"Yes," Sally said, "I am."

"And am I....?"

Once more, she rolled her eyes to heaven.

While we waited for Cuff's return, she told me Constable Withers had been out to the boat yard asking her brother about Cormichael. Thrip told him yes, that if the man were dead it would suit him all right, the way the scum talked about his sister; in the meantime, why didn't the Constable go looking for someone worth his time, his man Orkum for instance.

The sailors didn't bring Cuff back that evening as promised. Sally was beside herself, sure now that the Admiralty thought him too valuable to be loose among the Newport mix of rebels and Tories, that they meant to press him into permanent service as their own translator. She was ready to black her face against moonlight, pad oarlocks, and row out in the dark to chop the Rose's cable. Let the bully ship founder on the Point, she said. Cuff could be rescued in the confusion

"Yes? And let them drop a cannon ball on your head?"

We walked together, back and forth along the waterfront, with no destination, I thought.

"You'll soon be sleeping rough, eh?" she asked with honest concern.

At my urging, she returned to her childhood adventures. Intrigued by the story, I hardly noticed she was leading me off the waterfront up through the town to Cuff's lodgings, while revealing more of her and her brother's history.

<>

Escaping from the dishonest Jameson's control, she and Thrip had slogged through rain all the way to New London, hungry, and a sorry sight in muddy clothes; thus lucky, they believed, to be met with uncommon friendliness in a prosperous house on the waterfront. "Just call me Joshua," their new patron told them.

Hearing all about Jameson, Joshua said another letter must be written to the Philadelphia Quaker Benezet about their false guardian. Joshua seemed all heart for the orphans, promising schooling and work to support the siblings, and giving them quarters in his attic. Sally, suspicious of such enthusiasm, woke on their second night in the house to commotion below her dormer window. Two Negroes were being led up from the docks into the house. Before dawn, she watched as they were marched by lantern light back to the waterfront, and onto another boat.

"We can't stay here," she told Thrip. "He's doing the same as Jameson." She feared she and her brother might be sold into some indenture. This time they walked away at night. If they could get out of Connecticut without being seized, maybe they could find their way to the Philadelphia Quakers. Benezet was the name they clung to as haven of last resort.

We'd come to Cuff's quarters. Here Sally pushed free of my attempted embrace, and let herself into the house for the night. She wanted to be close to the town wharf the next day, to watch again for Cuff's return. Never mind what people might think of seeing her walk out of his rooms in the morning.

I ambled back to my own rooms on the point, wondering what next for me.

Back at the town wharf at first light, I found Sally already there. We watched the Rose lower its longboat with four oarsmen and two passengers - Cuff and a larger black man beside him. There were men around us by then cursing Cuff as the Quaker's fancy African who'd just betrayed them, conspiring overnight with the British General. They taunted him as he climbed onto the dock with the big African in tow. He ignored them; they followed him up the pier. Someone threw a stick, hitting him in the back. He never slowed, ignoring me and the pregnant Sally as well. He was late for his class of black children.

<>

Long before I'd been fired, the *Mercury* was receiving a stream of contradictory reports on the movement of troops and frigates. The Admiralty was masterful at this, passing the false and a bit of truth through their fast friends at Trinity or even a reeling sailor tossed out of the alehouse. Whether the jiggered news originated low or high it came through Southwick's door from respectable men and women who had heard for a certainty what was in store for us. And had he heard that....? And just what had he heard? The British fleet had left Boston. No. Troops were moving but the ships still there. No. All were on their way to Newport. No, no sign of any troop movement.

<>

Cuff found me in my rooms, a half-empty bottle of rum in my hand wondering where-to, what brig sailing for what port, and what I'd tell the ship's master that might save me from British chains or a colonial jail. Normally Cuff would take his news to Sally, but she was showing now, and he was nervous to be seen with her.

He said the men rowing him out to the Rose had been pulled from their hammocks for the chore, and were worse than rude, mocking his black face for 'talking white.' On board the Rose, General Wallace had been ingratiating and menacing by turns. He was in his quarters taking rum in his tea, inviting Cuff to sip the same. Wallace called him a decoration on his black continent. Said it was a good thing for him he'd fallen in with the right sort on the island. If it couldn't be the Anglicans, he was well met with the Quakers, who were showing more common sense than the general population. Eh? What did he think?

Getting little reaction, he turned on Cuff, threatening permanent duty on the Rose if he tried any black tricks in the galley. That's where the mad African was chained for cook's chores, and where Cuff was taken to interpret and explain what would happen to the big black if he didn't shape into duty. The man made a sad figure, sprawled on the galley planks, chained to a scupper grill. Beyond him, leaning over the galley sinks, linked together in their own ankle irons a paired revelation, the missing, never-drowned Ram and Thrip's sawyer Orkum, staring daggers all around.

The Lieutenant, there to preside over the interview, kicked at the down figure, ordering him to stand, but the African only shifted to allow the officer past him, as if he'd understood nothing. Cormichael lunged toward Cuff, slashing at him with a paring knife, but was tripped by his ankle chain. Thwarted, he took a swipe at Orkum's leg, and the mute sawyer gave him a vicious kick in the ribs with his free boot.

Cuff feared that neither the Ram nor the mute would ever escape the Admiralty's grip. In fact, that one was apt to kill the other, and the survivor doomed to ride the ocean for life in the British Navy; they'd never be seen on our shores again. To the man sprawled on the deck, Cuff had spoken a mix of Igbu and Portuguese, all nonsense to the Lieutenant, who was eventually convinced of the captive's violent insanity. Cuff translated the strange noises coming from the big African's throat as curses on the ship's timbers. He said the man could not be unbound without risking the lives of those around him. "You'd have to shoot him," Cuff told the Lieutenant.

Before he'd finished interpreting he was ordered to take the African to shore where he'd be the colonists' problem. It wasn't hard to convince General Wallace the man was 'mental.' On shore, he could be a trouble-maker among the remaining Newport slaves, maybe a royal asset.

You could trust Cuff to rattle white confidence until he'd had his way. He brought the faking black off the Rose with him, and Thrip put him right to work in the boat yard, replacing his lost sawyer. His name was Starboard, and he spoke English as well as any black on Aquidneck Island; but only when he felt like it.

<>

Jobless, and the target of men looking for the right moment to capture me, I went cautiously out the shore path for just a word with Sally. I saw Starboard in the saw-pit doing the up-and-down with Gummee, ripping planks out of fir logs, smiling and grunting along with his new partner. Sally wasn't there.

FOURTEEN

TWO FOR THE ROPE

Ezra Stiles seemed oddly pleased that we had something in common now. It would have been cheaper to buy insurance on a slave voyage in 1775 than a policy on either of our lives. We were both on the Admiralty's list of rebels to be taken back to England for hanging when the time was right, I for journalistic sedition; Ezra for his traitorous sermons.

A power balance kept all alert, with enough marines in the road and on the ships to force cooperation with the provender demands, but enough rebels still in residence to make them think twice before walking out with a colonial lady, even ladies attracted to a red coat. Tories and Patriots passed on opposite sides of the road, downcast or glaring.

Stiles was calling himself a "noose Yankee," making light of his danger. He'd already shipped his furniture and library off-island. Then his wife fell ill and slipped backward, all the way to death. I saw him in the tavern, his religious defenses all a-shambles again, divine retribution gone mad. He slapped the bar, and began to massage its mahogany grain.

With his wife dead, Stiles was putting everything worthwhile into the past. The glories of Newport were finished. "It's gone. The paradise of New England is no more," he said. He was still preaching to thirty families. But if Newport was finished, why were Rhode Island troops digging trenches beyond the Point, moving cannon there to cover that end of the harbor?

<>

Southwick was tying up loose ends at the *Mercury*, publishing last-chance notices, even using space to advertise his own discards, things he didn't want to carry off the island when the time came; a complete set of maps of the world, his Seaman's Daily Assistant Manual, sextant tables and a mariner's compass, rectified.

Sally walked into the paper's office the same morning the items were advertised, just ahead of a coasting captain with a new world-wide ambition. She'd already settled with Southwick - a whole pound for the navigation materials. She wouldn't let the pleading captain have them for twice that. They were for Thrip and his sailing pupil Castle.

She made no secret of her pregnancy. Swollen above and below, and walking through town, sash high and shiny black hair floating free. The town, beleaguered as it was, as if a future mouth to feed was a worthy concern, ran yet another warning out notice in the *Mercury,* again calling Sally "a woman of no fixed address," though everyone knew she lived outside the town in that black and white jumble at the Warren boatyard. In Pitts Head Malbone Jr. asked me, "who's the father," as if granting me first claim. "Or do you know?"

Thrip threatened to shoot Southwick if he ever published Sally's name again, then came looking for me. I wouldn't open my door till he threatened to smash it off its hinges. Seeing the half-filled suitcase on my bed, he demanded, "Where the hell are you going?" grabbing the case, spilling clothes across the floor. He threw the case against the wall. "Will it be your child?"

I was picking things up, packing again. He grabbed my collar and said he'd cut my thing off if there was anything more about Sally in the paper.

"Don't work there anymore," I said, pushing past him. "Fired. And evicted from here."

"The hell you say. You're not going anywhere."

He stomped off without another word, but he was back again the next day. I was still in my room brooding, the half-packed case open again on the bed.

"You'll be coming with me," he said. Not an offer, a command.

Clothes gathered, case in hand, I followed him off the Point and through the woods on the shore trail. Thrip's sudden patronage, not to be questioned. I was floating along, my bag no weight at all, half way to the shipyard where Sally Warren lived, when a bullet sang past my ear and a sapling split open beside me. I veered off the path, calling "Get down!"

Thrip never flinched or broke his stride, but over his shoulder asked me,

"Why should I? They're shooting at you. Keep walking. If they wanted to hit you, you'd be dead."

That afternoon I made peace with Thrip, the unlikeliest landlord on the island. I'd be doing the odd chore, he said, sleeping in Orkum's bunk, at least until the missing man returned. Thrip had discussed it with the others, he said. "Never mind that."

The others? Castle? He despised me. Gummee? Couldn't speak. The new man, Starboard? I was nothing to him. The rescued Sarah, whose sights were already fixed on Castle? I'd only be a nuisance to her, an extra place at table for the kitchen duty she'd taken over from Sally. And Sally herself?" She wouldn't want my eye following her around the house. The truth? Thrip wanted my beard in his household to answer his sister's condition. For all his apparent tolerance of her wandering ways, there were limits.

With no second thought I said yes, I'd be pleased to work in his yard and sleep under his roof. Thrip circled my wrist with his thumb and forefinger.

"Never mind," he said. "We'll put some meat on you."

That evening I went back to the Point for the rest of my scant belongs, bedding and a few books, and moved into the room then shared by Gummee and Starboard. I made up the cot beside their stacked bunks, and took a quick bound up the stairs to see the second-floor arrangements.

Sally had a room to herself, narrower of the two upstairs, a peahen pattern on the bedquilt, and hand-glass on the bureau. The adjacent room had a double bed, which must have been shared by Thrip and Castle; bed tables on either side held twin candle stands. On one side, "Cordimer's Principles of Navigation" and a carving in progress, an African head in walnut, resembling the dead ship mate again, a chisel beside it, and chips on the floor. Downstairs, young Sarah had a bunk built into the wall by the fireplace, convenient to kitchen duty.

That evening as Sarah served us turnips in broth, my first meal at their table, Thrip tried to lighten the mood with grog for all. It was no good, no antidote to a dark mood in a full circle, silence all around with baleful glances from Sally to her brother for planting me in the house, and all that might be surmised from my sleeping under the same roof.

I should have known the way to keep her favor would be difficult, living right under her nose. But I walked in, willy nilly, still drunk on the air beside our stone wall as I thought of it, where a flint rock rose above the general margin, the mark of pleasure's retreat when we walked the North Road.

Where Thrip had failed, I tried again with a story of a man who'd come into the *Mercury* office a few days before I was fired, a visionary from Philadelphia. Dead and separated from his body, for a time, he said, leaving the air around him full of angels, good and bad, sometimes circles of sparks across his palm. Among these, his own guardian, green, and an evil one in a circle of sparks.

I held my hand up as the man from Philadelphia had done and Starboard, frightened by my disrespect for spirits in the room, reached across the table and swatted it aside. He went outside, followed by Castle and Sarah. I continued for Sally's benefit, but she, too, excused herself from the table.

<>

After I left the *Mercury* Sol Southwick was telling people I'd tried to push him toward royal appeasement. Such a liar, saving his own face, now that the *Mercury*'s news was tantamount to advertisement of a coming war.

MILITIA LAW REVIVED, FORTY THOUSAND FLINTS AND THIRTY BARRELS OF POWDER ORDERED. NEWPORT CANNONS MOVED TO PROVIDENCE, TO-LET NOTICES DOUBLED, AGENTS LURKING AT POINT JUDITH. PIER AND FERRY HOUSE SOLD AT HALF PURCHASE PRICE.

Southwick pretended the *Mercury* had just learned that French Canadians and six Indian nations had refused to join the King's troops, though I'd reported this weeks before.

In January of 1775 came an eye-witness report of twenty-four British ships -502 guns - in Boston Harbor. Thirty-five hundred men -men and ships whose shifting whereabouts had Newport's full attention. No phantom force this time but a manned armada that might overwhelm the town at any moment. Southwick gave a column to a mutiny of the British 10th Regiment, their stacked rifles to be confiscated. Then carried a correction when the same regiment was seen under arms, marching from Boston to Haverhill.

The *Mercury* said the colony's island commander Babcock had gone too far when he ordered the one remaining Newport cannon be fired at Wallace's three-ship flotilla. Southwick wrote "*He left common sense at the breakfast table.*" He ate those words when the three British ships weighed anchor and set sail on western wind, as if our guns had driven them from the harbor. Narragansett bay was left un-patrolled.

Tory ladies wept as their unprotected husbands scurried out of sight. The colony legislature put the militia's General West in charge of rooting out other loyalists including the pompous Governor Wanton, the one whose face and wig reminded us of a sheep's ass. He was exiled to the farthest corner of the colony.

<>

Gummee and Starboard had been fighting for supremacy at either end of the rip saw with inevitable binding. There was cursing with each counter-tug, a complete halt, with blame thrown back and forth. Thrip's solution was to put me in the pit under Gummee.

With sawdust falling into my sweat-stung eyes, unable to decipher Gummee's mumbling, I nevertheless fell into a rhythm, letting him set the pace. In the middle of this first boatyard test I looked up and there on the edge of the pit was the rest of the crew - Thrip, Castle, Starboard, even Sally - all laughing at my exertion. I thought Thrip might have put me there only to be humiliated, but they all went back to work without comment.

Gummee jumped down with a cup of water for me, then motioned for me to climb up and take the top position. We finished the day trading places intermittently. I was exhausted but found I could survive this. At dinner, all but Sally nodded acknowledgment of my new place among them. She did aim a few words in my direction, said she'd never yet seen a newspaper man who wouldn't carry his knack for exaggeration to the grave. Well, progress, I thought.

“Don’t leave the boatyard,” Thrip said. “Don’t go walking in the woods. Let them think you ran off somewhere.” As if he were harboring a criminal. Most of our provisions were coming down from Providence on the Tall Sally with Castle, a practiced sailor by then, usually making the run himself. There were milk, eggs and pork from a farm on the North Road left for us under the fence by the burying ground. Cuff picked them up when he brought us the paper and town conversation.

With the British force shifting up and down the Coast, one colony’s celebration was another’s misery. Nothing was going to be the same. Wallace and his ships might have left us for a time, but we knew more would be back, that next time an occupying army could spill out of them, and we might all be running for the mainland. Nor was everything settled in the boatyard. I wondered what use I’d be when the sawing stopped, when enough planks were ricked and drying to cover the next hull.

After Thrip launched a fishing boat, he started on a longboat for the spermaceti merchant Rivera. Again, I watched the artful double twist of a new hull, keel to gunwale and stem to stern. With sawing finished for a time, I jumped in when something needed holding in place or took a turn with the augur. I was afraid this make-work couldn’t last.

“If you don’t need me here," I told him, "I could work at the rope yard.” No matter whose boats lay in the harbor there’d always be a market for rope.

“No, “Thrip said, “you’re still alive, and look at the change,” this time wrapping his hand around my forearm, more convincing in his fear for my safety than his estimate of new muscle. Sally told her brother, “he’ll take his ink disease to the grave.” She must have been thinking I could be more useful to the freedom trail if I lived at a distance from her.

Whatever they thought, I knew I was truly sick of meddling in other men’s business, of paying a shilling for a note stolen from a merchant’s rubbish. Tiring of my questions and useless attendance on his work, Thrip relented, sending me into the woods with Starboard to cut crotched timber for another boat’s ribs, a boat that might never be built. “Take a musket.”

<>

Under bed clothes reading by candle light, I came to the lines I’d been hunting for. “A writer’s labors are met with squint-eyed suspicion, idiot wonder, or grinning scorn." I got up, Hazlitt's essay in hand, and carried it upstairs to Sally's room.

"Look here!" I said.

"Be quiet," she told me, pulling me down beside her; pushing the covers aside.

"This is only going to happen once," she said.

"Don't you mean once more."

"What have you got for me?" She blew my candle out.

A few moments later our privacy was invaded by British warships, Cuff burst into the dark house with news of a Royal flotilla blowing up the Sakonnet River on the other side of the island and British troops about to land in force. Cuff had been at the *Mercury* that evening, watching the paper's frantic last hours, Southwick and Jacob dismantling the press, covering it with lard, and digging a hole for the machinery's secret burial in his yard. As if all that could be kept from eyes of royal sympathy.

A day after the King's marines marched into town all the printing works were exhumed. A week later the new British *Mercury* was printing the names of local sedition; Ezra Stiles and I right there along with Southwick, though the editor would be allowed to return 'if he'd surrender to common sense.' His answer was an escape with Jacob to Massachusetts, where they were soon supported in a new shop and publishing under the masthead:

THE NEWPORT MERCURY
Printed in Attleborough. The Original.
Be not deceived by the British imitation

Stiles had moved his household off island on the ferry to Dighton where he found an open pulpit and new followers, thus fewer censorious eyes on Sally. She was a frequent walker into town, but as secretive about her doings there as her brother about the lines of his boats. As the Ram had said, she was doing office chores for a doctor with a surgery on Long Wharf. Sometimes she sat in the tea-house with sisters in league for black freedom, free herself to come and go there, encouraged by Royal marines who were calling to black ears through bull-horns on their ships, "Come to us. We'll sail you to freedom."

As her time came closer, her name floated through the coffee houses and taverns - 'isn't she the doctor's dandle?' linked closer by the day with Benjamin Church, named only a few months earlier as the colonies' Surgeon General; she was clearly partner to someone's fertile fornication. I could only hope it was mine.

Resigned to my presence in the boatyard, she accepted her brother's command that I should have a disguise. I sat stone-still on a make-shift barber stool with her growing cargo pressed against my side. "Eyes front," she said, then out of the blue, she asked, "How can a stolen man steal anything? Whatever he takes is rightfully his." Her scissors pricked my neck. "Hold still," she said, "or I'll cut you again." She tapped the scissors against her belly, her swollen tummy-drum. She picked up a razor took hold of the bit of hair I had left, and began to shave me bald.

"You've a head like one of those Greeks," she said. "Look here," feeling a prominence at my temple. "I doubt there's much I can do about it with all the words stuffed inside.

I whispered back, "If you named me, I'd not deny it."

Her scissors pricked my neck again.

"Did that hurt? She wasn't going to talk about paternity. "Hold still, or I'll cut you again."

I wasn't moving, but fixed on the pressure of her belly against my arm.

"God's sake, man, you don't know me.

"I know everything but what you won't tell. Why don't you finish your story?"

The others - Starboard, Gummee, Castle, Sarah - fascinated by my scalp's transformation, were all there to hear how she and Thrip had fled by night from their would-be guardian in New London, walking all the way to Philadelphia where the Quaker Benezet had fully opened their eyes.

Benezet overwhelmed them with kindness, and news that surprised them. Their friend in New London hadn't been selling freedmen back into chains. His waterside home was a port-of-call on an ocean road to freedom.

Sponsored by Benezet, Thrip was apprenticed to a shipwright in a Philadelphia boatyard, and Sally's lessons in rebellion began. Not with the Bible as text this time. If *Genesis* had been my early rote, hers was Benjamin Lay's *All Slave Keepers*. She, too, knew much of her early lesson by heart. Shaving my head, she was reciting: '*elders keeping slaves, leading more to hell than they will every bring to heaven....* I've cut you, hold still, *whipping Africans, the mark of the beast and number of his name on their foreheads, they govern in iniquity.*'

The history Benezet taught Sally was a sequence of slave revolts from Venezuela to New York, with Jamaica, Antigua, Barbados, Carolina and Virginia between. His heroes became her heroes - Cudjoe, Tacky, Prince Klass, Tomboy, Chalkey - and their martyrs' deaths, hanged, drowned, drawn on the wheel, burned at the stake, and heads cut off and set on poles, to decorate a lane in the islands

Sally said as much hair as she'd cut from my scalp must grow out as side- whiskers and beard, that a bald head alone wouldn't fool anyone.

While face hair grew out to disguise my mouth and jaw, Thrip would keep me at work, hidden in the boathouse, until Tories and the Admiralty might assume I'd fled to the mainland. Thus, restricted to the boathouse, I assumed I'd be fetch-it for the motley crew, given the monkey chores.

But Thrip had other plans for a possible brother-in-law, and I was eager to please him, apprentice all over again, type forgotten, ready to learn the use of tools that smoothed and fashioned wood into floating arks. I looked around at that odd circle of doubting faces.

Sally, affectionate only by fits and starts, was not cruel in her wandering, never dishonest with me, but still the one most apt to tease at my "spelling problem," her definition of any writerly bent. We were all suspects of one sort or another on a British-held island, but I was the one assumed to be most in danger.

Sally had been called out one night by drunken patriots, threatening our compound with torches, calling for Dr. Church's "traitor hooer," to give herself up. Thrip, an old hand at this, straightened their crooked story from his bedroom window, pocking another retreat with scatter shot.

But the British *Mercury* roiled the boatyard and shook the town, publishing Dr. Church's ciphered letter to General Gage, which it said, had "passed through the doctor's whore in Newport to the Admiralty." Any school child who knew one through ten and his ABCs could have solved the simple code, the paper reported, and soon enough General Washington had a reading copy. Church couldn't deny what he'd written:

A continental army may be raised to take Canada.... The view to independence grows more and more general. I wish you to continue writing me in ciphers by way of Newport. Send your letters to an alias, enclose them in a cover to me .... so that I appear a perfect stranger to you.... Sign a fictitious name and send the packet to some confidant in Newport to be delivered to me.... Take every precaution or I perish.

B. Church

"Damn you all" Sally screamed into her potato soup after a troubling visit from Cuff who told us how two Quaker elders in town had asked after her health and her date of delivery, pretending sympathy with her reported link with the British. Did Cuff know, the elders asked, if Sally had passed the coded letter? Then the real purpose of their curiosity: would he inform them of the baby's arrival, and other particulars, its size, and if it might have hair at birth, and the color of the hair, any clue that might point to a father?

"Damn all of you," she said again, looking at her brother, then at me, nodding at each of us in turn in a way that accused us of the same insinuating curiosity, the whole town's interest, not just the spying charge but the coming infant's complexion. Sally walked out that night into a freezing rain; Thrip couldn't stop her. She got all the way to the British patrolled wharves. From my bed, I heard her come in much later. Thrip was waiting up. There was screaming about a torn dress. Thrip damned the one who'd put bruises on her. The screaming gave way to a long groan.

"I'm bleeding," she said.

Their voices fell to a fearful whispering. I heard her say she wanted no doctor, she'd be all right in the morning.

"But wouldn't you tell Palmer?"

"Why?

I rose up on my elbows to hear more clearly

"I mean that's the way it's told."

"What way is that?"

"Well, you've given the man more than a bit of mouth."

"Your mouth's run off with your wits."

"If you're bleeding, won't you get up to your bed? .... And if you'd save his neck, warn him again not to leave the barn or the house, unless it's for the privy. I'm doing what I can for him. He's only spared because I've told the Lieutenant I need him."

"The Lieutenant believed you?"

"Of course not, but he won't cross me till his boat's in the water. Then they'll come for him. They won't bother taking him back to London. They'd rather hang him in the harbor. We'll know then, which way your heart leans."

Sally was screaming. The whole house fell out to her commotion. It wasn't her brother she was screaming at, but a wicked, cramping pain. Sarah helped her up to bed. Introduced again to my fragile existence which had been hanging on his patronage it was hard to hold my tongue. This was the first I'd heard of a Lieutenant or a ship Thrip meant to build for him.

<>

In the morning fog Sarah carried a dead baby in Sally's blood-soaked sheet to the end of our pier and gave the bundle to the outgoing tide. Sally wanted only Sarah tending her next bed-ridden days of mourning, and then no one but Sarah watching over her slow, pale, recovery. She was staying clear of the town, where there'd be no more sympathy for stillborn misery, only scorn for reckless negligence twice over, and the ugly suspicions of bitter souls under British siege.

<>

We should have known my thin disguise and the locked doors we worked behind would be insufficient to keep British irons off my legs. They knew where I was. One day Cuff brought us the report that I need only present myself at the Colony House, home of the new paper, and declare myself reformed. A copy of the *Mercury* in Cuff's hand could have been proof of their sincerity, an inky embarrassment. The new British printer was clearly incompetent.

Whether it was a fool's bait or a traitor's opportunity, I'd never put my head in their laps. For the time, I was happy in labor that relaxed me, work calling only for coordination of hand and eye, and stamina, leaving me proud of hours well spent, smiling into my evening grog, free of all those doubts that plague an introspective life of editorial judgment and composition.

<>

I thought Sally spent an extravagant amount of time with Castle, mothering his complaints - headaches, toothaches, stomach aches- anything that brought her soothing hand to his cheek. And Castle, like a hound with his fill of one hand's stroking, moves on to the next in the room, turned to our other witching presence, the black beauty of the boatyard Sarah. Her affectionate attentions might include her couching warmth beside him on her cot by the hearth, a tea of sassafras or the African-informed potions, root and leaf cures, learned from a black lady on her Providence plantation. It was her hot broth that quickened Sally's pulse and interest in life.

Sally, old enough to be Castle's mother, and Sarah, six years behind him, both treated Castle with familial tenderness, offering affection as a mother and little sister might have done. They fussed without rancor over the shipwright and navigator in training, all under the protective eye of the proud yardmaster Thrip,

Lazing on a balmy Lord's Day with a royal schooner preening on the bay, Sarah and Sally, sat with legs dangling at the end of Thrip's pier. With Castle bare-backed between them I came quietly up behind and saw they were playing naughts and crosses, not with markers but marking Xs and Os with their fingers on the cross-hatched welts on Castle's shoulder. He was naming the winner by his back's sense of their gentle tracing. I, who'd seen the board of play drawn with a whip, backed silently away.

<>

With the town overpopulated with soldiers, and our colonial troops in retreat, a few stealthy patriots remained, along with those wives still keeping house where disobedient husbands had decamped for colonial duty. Newport entering Winter was losing appeal, even for the revived Tories, with frigid air falling from the North and firewood scarce. The British controlled all provisions landing in the bay, save those snuck ashore in some fog shrouded cove.

I was put to work again in the saw pit under Gummee. Thrip said the new planking was only for a trot-line crabber, no matter his client might be a royal provisioner. But we were cutting fir planking four hours daily, accumulating stock for far more than a crabbing boat. When Thrip put Starboard and Castle to work beside us in the pit, more than doubling production it was clearer still there was another commission. The sawing competition only made us happier, as the pile of planking - all ricked to dry- grew with no apparent keel or ribs to carry it.

I was never quite sure if another Tall Sally run up to Providence, with Castle or Thrip at the helm, was an example of the boat's speed or British permission. I knew there was a hidden compartment under the deck for contraband, also that sometimes a lady was brought down the bay for an officer's amusement. I accepted it as a matter of comfortable survival that Thrip played a double game whose final toss would tell his truth. Meanwhile Cuff, whose honest confusion made him a believable figure to all, was a natural go-between. We were ever more dependent on him for a reading of royal tolerance of the boatyard

As an agent of the surviving Quaker community Cuff had the good will of the officer assigned to police our section of the shore. Thrip couldn't keep his barn locked against this Lieutenant Rush. The young officer, informed of Warren's talents, came armed and pugnacious.

"Open the barn, or see your doors shot off the hinges."

Once inside, he circled the floor like a hound marking his territory. Stopping, he looked down at me in the pit, then slowly took in the whole crew. He inspected our stack of drying planks. "Too soft," he said, circling the saw pit for a second time, staring at each of us again. He took Thrip outside along with Cuff, and the rest of us went back to work. From the way Thrip spoke to him, you might have thought he'd never seen the Lieutenant before.

When he came in and closed the doors again it was as if nothing had happened. Sarah and Sally worked on either side of a vise, filing the teeth of a rip saw. Castle and Starboard sharpened chisels while Gummee and I did the long-stroke, the back-and-forth rip, standing over and under a fir log, keeping time to one of Starboard's deep forest chants. Thrip, aware of every stroke, was back at his bench with pen and paper, in deep study of the next hull.

FIFTEEN

GOD SPEED

From that day forward our work had a purpose. Thrip said we were making something unlike anything on the bay. Faster than anything close to its size, a wonder-vessel with a secret beneath it. Our hands would be busy, but our tongues must be still. And all of us knew the project carried the blessing of Rush and his Admiralty. From Thrip's vague description, it might be a secret piece of England's mission in America. Why should Sarah, Castle or Starboard have anything against that? I couldn't blame them. And I was familiar with Sally's indifference

But Thrip? I trusted he was only managing a charade for which he'd be well paid. Any grunting from me, he let me know in a hurry, and I might find myself hanging from any one of the hundred odd yards waiting in the Newport harbor. The Lieutenant's visits after this were only to inspect the work in progress. To see there was firewood sufficient to keep our hands warm and active, though his own soldiers were scavenging for wood everywhere on the island

All materials we required - sails, blocks, fittings - would be provided by Rush. The full insult of his control over our work came with his order that we not use any of the planking we'd been cutting for weeks - not up to his standard. We were told to load these on a barge sent up from town, to be delivered to the Colony House where they'd be cut to stubs for the marines' stoves.

Bad enough as a rebuke to our long labor, but worse to see Thrip's servility, so quickly complying with the requirement that planking for the new vessel would come from fir cut in New Hampshire and shipped down to us from Portsmouth on a tender detailed for the Lieutenant's private chore. And the Admiralty indulged his conceit. You could as well pretend to distinguish the tulip poplar honey of bees in Connecticut from the same trees' honey in Vermont.

Thrip was laying a thirty-five-foot keel but with a difference. Actually, a hollow form to resemble keel and keelson. The sorry sailor of this trick vessel trusting ballast that wasn't there could capsize in the first light squall. We supposed the hollow would be planked over before the Lieutenant's next inspection.

Rush came floating back to our pier a few days later on a barge loaded with his preferred lumber, but listing to the side of a heavier lading, rectangular bars cut from granite. The Lieutenant watched in smug admiration as the stones were laid in the keels' long trough. Once in place, they were covered with the conventional oak keelson. Under the Lieutenant's eye we were building the first weighted keel ever laid on Aquidneck, maybe anywhere in the colonies. A royal secret, but ours to keep by Thrip's order. Everything we did now, he said, would depend on our sealed lips. And the new craft's faring lines would be hidden in the shop until launch day, but that had always been Thrip's way.

My pleasure in labor under Thrip's careful instruction, my ease taking to woodcraft, surprised the others in the yard, even Sally. I was losing my fear of the Lieutenant's regular visits. It seemed we were working at the King's pleasure with Thrip promising Rush we were building a unique craft which, when finished, would outrun and outmaneuver anything on Narragansett, in opposition to all I'd written at the *Mercury*.

In Newport and Providence they were already condemning the treachery. Solomon Southwick for one, who sent a note from Attleborough, via Providence. "What of freedom's fonts now? Who are you serving, Palmer?" If I cared to answer him, and I didn't, I might have told him he didn't know the half of it, though our ready compliance with Rush's orders might be inferred from each nicely curved rib of the new boat.

The Lieutenant supported us in every particular, even fussing over our victualing, with concern about our health. It was his cocksure posing, the certainty of his force's victory over the pathetic colonial militias, that made him odious, that and his flicking tongue punctuating his pronouncements. "You'll finish within six months," and out came the point of the tongue.

He said when this uneven conflict was a silly memory he meant to live here on Aquidneck, "God's seaside haven." Not with me, I understood. No, for Rush I'd be like the Jews, conveniently kept around till Revelation. Then, like them, I'd be sent to hell by way of a rope hung from one of those idle British yards in the harbor. Rush was thinking when this brief unpleasantness was over his model of speed from the region's cleverest shipwright might pass to his personal use as the Admiralty shed its colonial impediment. He saw himself running before the wind in front of all that moved on our bay.

Behind the Lieutenant's back we were calling his craft 'The Mad Rush'; to his face 'God Speed.' Thrip's sketches of the boat were cartoons of naval audacity, drawn while he laughed in his sleeve at Rush's naive enthusiasm. The only specified measurement he meant to keep was the thirty-five-foot length, ten feet longer than the stone filling in its keel.

The Lieutenant kept repeating the phrase minted on his emerald isle, and sworn by as a golden rule of naval architecture; "in like a whale, out like a cod," meaning a seaworthy boat should meet the water with a blunt prow and broad beam before the lines narrowed and tucked for speed. However little relevance this had for the ship Thrip was building.

All proportions followed from the length, guided by Thrip's eye and the sleek lines suggested by his rough sketches. Numbers could only be a nuisance, he told the Lieutenant. He'd rather not be constrained by arbitrary limits, but free to shape the craft as intuition advised. Sheer plan, deck plan, and body plan, all in his head to take shape organically with the obvious bilateral symmetry. "That should be clear to any child. I can't promise you inch, foot or yard," Thrip told him. "You asked for a secret, didn't you? The length will be thirty-five, and the beam less than two of you. Measure the rest as you please when it's floating."

He pulled his drawings away as if even these were more than he cared to share. If Rush wanted to withdraw the commission that was the moment, but keel and keelson were laid, and mold stations in progress. Money had passed, and his recommendation of the Warren yard's exception was on record with his Admiralty. He'd promised them something new.

Rush's pink anger fell away below his collar, he apologized for a windy dyspepsia," and, recovering poise, he began to reassert authority.

"I'm assuming your acquaintance with the work of Edmund Gunter."

No response.

"Mathematician?"

Thrip dropped spittle and rubbed it into the ground with his shoe.

"But we all profit from his contributions, Mr. Warren. The variance in magnetic declination? His scale used in navigation? In calculating the hour? The azimuth? Gunter's quadrant? Surely! Gunter's scale, and the sliding rule that followed? Oughtred's little invention, yes?"

Thrip spat again. The Lieutenant's superior prattle took a confidential turn: "We've not discussed mast or sail. There'll be one secret below, and one above on our ship, Mr. Warren." From Thrip's sketches we'd assumed the boat would be two-masted, a Chesapeake-style clipper with its wheel behind the mizzen. Perhaps not.

Rush began to speak of a boat, which if need be, could be handled by a crew of two, and Thrip seemed intrigued. I wasn't sure from one day to the next whether Thrip was engineering a floating coffin or a craft that could only boost his reputation and the Admiralty's prestige. I'm not sure whether Thrip himself knew.

Rush began to connect the pieces of the pompous lecture, which brought him to "a sliding topsail" that should give his boat a new advantage. He had a little drawing of the way a topmast would slide on a pair of iron rings wrapped around the mainmast. "That's it," he said, taking credit for the invention though it was as unproven as his stone-weighted keel. Not just a proposal; he insisted upon it if the project was to go forward.

Whether a Winged Victory or Rush's sea going coffin I'd never been so eager for the emerging shape of an Everwood essay as for the shape of God Speed's sleek hull, passing from early sketches to rib and planking, forgetting for a time that the enemy was our paymaster and that Rush's bidding might be the Warren yard's shame. No week passed that some patriot slipping past a British cordon didn't fire toward the boat barn.

<>

Cuff Charleston had a standing invitation - call it a command appearance - to dine with General Clinton and several of his lieutenants every Wednesday night at Pitts Head, which the British used as an officers' club, off limits to the regulars and sailors. Cuff was the sieve through which news passed in two directions; a mesh course enough to pass any information critical to our survival.

The General, we were told, delighted in Cuff's company, pleased as a child with a trick pony when he found the man could pun in Portuguese, and trace a word's travel out of eastern Europe across the world - past the Guinea Coast, surviving a variety of spellings, to wash ashore in the colonies. Cuff's lessons might run on till he feared he'd passed the General's patience. For example: Slav, that European race reduced to servility by conquest, moving over land and water.

Sclaue, sklafe, slaue,
Esclavo, escravo, shiavo,
Slave

like a bit of poesy, which he said had been taught him by an Anglican scholar in Charleston, a man from the English university.

"And the word was made flesh!" Cuff reminded the General, as if instructing him from the text of a new-world Bible. "And the flesh was black."

"Oh, this fellow!" Clinton said. "What shall we do with him?"

A thorough novelty to the General that a man of such a searching mind might wear a black skin, and speak in so many tongues. Cuff skirted the General's suspicions, assuring him of a royal-favoring "inner light" that informed the Quakers who now gathered in a house on the Point since their Meeting House had become a barracks. And with Thrip's approval he kept the General alert to the project under way in the Warren boatyard.

Cuff told Thrip, 'he wants to know what depth the vessel will draw before lading.'

"Tell him 'more than a foot and less than a fathom'."

Cuff, wise to the narrow path he trod, wouldn't pass an insult in either direction. He told us about grumbling British regulars with numb feet and fingers, all fed on a dole of onions, and potato broth with their half-pint of grog. They were dismantling wharves for firewood, and already thirty houses had been chopped to kindling, with another destroyed every day. First Congregational had been spared as a barracks; the pews and pulpit of Stiles' Second Congregational had been burned, the door smashed to a carriage-wide opening, and the church turned into a stable, its bell rung every morning for reveille.

In fact all Newport churches were taken for barracks or less dignified uses. Resentment for Tory Anglicans grew to a hatred in full as word of the depredations spread through the hinterland.

SIXTEEN

CONNUBIUM

It wasn't like Sally to ask Cuff what the various church groups left in town were saying about her. "Funny how your name never comes up," he said. Such a lie! Like all mysteries, our remote boatyard carried a mythology which had Sally in the part of a witching and wayward Goddess in a licentious compound. What else did these Newport stragglers have to discuss, the ones who lingered in the frozen town in hopes their presence would prevent the destruction of their homes?

Sally was healthy again, awake to the charged air between her and men whose attention would naturally wander her way, no matter what pose of indifference they took. Like our regular visitor, Lieutenant Rush, who played for her favor with the gift of a novel, as if she could be influenced by a literary trinket. She was kind to a fault with the modest and retreating Cuff, and the black giant Starboard, whose lowered eyes in her presence she met with a gentle hand to his shoulder.

Not as naive as I'd once been, but I could still be whistled away or back again. I'd listen to any song she hummed, and be freshly charmed, though more a pained observer now, suffering to see how she gave her longest glance to young Castle, who was becoming a shipwright complete and Thrip's unlikely navigator in training. At Thrip's coaxing he was memorizing the hidden harbor bottom, along with the shallows and shoals of the bay all the way to Providence. In this way, he was Thrip's proudest accomplishment next to the swift vessels he built, each faster than the last.

Considering his youth, it was hard to credit the ease of Castle's accomplishments, not just ship-craft and navigation skills but carving wood with unusual artistry. By his own calculation he was twenty-three, with Sally forced to admit she had wrinkled past his fancy, though he still welcomed her comforting hands on the little miseries and melancholy informed by his stolen childhood. His whole stolen life for that matter, which had only been returned to him at the sufferance of a guilt-ridden Quaker man, and only so far as the colonial shoreline.

Sally, chastened by her second miscarriage, in a confessional mood, was gradually opening her life to me. She was not the harlot the remaining town people supposed, and not a spy's moll, though a flirting vamp when it served her. The green silk gown she sometimes wore into town was the costume of unconsummated sporting. She tricked herself out for the fantasies of men who might assist the black escapes she managed. And these were not interrupted simply because the English sat in town. Her early story of a husband lost to the throat distemper was a fiction told to excuse her indulgence with a false-hearted man and her swollen arrival in Newport.

More, the foolhardy walk to the harbor on the night of her miscarriage had not been to meet with the accused Doctor Church, recently condemned for treason, but to see another doctor whose surgery she cleaned for free medical attention. She wanted more of the capsules he'd given her against a recurring fever. The bruises she'd come home with that night were not at the doctor's hands, but a drunken sentry, who tried to pull her out of the rain into a warehouse.

No Jezebel, but no saint either. If her intimacies had been color blind, to my eye this was not the permanent stain others considered it. Erased in a moment if she turned my way. Was she really Thrip's sister? Half-sister? No kin at all? She didn't know for certain. Enough for me that they honored each other as full-blood siblings, standing together against adversity, no matter what she did to raise Thrip's eyebrows.

From the days I'd first seen her on the Piety, Sally's real calling had been service to the dark skinned, the most recent arrivals from the African riverbanks, and if her love tended in that direction as well, I'd freed myself from the shock of it. By temperament she wandered; I was resigned that she might never settle.

Thrip's effort to raise me in her eyes was transparent. But if I was coddled, I was also a quick study, not likely to make the same mistake twice. And Thrip would be at my side in a moment, before I could ruin a morning's work with a faulty measurement, or gouge too deep in a downward grain. Sometimes he called Sally's attention to my work, as if to say, look at this, you could do worse than this fellow.

Castle could be left in his own charge, Gummee and Starboard were content in the pit again, while Sally and Sarah were usually at the bench, sharpening saws and chisels, or splitting and rounding locust pegs, both amused with the awkward conceits of the men around them. Reduced by war, we were the only men in their lives, and they took part with a will in our not-so-secret labor for the royal navy.

It was an odd time to feel so complete in the daily circle of life. Breathing the perfume of fir and oak, our clothes smelled sweetly of the work. I was content, even as the destruction of Newport by royal troops spread to outlying orchards laid down for more winter fuel. When we used the privy, we could hear axes sounding in the forest above us and down the coast; everywhere all available firewood scavenged from the land. Not a piece of driftwood left on the whole island's circumference.

We were tucked away from the wasting town in our strange social cocoon, protected by royal sentries along the shore path. "Your little black and white connubium," Sol Southwick sent another scathing note. "Ashamed I ever hired you," warning me of a hard knot of men gathering every day in a Providence tavern with nothing to shoot at, but threats for escaped Africans and their white protectors who had work in this day and time, building a ship for the King's Navy.

The boat was taking shape, stem and stern timbers set to the keel, and mold stations sawn with precision, each station remade several times before Thrip deemed it ready. The craft was wonderfully sleek, even in skeletal form, a water-dart that could ride, crest to crest, over a thirty-foot trough. With narrow beam and short freeboard, you could imagine it heeling to the rail and beyond under its extended mast and sail.

Again I wondered would it be the Lieutenant's coffin, or unmatched speedy clipper? Thrip stared at the work with ambiguous fascination, as if it might actually stand stiff to the wind, but doubting there'd be a broker who'd insure it with all its upper reach of canvas, not even one of those who sold protection on a slave voyage.

<>

There was a small keg of Guinea-proof rum, brought us by Lieutenant Rush on the same barge that carried new wood for the God Speed's ribs. The keg stood by our front door, far from hearth flames. Only Thrip was allowed at the bung, pouring each of us a pint of grog before supper.

The rum made Sally introspective. It had the opposite effect on Sarah, who'd sing love plaints from an African forest to Castle across the table. You could tell the words embarrassed Starboard. They made Castle look away from this rare girl of ebony skin who was taking his heart. There were times when the three blacks left the table, going off for a chat in a mixed tongue, idling along the shore beyond pale-skinned observation.

<>

MEN ARE SO FEEBLE IT'S BETTER
THEY BE LEFT TO THEIR SUPERSTITIONS
THAN TO RUN WITHOUT MORAL REIN

For some months the provocations of the Frenchman Voltaire (see above) have been foisted on that occupied town Newport by the unwitting proxy of an illiterate derelict. This man, camped in the street by tavern or steeple house, is ignorant of the news he carries. A provocateur, once employed by the Mercury, pays the man at the tavern door, knowing full well the fellow has crippled himself with spirits.

I slapped my forehead. It was Voltaire's wit that Walter Shifflett had been carrying from his Alms House to the tavern door. The Frenchman who hid behind irony to avoid his own country's noose might have been my own doubting double if I'd only had his wit. And Southwick could as well have spelled my name outright as Shiflett's source. I had passed Shiflett a few coins, but never the words on his signs.

<>

There came a day when the others could admire the wood I shaped. A curve begun with adze, then fashioned with draw-knife, smooth enough to be furniture, far beyond a boat's necessity. The whole Warren cadre, black and white, took a growing pride in the perfection of the craft we were building.

It was in the middle of these oddly blessed winter weeks that Ezra Stiles made his way to the Warren compound. With British permission, ostensibly on the island on a mission of mercy, assisting a parishioner stranded by age and health, but actually to judge for himself the sin and perfidy of our renegade boatyard.

He'd been told the Warren compound under my influence had become a social experiment and a traitors' camp as well. We were degenerates to scolds like Stiles and the town's late inhabitants; whether we were loyalists in England's sway, or patriots keeping our heads down north of the bay. No matter the extenuation, war and the daily reverberation of British cannons firing on towns as distant as Dighton, there was the mystery of the two-hearted craft under construction, the frigid nights with the imperatives of survival and desire, bringing condemnation on us from all sides.

What alibi could excuse the loss of prudence to passion, that the shivering misery of that winter be healed by one couching warmth and another? Ever since Yale my needling had festered in Stiles. It might bolster his self-esteem if he could witness the shame of a hypocritical traitor, the Everwood puppeteer sleeping in sin while he, Stiles, carried on as upstanding widower patriot.

He showed up at our lunchtime. Thrip locked the boat-barn door against his inspection, but let him in the house to share a bite - dried apple and a loaf of bread with a bit of mold at the crust. The preacher covered the embarrassment with a couplet:

'No matter the bread's gone green
If it sops the laird's poteen.'

"No poteen here," Thrip said. Rum or go thirsty," his charity gone out the door with the rim of spoiled bread. "You take care of him, Cotton, he's your kind for scribbling, isn't he?"

That was true, if Newport had a constant chronicler before the war it was Ezra Stiles. When he left us, and returned to Dighton his report on the boatyard might fill several more pages of his journal. Unless we gave him nothing to write about.

We did make an odd party that day, the learned Reverend and the full Warren menagerie, Gummee and Starboard sulking at the intrusion, Thrip without a word to throw at a dog, and Sally with a shawl covering her face against Stiles' inspection. On the way up to the house, he'd pulled me aside, nodding in her direction.

"What happened?"

"She lost the child in nature's own way."

A stranger party yet when, after eating, the preacher fell into a memorial mood again, predicting a sad end for us with "Newport already in the coffin. We used to have a little republic of letters here," he said. "Curiosity, debate, wandering, seeking." Though he still condemned a drifting faith. As if the privilege to drift and return wasn't the saving grace of his own flock, and what kept the Anglicans stupefied, the plague of the dozen tolerated "superstitions" that prevented any one doctrinal control, and the political control that would have followed.

"I had seventy Africans in my church," Stiles said, trying to raise the others' heads. "I taught the catechism myself."

Sally came out of her shawl. "And where did they sit on Sunday? In your African heaven."

"When I left Newport," he said, "I set my servant free."

"When you left Newport," she said. "You had no more use for him. He could have been a cat turned out in the street. Of course he followed to your new doorstep."

Stiles looked my way again to talk about blasphemy carried through the streets. "You saw this?" He had a copy of the Shifflett notice, but his eyes were moving to Sarah's cot by the hearth, to the staircase, to the bedrooms above. "You people aren't the first to try this, you know?"

"Yes," I said, "Hallowell's in Boston built for the British ten years ago." The Sultana, a small schooner for coastal chasing. 'A turtle,' in Thrip's opinion, when it showed itself on Narragansett.

"I don't mean the boatyard," Stiles said. "I mean what goes on in the house? Where's the privacy for the women?"

"We hang a sheet for Saturday bathing," I told him.

"A connubium?" he mused. "More like a fornicatium," then shifting from pastor to patriot, "The British won't win. They're corrupt in court and Parliament. They don't know this country. They'll be snipe in red plumage for any colonial fowling piece."

"And what are the colonial corruptions?" Sally asked.

"I could only guess at yours, Miss Warren."

Thrip came out of his seat, but Stiles was already moving to leave.

You couldn't explain to a man like him the balance between prudence and passion in a heartless winter. He'd only be guessing at what he missed - Sally's invitations to bedded comfort, even in broad daylight And Sarah the same. Sometimes the two of them couched together. The grunting urgency from the fully dressed inhabitants with all candles snuffed and the fender gone dark, when the slide of stockings on the stairway might be confused with the rustle of mice as anxious to share a ball of wool under the stairs with sisters and cousins, gray or brown as we were to nestle in a bed's warmth beside another body of any sex or color.

On close inspection, the detail of our nights would recede from scandal into a dull anthropology of fellowship and survival in a frigid house. No way Stiles could imagine, much less forgive Thrip accepting the swarthy Starboard upstairs into his bed, bundling with the huge African, making a pair of leather-covered nesting spoons in their britches and vests. Leaving Gummee an extra blanket in the side room where he rolled himself into a woolen log.

The night-shift in the house was not discussed, hidden by winter dark and a natural discretion. Though Thrip's example licensed the rest of us in any direction we might choose. Sally despite her natural attraction to Castle was not selfish. She saw that Sarah and the boy had bonded in love. She touched him only if he came to her for attention, and only in front of the girl who, if she was worried, could still smile on the restrained affection.

<>

In the middle of that winter Cuff brought us news that Voltaire's witless messenger Walter Shifflett had been murdered, shot down on the lawn in front of Trinity Church. Two British marines fifty yards below him on Thames Street, wagering which would be first to put a musket ball through his sign, had found his head instead. No courts martial for their whimsy. Defending the faith against another sly blasphemy, their only reprimand - “you will take his body to the paupers’ graveyard.”

Prescience Townsend came wandering into the boatyard and found me alone. Tears poured down her cheeks as she took my hand and led me into the woods. I thought she’d left Newport weeks earlier for Philadelphia. No, she’d been staying away from her family, living in a cabin on the Malbone estate.

Nothing, she said, could excuse what she’d done. She’d made Shiflett’s signs, all that French blasphemy, and he’d carried them in return for her regular delivery of soup to the Alms House. She'd hoped I'd pay more attention, that the *Mercury*, with my prodding, might have seen a usefulness in exposing religious hypocrisy. She faced me, put a hand on my shoulder, her eyes questing. I only stared at the ground. She pushed herself away, gathered self-respect, and said, “your woman makes quite a spectacle of herself,” before turning away for town.

<>

On a Lord’s day Thrip had gone off with his sister to the Quaker farm, which favored us with a weekly ration of eggs. Starboard and Gummee were in the neighboring cove, crabbing for our supper. I was upstairs on Sally’s bed with my head in a book, pretending I was the fictional Rory Random seeking the favor of a lover, when Sarah and Castle entered below. Sarah was whispering. Castle was brimming with Starboard’s account of an island where white and black took what they could from the sea for a shared livelihood. A fantasy island, I supposed, a bedtime dream for the young sweet-mates.

Castle called up the stairs, “Anyone here?”

I lay silent, not thinking to spy, only to continue reading without interruption. In that house, even the blind could not help spying, the way sound traveled up the unfinished stairway and bounced off the walls. I lay back, more roused by Rory Random’s romantic predicament, than the tryst below.

I hadn’t thought to watch, though it would have been easy enough to see them between the floor boards. I could hear their happy battle in a game of Warri, the rattle of acorns being moved along a board of nesting divots. Groans and laughter as the game progressed. “That’s my place,” Castle complained, “You can’t stay there.”

“I don’t like playing this,” Sarah said.” I don’t like to think against you. Do you know the stars yet?”

“Why you worry me with that? Don’t be my worry. I’m happy with you. I’m happy with this.”

Sarah laughed, and I heard the acorns spill to the floor, then the murmurs of a match that could not be played on a game board. I wished myself away, as if my reading could pull me back into a novel's world. A short while later Castle came bounding up the stairs. Through the door he could see my feet at the end of Sally’s bed.

“The Palmer man's lying here,” he called back to Sarah.

"What? He dead?"

<>

The next time Sally licensed a night upstairs with an evening hand to my arm, I left my bunk after Starboard had climbed the stairs to Thrip’s room, and after sounds of sleep came from Gummee’s wool cocoon. Light-footing up the steps I found Sally shivering like a shaven puppy.

“What were you waiting for?” she asked

“For the rest to fall asleep.”

“This isn’t a secret,” she said as I fumbled with my buttons.

“What are you doing? No,” she said. And I understood that my fastened trousers would be part of the night’s contract enforced by the wool sheet, which she wrapped around me as I stood beside the bed. Fallen onto her straw tick, with arms mummified, I could be used as a full-body warming-pan with no wandering hands. And in my turn, I was warmed by the one I coveted. For a season the frigid air in that house held us all in a companionable grip, but as one season folds into the next, and habits shift with the heart’s inclination, our house could not be held to the first pattern drawn on it.

SEVENTEEN

EBONY SALUTE

The skeleton of the boat we were calling The Mad Rush in honor of the Lieutenant progressed over the keel, and once again drew his approving eye to its graceful naked line. Pliant strips fastened at the molding stations began to show the shape of the boat; you could imagine the full beauty of the hull-in-waiting. No undue haste; we're on our own schedule Thrip says, stretching the Lieutenant's patience. "Imagine we're making a great big violin."

The ribs were each a labor of love; over-lapped timbers of oak pegged together, spaced every foot and a half, six pieces each, all chosen for grain that would follow the hull's curve. Each rib bolted to the keelson at the base. And the longer this unnecessary precision took, the more Thrip asked in payment from the Admiralty.

He led us by example. Though he praised my work in front of Sally, he criticized when he had me alone: "A printer still. You'll have my sister pulling splinters all night." But the further the *Mercury* receded into my past the more I was accepted by the crew, if still skeptical of my previous employment. Like most of the world they believed a printer's font was only an unsolved anagram waiting for the Devil's arrangement.

I spoke less and listened more, and Thrip boasted of my progress. "You'd think he'd been born on an island." But if I became too confident, he was just as likely to say 'You'd best go back to spelling.'

<>

When Lieutenant Rush came next to the Warren yard the dark mound under our privy seat stood up, an inverted frozen cone, the point rising to threaten his ease. He promised to send the Admiralty's honey-wagon to carry off the muck, but no horse or wagon could reach our yard;

all trade came and went on boat or barge. He was piqued; still no planking on God Speed.

He came again a week later and saw The Tall Sally, dashing back and forth off our pier, reefed for a stiff breeze coming off the west bank. Only Thrip had the Admiralty's permission to sail the bay at will in return for his service delivering the lady from Providence paid to divert General Clinton.

"Is that your African out there in your boat?"

The next time he looked the Tall Sally had put the north end of Prudence Island behind her. If the British cruiser behind continued on the same course, it would soon be hard aground. Forced to tack, it came about, standing to the South.

"If you can't win," Thrip told him, "you pretend you weren't in the race," reminding the Lieutenant of the speed still sitting on the blocks in the boat barn. But the ship was confoundedly bare of ribs again. Thrip hadn't liked the shape of what had already taken months to produce. If Rush wanted the fastest thing on the bay he'd have to be patient.

<>

With the Admiralty still promising freedom to any black who'd run from a rebellious patriot and join the royal cause, we were woken one night by Cuff and a Quaker's slave who was, in fact running to freedom, not to the British who would press him into service, but to Northampton Mass. along Sally's freedom trail.

Unspooled from my confining blanket, I was downstairs with the rest of the household when Thrip opened the door to the unexpected visitors. There was a hurry to get the runaway stowed under The Tall Sally's deck before a British chasing party might come after him. They'd been promised the boy would report for duty on one of their brigs. The same night two of their marines were lured ashore by a false call for freedom from Brenton's Point.

The marines were taken prisoner, and already off the island as a British frigate and her tenders circled Conanicut, raking it with fire, burning Fort and barracks. There were flames on all sides when the enraged General Wallace took his ships to Prudence Island and set fire to the houses there. He sent ashore the names of forty English ships that would arrive in the Spring. 'Take that to your assembly in Providence,' he wrote.

<>

We'd had the Lieutenant's commission for nine months, making progress by calculated fits and starts. One week Thrip showed Lieutenant Rush stem and stern posts, and three finished ribs. The next, the stem had been removed and ribs lain flat, all labor stopped while Thrip made further calculations. When Rush came again and saw no ribs in place and Thrip still fussing over the boat's lines he walked out of the boat barn, consulted with an aide beyond our hearing, and returned to say that since nothing was happening, some of us might be better employed on the flag ship in the harbor. "Maybe you noticed Mr. Charleston hasn't been around for a while."

Rush took the chisel out of Castle's hand, ran the blade over his own thumbnail, producing a tiny white spiral. He walked up to me with the well-honed tool, and said, "This could take the hair off your face, Palmer. Or did you think you were fooling someone behind the whiskers? You should be doing your royal duty in the print shop.

Thrip told him 'hands off,' he couldn't spare me. He said the delays had always been with speed, seaworthiness, and Rush's safety in mind. When the Lieutenant left, Thrip gave us a choice; finish the Mad Rush with deliberate progress, or delay past the lieutenant's tolerance, then run off-island to enlist for the colonies. No one chose to leave. We continued in the pay of the enemy. And it was never out of mind that I could be shot by patriots before a royal troop could hang me.

<>

Cuff Charleston's disappearance, his arrest, was only partially the Lieutenant's taunting fiction. Sally ran with open arms to greet Cuff at the boathouse door, and all work stopped as he described the misery in Falmouth, Maine, the houses razed, and colonial craft in the harbor burned to the water line. Cuff had been taken against his will on an armed transport, and shown the devastation, then brought home to Newport to give the news to any blacks still waiting to choose a side.

The marines, instead of razing Newport, the town they slept and mustered in, were only dismantling and burning it piece by piece, their anger building with each act of defiance. And I could see how an insult could be sent up a chain of command by the self-aggrandizing vanity of a junior Lieutenant such as Rush, who might call for the boatyard's destruction.

The Fall of 1777 was a long season of disturbing news always brought to us by Cuff. He was as well informed, Thrip said, "as a Boston barber pole." After a battle at Chad's Ford in September, the Brits were swaggering on their way to take Philadelphia. General Washington attacked Howe's force at Germantown. The British M*ercury* said the French had soured on the colonies, unconvinced of their determination. In October Colonial troops kicked Hessians out of Red Bank. But little to savor in this with the English still holding Philadelphia

All that was all old news when Rush came next with the General we hadn't seen before. Prescott. We could hear the Lieutenant telling him of our progress .... moving ahead .... all mold stations in place, the lines now acceptable to the shipwright... best at his business from Charleston to Falmouth.... you'll get no argument there... we're lucky to have these chaps' cooperation.... accepted the reality of their situation.... on board with us now.

Rush was in Prescott's face with his enthusiasm. We could see how much of his reputation the Lieutenant had invested in the unlikely craft, how far his boredom in America, away from his London ladies, had taken him-beyond caution, encouraging Warren's risky reach, though explained to the General as "stability with unmatched speed, the sliding top-sail, the hidden ballast!"

"A figurehead of course."

"Not one of those to make a sailor stiff. Robed below the bosom I should say."

Such a laugh they had before the General left.

"About the figurehead," Rush said, "I want something a midshipman could salute, and a clergyman admire."

Castle was the sculpting talent in the yard. A little studio was arranged for him, that is to say a curtain was drawn across a back corner of the barn for artistic privacy, and for an hour or more each day he worked behind it. Thrip had given him a big black piece of wood from South America to carve. At dusk, he draped his carving under canvas, emerging from his curtain with raised fist and chisel.

Sally was the compound's barber by default with no training, but a sharp pair of scissors and a curry comb occasionally dropped into boiling water against an outbreak of impetigo. She had a sweet eagerness to groom us all. Castle, who came to the boatyard with a full kinky bush, was coaxed to an early cut down to near baldness, and Sarah, in solidarity with him, asked Sally for the same.

For Gummee, bald early, there was no choice. Starboard, who kept a monk's silence if a hand signal would do, pointed to the first joint of a finger, and Sally kept him trimmed back to his inch of wooly white. Her own shiny black hair, was washed weekly over the fireside tub, a dripping, immodest spectacle hanging below her shoulders, to be dried at the hearth.

Thrip was "a shaggy beast from North China" in her opinion, with hair gone wild to prove his indifference to the manners of the occupation force. The pointless disguise of my shorn scalp was long past. With hair grown back I was always content to have her fingers in it.

<>

Our mystery craft Christened God Speed began to show the full daring of Thrip's imagination, the remarkable stretch of hull measured against the narrow beam, the sleek twist of the hull above the water-line, from the tight V at the prow graded back to flat bottom amidships, more suggestive of a wave-coursing arrow than any sailing vessel Narragansett had ever seen.

Castle and I, trusted with the shop's two augers, were put to drilling through the planking into ribs for the binding pegs and nothing would do but an exact right-angle to the hull, and a perfectly shaped round of locust to fit the hole, then hammered tight and sawn flush until the white fir boards appeared to have an orderly case of locust measles.

<>

As the wind warmed, and February gave way to an early Spring, the geese flew again over the Sakonnet channel, a signal of the earth's turning. I was released one night from my spooled sheet, allowed again to explore my bed-mate's soft surface. It happened not with a spoken word, or even a murmur, more like Sally's own slow turning to a natural compass, and a coupling of incidental convenience; then, a recognition of new compatibility, and a long-postponed contentment. The pleasure turned into narcotic habit. In the after-mist of another day's labor, and another night's gentle invitation, I might drift into a dream of the curve of the God Speed's own bosom, the once rough-cut fir tamed to a complaisant and ready smoothness by a gratified hand.

<>

Knees had been cut for the cross timbers, and the deck was laid forward to the mast partners when Cuff came with the astonishing report that a squad of colonials had got past British guard boats and snatched General Prescott from his headquarters on the west side of the island. Without the general's support, we didn't know if Lieutenant Rush's orders would be sufficient to keep God Speed on the blocks and moving to completion.

Without his supplies, our craft would remain a queer duck, mired in its staging, with no tackle, iron fittings, mainmast, the mysterious sliding top-mast, or suit of sails. But Thrip cut and fitted the rudder and tiller, and we built a cabin forward of the mast station. Soon enough Rush returned, more anxious than ever for progress.

There was no stinting in his response to Thrip's requests-oakum, blocks, cordage, and the tall pine from which we'd shape the main mast and sliding gaff. The mast itself to be as long as the deck, and the sliding piece another dozen feet above it. We could hardly imagine how overpowering the coming expanse of sail would appear when raised over the narrow-beamed hull, but every so often Thrip would leave his work on the rudder to pace the length of the mast again, as if he knew the Lieutenant's dream of speed had gone far beyond a shipwright's obligation to caution. For his own peace of mind Thrip ordered a modification.

We'd finished roughing out the mast, when he stepped off its length yet again. He spoke of the hot-blooded horse Indigo; uncut, skittish in the paddock, bred for a wild ride. The stallion had rolled and killed a Kingstown jockey when he had gone to the whip. But a boy from Tiverton rode him to three purses with a loose rein. By analogy we were asked to believe that a tiller in the right hand might keep the Mad Rush over its keel.

We drilled and chiseled a rectangular slot through a short section of the keel. Then built and boxed a stabilizer that could be lowered from the floor of the cabin. The Lieutenant scarcely noticed it on his next inspection, so concerned was he with the progress of his figurehead.

But the figurehead was the last thing on Thrip's mind; Castle' carving still under canvas. While the sails were sewn, there'd be ample time to fashion something, perhaps the Lieutenant's own image.

"Oh, nothing masculine," Rush said modestly, so proud of the bully's bargain he'd made with the Warren yard, procuring another little engine of our destruction at the cost of our colonial honor. His hand moved over the framed ports and hatchway, the rail joints without a wrinkle. He found no flaws.

We planned and rasped the boat's surface until a palm could slide stem to stern without fear of a splinter, Thrip asked the Lieutenant if he wanted sheathing

No, Rush, said, we'll not be planking the God Speed.

I imagined his maiden run at the tiller in a stiff breeze, close enough to our pier that we might pull him out of the water before he chilled past revival, or perhaps it would be too late to save him.

"What color would you say?" The Lieutenant wanted Thrip's opinion. He could get anything from the naval stores on Conanicut, he said. "Yellow, any shade of red, blue, green, white."

"Not on this one!" Thrip told him. "I haven't raised this little clipper for a painted hooer."

"No paint at all?" Rush seemed disappointed.

"Bay simple," Thrip told him, and she'd look the devil's own cousin in a chase for any who'd look up her skirts. For the upper hull, two coats of turpentine that would weather to a pale yellow. That to be set off by a few bands of tar and lampblack, one at the waterline. Below that, a mixture of tallow and sulphur where none but barnacles would be the wiser to her off-white bottom since she'd not show it to anyone. Not yet.

<>

At the supper table, we marveled at Cuff's war reports. Politically we were as separated by gender as the rest of New England; men pugnacious, women practical. But the thing was dragging on with the British armada stacked at the top of the Chesapeake, with seventeen thousand men trained to tight formation, debarked and stalking General Washington, and men-o-war, waiting for favorable wind to sail north and fire on the whole Rhode Island shoreline. But then they'd have nothing left to savor. Was that the logic behind this paralysis? If they burned the whole coast there'd be no stick left to warm them.

Seventeen seventy-seven and already Fall.

The British dallied, the patriot *Mercury* reported, letting the colonial army escape from Philadelphia. By rights they should have beaten our stumbling army and our two-hearted country. But Ezra Stiles had been right; their regulars were becoming vulnerable snipe in red plumage, lost in the thick American forests.

Thrip painted "God Speed" on the transom of the new boat on the Lieutenant's orders. That week I heard the love-couple Castle and Sarah whispering of their future. "You don't know where you be, up or down the chart," Sarah said. "How will you know which way? You be lost." He was explaining to her "at night one star stays home and we keep turning." He didn't know all his numbers yet, but Thrip had taught him tricks with the night pictures Orion and Cassiopeia

"And what if the stars be lost?"

"Let the sail down and sit where we be."

"Lucky you going nowhere," Sarah told him. "You staying right here with me and the English men." Why shouldn't she hope for an English victory if they were the ones promising black freedom.

<>

With three stripes of tar and lamp black around the hull; one just below the scuppers, one at the water line, and one halfway between, God Speed took on the sinister aspect Thrip had predicted for her, "a smuggler's going-out-of-sight boat in devil's dress."

Castle's creation came out from behind his curtain, and we sucked audible air at the black totem he'd carved from a fat pole of ebony, no busty maiden, but another likeness of the slave who'd come with him on the Piety, this time reproduced to a certainty with teeth bared and jaws clenched. The torso, shaped with two sharp nipples and rippling muscle, gave pride to the ebony penis below, unsheathed, gallant in dimension, erect to the vertical limit, flush against abdomen.

Castle stood impassive beside his carving. Thrip said nothing, but set to work on bracing under the bowsprit to carry the bold piece. Once attached, it was covered again with canvas to be concealed till launch. When Rush delivered the suit of sails, he was warned against a premature viewing of the figurehead, which might put bad luck on the ship. He'd wait another week to see his commission in its full glory, sliding down the ways. Passing his palm over the masking canvass he felt only a thick shaft where he'd expected a round handful.

"You've grabbed the wrong end," Thrip told him, saving Castle's surprise for launch day. After dipping in a tub of carbon-dyed water, the sails dried to a dark gray and the Warren boat was finished. Rush's "God Speed" was transformed in our conversation to Thrip's "Gray Ghost," a craft that would disappear against a dark sky long before it fell below the horizon, tricked out for remarkable speed with phantom cloth, and a stabilizer below, though we had secretly removed the ballast of granite from the boxed keelson.

<>

When Cuff Charleston disappeared again Rush told us, "I guess your black genius passed one secret too many." He said Cuff had been taken by a band of traitors who stalked Newport at night and slipped away to the upland with stolen provisions and the occasional prisoner to be delivered to Providence, hostages to be exchanged for patriots held in the Newport jail. The Lieutenant was lying or misinformed.

In fact, Cuff had been taken up by a British spying party at a tavern on the Providence waterfront, put on a coasting schooner and carried down to New York harbor, this time to be translator in the interrogation of another black claiming ignorance of English, but suspected of spying for the colonies. Cuff had been taken to the prison ship Whitby where the hapless Negro would only answer in whispers, and only in that mix of Portuguese and Igbu common to slaves raised from childhood at Cape Castle.

The prison ship was a black hole of depravity as Cuff described it. Through its barred ports you could see shallow graves along the shore, some of them giving bodies back to the shifting tide; and more graves being dug as Cuff's interview went on. It was a long session, completely dishonest in Cuff's translation to the British, and a comedy of mutual loathing.

Death on board the prison ship came at night, the prisoner told him, a panting asphyxiation when the whole population of the ship was locked in the compartment below, wandering in the night like walking ghosts. The dead were brought up in the morning, lowered over the side, and rowed ashore for burial so that more could be pushed down the hatches. Death made room for all. The Captain warned Cuff, a similar ship would be lying in the Newport harbor soon enough.

From my vantage in the boatyard I saw only a portion of the next sea chase, when twelve French ships off Brenton's Neck got by the batteries on Conanicut, and set fire to the remaining British ships in the harbor. We thought we might be rid of Rush, and in possession of our own English prize, our Gray Ghost. But Lord Howe's armada appeared in the bay, layered in flanks, ships behind ships, impossible to count. The French dozen came firing down the straits, escaping to sea, with some of the British disappearing after them. They never engaged, scattered by a storm that washed away what was left of several Newport piers.

That week nine thousand colonial troops camping in Tiverton were ferried onto the north tip of the island, a motley of white, black and Indian, hoping for the support of a French commander who wanted nothing to do with this "flock of ducks in cross-belts." They never made it into Newport. Lieutenant Rush was still our arrogant paymaster.

EIGHTEEN

DO YOU LIKE THE WAY SHE RUNS?

No fog for launch day in mid-May. There was full sun with a light breeze coming off our shore. Rush arrived before noon with several marines in tow. We were months behind his expectation, but right on Thrip's schedule, with odds on the war's outcome close to even by then, and the Lieutenant less cocky. I couldn't tell if he was more amazed by the radical dimensions of the boat, the sky-full of canvas over the arrow-like hull, or the 'stiff African' he discovered under the sprit. Putting a tight face on his anger, he said,

"A stiff nigger, is it? We'll cut that off."

Then maybe a sense of disbelief as his Union Jack climbed the mast, and kept on climbing till, thirty-five feet overhead, it tugged back at the light halyard in his hand. And for the first time he saw the box built over the keel with its retractable stabilizer.

"I thought it was your idea," Thrip said.

Mollified by this shift to his credit, he asked, "These barrels?"

Below deck there were six casks amidships.

"Ballast," Thrip told him.

The Lieutenant kicked at one to try its weight and was satisfied. Most were full of water, though one contained hard tack and salted cod. He ran his fingers over the beaded molding of the glazed cabin windows. He might have been admiring the care lavished on his new bay charger, or considering all the wasted time at his expense.

"Are you ready?" Thrip asked. "Are these men your mates?"

"Would the King try the meal before his cook? No," Rush said, "You run her out. Or let your clever African go. See if he's as smart with the tiller as he is with his chisel. Send him up to the tip of Prudence and back."

Whether out of fear or doubt in his own incompetence, the Lieutenant was walking perfectly into his part. While Castle cowered back toward the house, as if he suspected white men were plotting his place on another fateful voyage.

"Get back here!" Thrip called.

Still playing his part, Castle came slinking back down the path in feigned submission. But Sarah began to cry in genuine fear, throwing her arms around Sally, begging her not to let them send Castle out on the death ship, proof enough for the Lieutenant that his caution had likely been wise. He walked to the end of the pier for another look at the black totem glaring from under the sprit.

"You're going too," he told Thrip.

"No! It's your God Speed now," Thrip said. "If you don't want Castle proving the boat, take her out yourself. She's paid for. She's yours." The boat was riding against the pier, facing directly into the freshening breeze, the sail crackling, daring someone to turn it into the wind.

"All right then," the Lieutenant said, "he'll take the other darkies with him, the young wench and the big boy. What are they worth to you, the three of them? We'll find out."

Sarah ran toward the house. She was yelling some African abuse at the white men, then "He don't take me on the water! No, don't take me!"

Starboard went after her, and she was pulled back to the pier, and lifted onto the boat. She couldn't be made to stay in the cabin but sat forward on the deck, her back against the mast, staring straight ahead, frightened to stone.

Starboard moved to Castle's commands, freeing the lines, then pushing the bow clear before stepping back onto the deck. As wind filled the canvas he tumbled against the cabin. God Speed heeled dangerously, giving a glimpse of her pale bottom before Castle gave her leeway, and she came upright in the breeze.

Starboard bumped his head on the hatch going below to drop the stabilizer. An awkward lurch from the pier turned into a smooth glide out of the cove. She was standing tall against the wind coming over her eastern fore-quarter. A moment later Castle gave her a northern heading. She laid over at a rakish angle, not bucking in the choppy swell, moving smoothly as a pacer. We could see a mustache on the prow.

"Five knots," Thrip guessed, "with the wind at a front quarter. So, what would you say on a broad reach? You'll see in a moment. She'll come about with no stammer."

Instead of doubling back, Castle was falling off the wind, past the northern tip of Prudence Island

"Damn!" the Lieutenant said, suddenly satisfied that the boat was bay-worthy. "Damn!" cursing the Africans for stealing more of the virgin launch.

"Why doesn't he turn back?"

"No luff in his sail." Thrip was admiring the seamanship, not the boat, telling the Lieutenant the boy had advanced beyond his instruction. The boat was proving itself too, his obligation to the Admiralty fulfilled.

"Do you like the way your lady runs?" he asked Rush. She was past the top of Prudence still gliding smoothly when Thrip leaned to Sally's ear and said,

"They're free," as if the three on board hadn't always been off the leash in the Warren yard.

"Why doesn't he turn, damn him?" The Lieutenant knew something was wrong. We could barely make out the gray sail by then, but God Speed was coming about beyond the point. Rush had a glass on her for a minute before she disappeared again, going south and out of sight behind the island.

For a quarter hour, we peeled eyes to the slice of mainland visible between the southern tip of Prudence and north rim of Conanicut, where the boat should appear as she turned toward home. It was taking much too long.

"He's only tacking for sport behind the island," Thrip told the Lieutenant.

No sooner said than God Speed showed her full, gray profile again, between the islands, nothing reefed, heeling to starboard, racing south and soon out of sight. Behind Conanicut, flying her British banner, unopposed.

"They've stolen her!"

"By God!" Thrip said. "I think you're right. The little devil!"

"You bastards!" Rush said.

With the three marines, he went loping back toward the town to give the alarm.

<>

As we learned later, that was a night filled with a navigator's favors. As twilight gave way to a blue-black star-filled firmament, in which the big ladle's far edge made a clear pointer to Polaris. A light wind out of the northeast would require no reefing, but foretold a big swell further out to sea, where I imagined Castle and his crew of two had dropped, hull and mast, below the horizon. Frightening to think he might be holding his rudder to a landfall across the ocean, aimed as best he could at the Guinea coast, tacking on a course east by southeast, on his way home.

No sign of God Speed in the channel. Lieutenant Rush returned to tell us the boat had not turned down the coast, but was seen heading out to sea. Chased, it disappeared in the mist. "That boat could never make it," he said. "And well you knew it."

The boatyard would be put under guard, he said, and we were under house arrest. The charges, treason and theft of a British ship, more than enough to hang all of us. "The woman as well. If any of you run, you'll be shot."

Sally interrupted his promise of the rope, recalling one of the marines who'd come with Rush to inspect the finished boat. "The blond one with the cowlick. Asked me to your next social," she told the Lieutenant.

"If he dances with you," Rush said, "He'll be dancing with a ghost.

Thrip reminded him our privy had never been emptied as he'd promised. "Of course," Thrip said "it was only a gentleman's agreement, nothing a Britisher need bother himself with," and Sally said, "Ask your marine what gown he'd have me wear? Will you be at the dance yourself?"

"I ought to shoot all of you right now," Rush said, promising that when the boy and buck were captured, if they hadn't drowned first, they'd work for the rest of their lives in a navy galley. "You'll never see them again."

There was the dagger flick of his tongue, and he was gone.

<>

Sally retired to her room, and I dared not follow her. She came down a short time later with red eyes and short temper, but it was only to warm her own supper of broth and cress. Shift for yourselves, she told us. She'd known what was afoot, that Castle, Sarah and Starboard would be the first crew, and had been told not to bring God Speed back to the pier. But she never thought they'd head into the ocean. In fact, Thrip had told Castle to run down the Connecticut coast to Fishers Island. There they were supposed to disguise the boat, remove the sliding topsail, and refill the keel with stone ballast. Only to bring the boat home to the Warren yard if the British had been chased for good from the island.

We all knew the boat could turn turtle in the first squall, that the over-hatted craft would capsize in an ordinary mid-Atlantic storm. Sally watched with suspicion as her brother ate, wondering if he'd suspected Castle would steer himself and the others into the wide Atlantic. Even with the best of luck, unlikely that he'd strike the African hump. And worse luck for him if by miracle he made landfall near Cape Castle, the last place to flaunt his black totem or his own black face.

Sally retreated again to her room upstairs with no candle. I had my grog while Thrip poured himself a second and third of the same anesthetic, shorting the water. Gummee's mumbling became the drone to Thrip's tongue-thickened muttering, "thought he had more sense," then "I don't believe it .... he wouldn't do it.... they're fine. Go ahead, man. Tell her they're safe." He was looking at me, pointing at the stairs.

In her pitch-black bedroom Sally was face down in her pillow, still dressed, on top of the bedclothes. We must have lain against each other for a quarter hour or more before she began to unbutton herself. And without a word, she did the same for me. I knew I was not meant to speak of what had happened that afternoon whether there were lies or secrets to be kept or told in the diminished house. But when we were adjusted to a mutual contentment, she gave effort to our coupling.

I don't know where her mind was in that soft struggle; she never spoke my name, but gave herself to my lingering pleasure, then said the most surprising thing. "If you need me again, you can wake me." Content as a nursed infant, I slept straight through the opportunity.

<>

We were barely awake the morning the red-coated deputation came to march us into the General's quarters on Spring Street to answer the Lieutenant's charges, to have our case heard before a makeshift military tribunal. The court's proceedings just a formality, we understood. The gibbet was up and waiting for us at the top of the Parade, and muskets at ready arms, front and back in the hearing room. On the way to our arraignment and trial, both to be accomplished in the same room in the same hour, they marched us past the rebuilt gallows, in case we thought our case was not already settled.

With war's outcome uncertain, we were ready examples to frighten others into a surrender the red coats had not achieved by force. In a gesture of judicial legitimacy, they had thrown some sheep's wool over the head of another lieutenant, and he had appointed a recorder to keep an account of the case.

We were asked, one at a time, for our pleas.

All 'not guilty,' though when it was Sally's turn to answer, she told the wool-headed justice there was a marine, a cow-licked blond boy, a deputy of the accusing Rush on the day of the alleged theft. He was in the room. Could this man be called?

Without objection. Seated as a witness, he turned his pathetic eye on Sally.

What had he seen at the boat yard? What had he heard?

"When the sail was raised," he said, "the shipwright offered the tiller to Lieutenant Rush. But the Lieutenant didn't trust ..."

No, he was told. Not what you thought. Just what you heard. Just what you saw.

"Lieutenant Rush said no, he'd not be first to sail the boat. He told Mr. Warren to send his Africans out on the boat."

Then what?

"The black boy was made to go aboard. And a black girl. Another man as well."

Did they go of their own will?

"No, they argued against it," the testifying marine seemed unaware of the trouble he was making for himself, duty bound to truth with Sally smiling back at him. All this in the recorder's notes before Rush could ask the judge under wool for a deeper understanding of that day, the way he'd been tricked into what seemed at the time like sensible caution.

It seemed beyond miraculous, but our ropes were removed. We walked home along the waterfront, gallows-cheats.

<>

Thrip had a commission for something between a longboat and a small shallop for Jacob Rivera, who was out of sight, somewhere north of Providence, already looking ahead to post-war trade. He wanted something agile to run his local business in candles and spermaceti up and down the bay. Lieutenant Rush, in privy odor, had been called home to England, and we survived on reduced rations while British canons raked other colonial coasts.

If a troop of marines knocks on the boat-house doors, Thrip tells them we're building on speculation that the Admiralty will want this miniature tender with single mast to run between port and the flotilla. When colonials are about, we tell the truth; we're making it in expectation that a little troop transport will be just the thing needed to carry a few patriots up river-mouths to their hidden camps.

<>

Cuff brought us a copy of the new *Providence Gazette*, whose war news was seldom fresh, coming from back issues wherever New England patriots protected type and press long enough to pull a sheet; from clandestine broadsides as far away as Carolina, and reports from stuffy London prints, long past ripe. This one says the British will leave Rhode Island to gather their forces in New York. And, by God, some loose-tongued red-coat in the social hall has told it true. Even as we read the report, we watched the occupying navy sail down the straits and out of Newport, every last British spar and topsail falling out of sight? And the boldest of the Newport Tories went scurrying again, their doors locked in vain, carts loaded in haste, and mounts whipped out the North Road, cheered on their way with:

"Bad cess to you, and thank you for what you've left behind," with a rotten gourd, for a dog-shit scoop hurled at a Tory as he boarded the ferry.

NINETEEN

SAIL AND SPAR

The British regulars had trashed the Colony House, that brick beauty, handiwork of architect Harrison; their fool names and ranks carved into the floors and stairway; walls and furniture gone for firewood. For a time, vengeance could be written with a finger in the smoke-stained hall: A Short Life To You, King George.

The Assembly and Supreme Court were moved for a time into the synagogue. The week of celebration was as well a week of subdued strolling through the sacked town, sometimes with Sally at my side, surveying the damage, the defiled meeting houses, rope-walk burned, stills smashed, shops looted, warehouses emptied, spermaceti barrels spilled onto the floors, patriot farms stripped of stores and livestock, a few alms house tenants wandering like ghosts in the lanes.

Hundreds were forced to off-island foraging, a community of dependents, surviving as they could. Taking strength in the generosity to be found in mutual deprivation, and an instinct to share with the poorhouse vagrants. The Warren boat-yard's livelihood depended for a time on a regular run to Providence in the Tall Sally.

Sally knew I'd scratched a few things on this and that scrap of paper, against my promise of no more journal habit. But she hadn't seen this, my letter that Cuff had passed along to the reborn Providence Gazette.

In the matter of a dispute between Misses Newport and Providence –

As rival sisters chasing the same fortune, your squabble has shamed you both; a display of bite and scratch, which leaves you marked as children. The long struggle between your advocates Ward and Hopkins is over. They work together now in Congress for your mutual survival.

Newport bears shame enough, but figures small beside faithless Providence, whose petticoats, defiled by the British, have since been lifted, without protest, by the eager hands of Browns, Russells, Clarkes and a host of other residents. Given money to build a well-gunned colonial navy and fortifications, these men and dozens more put their congressional gift to a fleet of privateers – sixty-five ships outfitted in the war's first year, all for their own gain. Not a sailor there would leave to join the colonial navy in Narragansett, even if the ships had been built.

Now the Misters Brown and friends complain there was no navy to cover their privateers' escape to sea. Providence, charmed by a life of ease, still favored the war fought for prizes over that fought for liberty. Three hundred thousand pounds Sterling laid at her feet; doubling her treasury in two years. Now she's the Revolution's wealthiest whore.

Another issue of the *Gazette* carried a report from Bristol, England. Sally pulled it from my hand, and read it aloud to Thrip.

Bristol
Mystery Voyage
Brigantine Mary Anne witness to St Elmo's Fire

The Brigantine Mary Anne, out of this port, on her way home from the American coast brings a logbook filled with misery. Not long at sea, her sailors witnessed a corposant of several hours' duration, a fireball moving up and down the mast stays, alternating port and starboard. The vessel's men begged their captain to return to the colonial shore before tragedy befell them.

A day later, in a wild Atlantic storm two sailors fell from a topsail spar to the Mary Anne's deck, dashing their brains. They were buried at sea. The ship's log was to be kept an Admiralty secret, but from marines off the vessel and roaming the Bristol taverns the "Intelligencer" has learned of the savagery of an officer in his treatment of a dozen sailors, who could not reef swiftly enough to save several of the ship's sails. With the storm subsiding, the vessel had just cleared the place called Block Island when the wheel stiffened, and rudder gave no reply. A grappling hook was dropped and belted aft in hopes of clearing the problem, but to no avail.

Two men were then lowered into the sea, and discovered a sail to be fouling the rudder, a tall sheet, a full triangle hanging from, and kept afloat by, a short spar of only a dozen feet. Once freed, the apparatus was pulled aboard, and hung to dry. The canvas, a piece of sea-going mystery, was found to be dark gray. It was cut and re-sewn into two square sheets, which helped to pull the crippled Mary Anne home.

The Admiralty wishes to inform the maritime community of this odd cloth and spar, prays for the souls of the seamen who perished under them, and asks that any with knowledge of a craft carrying such cloth come forward with her name and the names of her crew. It's thought the vessel must have been lost in the same storm that damaged the Mary Anne.

Mariners be warned by the fire balls named for St. Elmo (Ed.)

Sally and Thrip came from the house, stony-faced, passing me on their way down the shore for an argument charged with recrimination. Even thirty yards away and over the wind and slapping water I could hear Sally's anger, if not the words. But Thrip must have convinced her he was as stunned as she was by Castle's disobedience and recklessness. One moment their arms were thrashing the air, and the next, the two of them were locked in each other's commiserating embrace.

Arm in arm they came slowly back, talking of Castle's deception. After Thrip's careful instruction, Castle had broken his promise, as if Thrip's patronage meant nothing to him. The plan had been for him to head for Point Judith under the British flag, dodging any craft that would hail him, then with the Connecticut coast always in sight, dropping the Jack, he should dash west with wind likely at his stern to find the back side of Fishers Island. There he would run back and forth along the island coast until he saw a double flame, twin fires by night, or wait by day for a sailing dory with a black standard running out to meet his gray canvas.

And there, with a compatriot's aid, as arranged by Thrip, they would disguise God Speed in new colors and cloth, and, the three of them remain on the island for the duration. That is, until the British were gone from Rhode Island, and they were free to sail home to Newport. But Castle must have turned God Speed into the wide ocean with a vain notion of final deliverance.

Sally, though she took it hardest at first, did not dwell on the betrayal and predictable shipwreck as heavily as Thrip did. He went about for weeks afterward in a brown study; mumbling his disgust. Cuff, too, the one who should have known more than anyone else about Castle's intention, walked the shore in quiet mourning.

<>

Now French officers want to know all about our fabled boat yard, though Thrip's recent invention likely lies fifty fathoms deep somewhere off Block Island if the report of flotsam is reliable. Who was this cunning devil who made such a fool of the British Lieutenant? And why did men come spying on his work? The French just as curious as the British had been, if well warned against a Warren trap - the comely, inveigling sister, the accomplished black apprentice and his young black queen, the tongue-less grunt and the printer turned shipwright, all of them of doubted allegiance.

July 1780. The French! Fifty-five hundred of them, such a spectacle, remade the damaged town into a New England *ville de plaisir*, a glamorous if tarnished rendezvous. The Frenchmen made a treat for the remaining and returning ladies. As a class, the officers spotless by reputation. And *not effeminate in the least*, according to the Providence paper. Don't be fooled, it said, by the gold piping on their cuffs, their elegant epaulettes, or their rolling vowels. No, they were *as likely a band of human specimens as made anywhere on the planet.*

The sailors were even polite on the wharves. Well, a little polite. And the officers, men of such parts - musicians, philosophers, linguists. Thrip asked why they'd send their best here. But every nation sends its best on the glamorous adventures so critical to promotion.

General Rochambeau himself, quartered in William Vernon's home, spoke a passable Latin with the visiting Reverend Stiles, who'd moved from Deighton to New Haven as president of Yale College. The General's three *marechaux de camp* were resident in the confiscated house of that Tory in sheep's wool headdress, Joseph Wanton, exiled. The three of them in company with Quakeress Polly Lawton, the Redwood daughter, and the

Ellery sisters, all of them with chins high, snubbed Sally Warren as they strolled to greet the Chevalier de Chasteleux, a member of The French Academy.

<>

Cuff Charleston is "the black sphinx of Newport" according to Sol Southwick, back publishing a reborn *Mercury,* though there's many a white-skinned political juggler, men of a dozen faiths, just as cunning, hardly rinsing the British ale from their mugs before the crockery was wet again with the French grape, with a toast to resident *chevaliers*. And why should Cuff swear allegiance; he'd never asked to sail from Africa in the first place.

Deference to all was his way of survival, a habit of manners. Liked, in the main by all, he was balanced like others on the pivot of revolution. His method of evasion was not in a lie sworn, but in a thought withheld. He knew the underside of this new world where there wasn't a man from the heart of Africa or the Guinea coast whose story he couldn't sieve for truth.

When Thrip asked Cuff to go looking for any news of the lost vessel and our black mariners, he suspected Charleston had known more about Castle's intentions than he cared to share. He paid Cuff to take a carriage from Point Judith to New London, and a cutter from there to Fishers island. He was to find a man there who would answer to Zed, and learn why this man had never sent us news, good or bad.

Cuff did find his way to Fishers, learning that Zed had been shot dead in his dory, trying to slice the cable of a British ship in the mouth of the Mystic River. Cuff found friendly company to lodge with while exploring the island, gathering information that led him further off the coast to Block Island.

<>

For a time, I moved out of Sally's bed, not pushed so much as nudged by her fidgeting sweats, her struggle with the image of Castle under the waves. I could see him too, milky eyes staring, as wide as when they fixed me on the Piety as the agent of his torment? Arms and legs dancing, drifting down, past sea creatures gliding clear of his open mouth calling out to Sarah, stripped naked by the thrashing sea, not to be left behind; with Starboard, floating above them, angry, cursing their submission, their marriage wrinkling in brine while he held fast to a wooden rib until his grip failed in a drowsiness that became a final sleep.

<>

Cold again, December. I'm called back to Sally's bed, and not just as a warming pan. Thrip treated this with a reassuring indifference, welcoming my blissed drowsiness into the morning shop where we were putting a sail on a French dory. With all Newport patriotic now, as if there was never a doubt of it, and the French in no great hurry to leave, billeted among such admiring citizens.

But their Admiral de Ternay was dying of typhoid, and a funeral in preparation. Hard to believe how many priests accompany these several thousand soldiers. For the Admiral's funeral Trinity became a Catholic cathedral, full of chanting and smoke with the organ gone into a minor key for a whole day. Sally, corseted beyond comfort, most of her hidden in a black robe, wedged her way into the church, and was brought to tears by the mournful sound of the Latin and the grief of so many handsome boys. While a few Anglicans sniffed at the papist intrusion.

<>

Cuff was away so long we suspected he might have left for good, might have found a likelier home for his talents. But he walked into the boatyard a month later with a story so unlikely he was afraid it would be taken for invention. It had to be told start to finish, he said.

On Fishers Island he'd been met rudely by the agent Zed's widow.

"What's your kind doing here?" she'd asked him. "Aren't all you blacks gone to the British?"

She offered no rest or food, only a tin cup of water while she railed against his awkward arrival. Her husband had been a fool, she said, to get mixed up in the Warren schemes on behalf of the ungrateful race. And now coming so soon to the widow of a man worth a dozen Warrens! No, she assured Cuff, Mr. Warren's Africans had not shown their black faces on Fishers. Wouldn't the whole island know it if they had? She said Cuff would likely be shot if he lingered there, and she couldn't be blamed and wouldn't care.

Her anger, Cuff thought, was not real, but performed to some hidden purpose. Untroubled by her threat, he did lag. He sat on the shore with some fishermen, proving a fair hand mending nets, fabling their imaginations with stories of Newport extravagance, and the tale of a slave boy there who had learned to build boats, and had taken one from his shipyard, and carried his young black lover and another man into the Atlantic, giving their lives to the sea. Had they ever heard of such a thing?

No, but would he stay, they asked, stitching up nets and telling them more in return for bed and board? They kept him for a week on a diet of potato broth and fish stew, eventually delivering him to Block Island on a fishing trip into deeper water. They put him off at night on the island's far shore with some salt cod and a water cup hanging from a loop in his britches. He believed he'd find more cooperation if he looked like a servant on some master's errand rather than strutting his independence and education in such a backward place.

He crossed the island the next morning with the sun at his back, going at a pace not to be stopped or questioned, then turned back from the west shore at an oblique across the island, and found himself in a cove marked "Snake Hole," where he was stopped.

A small angry man stabbing the air with his pipe stem, told him this bit of shore had belonged to his family for four generations, and no nigger or anyone else was welcome there. What did he want? The man was looking behind him, concerned with what Cuff might already have seen.

"Any sign of a lost boat?"

Cuff let the man lead him back across the island to a harbor where a little packet for the mainland was waiting. Aware that submission served his purpose better than resistance he let himself be taken onto the boat for New London. His escort said he was lucky his African ass was still alive. "Look for the whale's jaws, darkie."

"The whale's jaws," the man called again as the packet's mooring lines were thrown aboard. And Cuff answered, "Your mother bore you through her ass hole," once in Ibibio, once in Igbu, and once in Igala. Approaching the wheel, hoping the Captain would speak with him, he was pushed aside. "Stand to the lea. Did they teach you nothing in Newport?"

If Cuff hadn't had a bath for two weeks, the Captain himself stank like an opossum's winter burrow, no improvement on the box of rotting bait fish beside him. Best they all stand to themselves, Cuff decided, each nose accustomed to its own neighborhood. He learned nothing more on the short voyage

<>

In Newport, the bay trembled, the docks and houses shook for a whole minute with the violent thundering cannonade, the French fleet's guns firing in honor of our approaching General Washington, commander of the whole colonial force. I watched from the top of the Parade, a double line of French troops saluting as he came between them from what was left of Long Wharf all the way to the State House, then to the Vernon home to speak with Rochambeau.

Afterward, with houses in spermaceti illumination, on to a ball where the General took the merchant Champlin's daughter for a partner. Our wandering Sally was in the hall, and might have had his hand, but overplayed her reticence. This Washington was not playing parlor games. The lady who came forward first to take his hand would have it. So, the Champlin girl and he danced to applause and fast fiddling.

There was a happy romp and dalliance; more faith promised that night than would ever be honored, because the next day the French troops marched westward, following our Commander Washington out of Newport. The town, drained of excitement, was reminded of the destruction on all sides, not repaired, only decorated for a while by French manners and gallantries.

TWENTY

A CONTINENTAL VICTORY

"Did you learn anything, or didn't you?"

Sally slapped her brother's impatient head, and led Cuff to a chair. She straightened his mussed shirt, and then would not let go of his hand, until he agreed to continue, at whatever pace pleased him.

In New London, he said, he'd been made to show his freedman's papers to three self-appointed deputies as he made his way beside the town's wharves, through back lanes, past rows of dark shops, boarding houses, a sign boasting "ladies of three continents," and several taverns. In one of these the barman pointed him back toward the waterfront. On the way, he found himself standing before a huge open jaw of bleached bone. He passed through the opening under a lettered shingle,

THE WHALE'S BELLEE
Simulacra & Curiosities From The Seven Seas
Bought With Discrimination. Sold With Regret.

The entry was lit with candles mounted on a leviathan's ribs connected by sheets of red canvas forming a tunnel and leading to a turnstile. A bell rang and the head of the proprietor popped up behind a counter. A tomblike salesroom was furnished all around with the advertised simulacra, bones and carved ivory. In a glass cabinet, a shrunken head from the Amazon was marked "Active Spirit." Next to this was a large leaf, insect-eaten to a lacy resemblance of "the face of Jesus."

Three pieces of driftwood, said to be likenesses of Joseph, Mary and Jesus, stood under a shelf holding skeletons of a hyena and various rodents. In another case were burnished puzzle rings of soft metal, and a potato, labeled "pregnant lady," but more like a miniature snowman. A barrel of cowrie shells was marked a shilling per dozen.

The proprietor Canty asked Cuff straightaway, "What do you want? What have you got?"

Turning away, he faced carvings of six Africans with long faces and drooping breasts, and beside these, the rude black pillar, the ebony figurehead, Castle's carving of his murdered mate from the Atlantic passage with tumescent arrow pointing straight up to his chin.

"Not for sale," Canty said. "That was carved by a Benin Prince. I wouldn't tell you what I paid for it."

Cuff could see how carelessly the ebony figure had been removed from the God Speed with a dull saw. How long had he had it? Years, Canty said. Couldn't remember how many.

<>

On his way home, traveling with incoming Tory prints from Philadelphia and New Jersey, on the Point Judith ferry, Cuff read an account of cowardice: French and Colonial Armies giving New York City a wide berth. Hiding or seeking? the correspondent wondered, maybe both. A game soon to be lost by the colonists, the writer predicted, wondering when their motley of sudden-soldiers would go home to porch rockers, and let the world turn its normal round.

Cuff's story of his Connecticut trip brightened Sally's world until Thrip snuffed the fresh light in her eyes. Where she'd seen the God Speed landing on the Connecticut shore intact (how else the extraction of the carving?), Thrip was sure it had washed up, a capsized wreck to be picked over for its fittings, blocks, and a few strips of teak trim. All that and the ebony figurehead, now displayed as an antique carved by a prince.

Thrip still couldn't believe the boy he'd trained with a father's devotion, if alive, would not have returned to his nurturing home, to work again as they'd planned when they plotted his theft of God Speed. Sally, whose affection for Castle began with her tending of his misery under the Piety's deck, nursing him through his quarantine on the smallpox island, and every illness after that, would never accept that he was drowned if it was nothing more than a probability.

<>

She said she might follow Prescience to Philadelphia where the Quaker Benezet had opened a free school for African children. His contrarian papers on African humanity were even upsetting the abolitionists, who maintained the inferiority of the race they meant to set free. She said she dreamed of sailing with Mr. Benezet to the Guinea coast. "Cuff, you come too," beyond the reach of slavers' longboats.

"You are dreaming," Cuff agreed. "You think the African is ready for you? You ask your custom of Africa? Who are you in Benin? Maybe they want to know what makes you so pale, and they cut you open for a look inside. When they finish, they put you back in your boat to show your ordinary heart to the village down the river."

Sally was discouraged in the boatyard, tired of the three men still working there, and the duty of meals, washing and cobweb control. Our night-pleasure was less frequent; she could be pleased by a soft hand on her back, but a full tangle had become a chore and might remain so till the chilly damp of the next winter.

<>

The oddest thing. Sol Southwick has resigned, turned the *Mercury* over to his editor-in-training, Henry Barber, who comes out swinging his editorial fist at Newport remnants of loyalist sentiment. LINGERING KING'S MEN for example, a headline set over a list of thirty names guilty of crimes against freedom; among these, the whole Warren yard.

The aging shop-boy Jacob had been passed over again. After all those years, still the drudge. I suppose it made him feel better, setting his ale down in Pitts Head long enough to tell anyone who'd listen that the new printer had been warned against hiring me back. That I might not be long for the colony.

<>

The French left before they collected their runabout tender we'd been building for them. It sat beside the Tall Sally in the cove where an empty berth reminded us of the missing ghost ship and its crew. Sally would stare at the mooring buoy.

"They're gone," Thrip told her, but Cuff whispered hope in her ear. He thought the Block Islanders were lying to him, hiding something. He thought the lost Africans might be held there against their will. His larger fear was that they didn't want to be found.

He told me, "If they're breathing, they don't want us knowing it." Lost from all knowing of their faces, they wouldn't want to be tangled with Newport again. He was confused. He did think someone might have picked them off floating wreckage, and taken them ashore.

Thrip had no time for this. He wasn't going to Block Island, but Sally, hanging on Cuff's fantasy, was making her own plans. I heard her tell her brother again she was tired of doing the boatyard laundry and ladling our potato broth. Thrip told her, "If you're going, take the Inkfinger with you."

"I'll be taking Cuff," she said. "I don't think the printer would want to go."

"You're not leaving without the Inkfinger," I said.

She laughed and came over to where I was sitting, ruffled my hair, called me a nuisance, reminding me, "on Block Island they walk with their muskets loaded. You'd be a rank stranger there,"

"And you?"

"They don't shoot women. "They take them home and see if they can make gooseberry pie."

Sick of this, Thrip said, "Why don't the three of you take Tall Sally?" as if there were a competent sailor among us. "Maybe turn yourselves across the ocean and find your own way to the bottom."

"There wouldn't be room on Tall Sally to bring all of us home," she said.

"They're under the waves," Thrip told her again.

She took my hand. Pulled me up the path to the North Road to be away from her brother for a while, and to mend "the Inkfinger's" feelings.

<>

Cuff wanted to go with Sally and me. The three of us were preparing our nerves and our kits to travel to the back side of Block Island. We had seats in a coach reserved a week in advance for Providence to New London, when all plans flew to pieces for a time.

Water-born alarms came from north and south, from the two ships of our ragged continental Navy-the Alfred down from Providence, throwing smoke, firing balls into the bay, broadside and swivel; and the Columbus, coming up from the harbor, answering with the thunder of her own guns, all aimed into the water.

A runner came up the shore path warning everyone on his way, move back, everyone to the middle, and that won't be far enough if the huge Liberty's guns were in play. He couldn't tarry, had to get the word all the way to the north end. The entire fleet, every British vessel on the coast was gathering to put themselves broadside to Aquidneck, circling our island, coming to blast every house and living thing to eternity. Their anger was Biblical, indiscriminate. Patriot's home or Tory's wharf, no difference.

Who told him all this?

"Captain Jennings in Pitts Head."

And who told Jennings?

The runner stared at me as at an imbecile, and continued his frantic errand.

<>

A half hour later, Cuff walked into the boat barn and told us the postal carrier said the English had laid down their guns in Virginia. The thing was all but over. A surrender to our Continental General, the one who a few months before had taken the Champlin woman's hand and done a turn around the floor. The Britisher Cornwallis, indisposed in his tent, sent a proxy. England was suing for peace.

Cuff said now you can start fighting among yourselves again. Such a cunning forecaster. You'd think there'd be mayhem, fowling pieces fired in the streets, bonfires, spermaceti flame in every window, and a constable punched up and down the Parade for spoil-sport interference. Nothing of the kind. No armistice had been declared.

There were die-hard Tories still spreading doubt and confusion. If there was revelry in Boston, Philadelphia, New York, the drumbeat was muffled and lost on its way to Newport. On the North Road, there was a cautious procession of carts and carriages returning to what was left of the town after the British had their way with it. Five hundred houses missing, almost everything made of wood gone, only two taverns serving.

Thrip and I stepped into one of them where reverential whispering was the only sound save the occasional interruption of the barman's question. Suspicion in the air. Debts to be paid. Tories and their sympathizers sitting at tables apart from patriots, baleful glances passed both ways, but patriots, the recently converted and the original, puffed with new privilege, now in command of the word "traitor." Newport was preparing for a final accounting. Someone called us "harbor bait," We raised our mugs to our critics on both sides and walked home.

<>

It was settled. We were going to Block Island, Sally, Cuff and I. Thrip carried us across the bay to Point Judith, and from there, we were taking a public coach down the coast. In Wakefield we were told there was no service from New London to Block Island; we'd have done better to take our own vessel straight from Newport. Further along, in Westerly, a deputy climbed into our coach, on his way to help New London sort a dispute there, which had spread to Fishers and Block Islands. In Mystic we passed a sign tacked on a tree beside the coach road. "Travel to Fishers and Block Island not advised."

Before Groton the lawman traveling with us wanted to see Cuff's papers, and was told in Igbu, along with a mimed deference, that his ignorance was the most interesting part of our journey so far. For this he thanked Cuff and, convinced of our respect, told us what we could expect to find in New London and the islands. "The actual state of affairs."

There had been the betrayal of Thrip's contact Zed on Fishers. Shot while cutting the cable of the British ship lying off New London. A feud had spread to the New London docks. The wife and son of the dead man, both ready with pistols. Patriots on the near side of Block, and loyalist fishermen on the back, at war on sea and land. You couldn't go to Block Island in a neutral way. Choose a side, front or back, we were told. "Either way, you won't be welcome." After thirty years of French, Indians, British, pirates - all using the island to their advantage - plunder or sanctuary, why would they trust anyone?"

<>

First thing in New London, we sat for an hour in a coffee house, ears cocked for talk that might instruct us. We were watched but not spoken to. Weary of a sailor's talk about his infected leg, Sally was impatient to see the ebony figurehead. She persuaded Cuff to take us to the Whale's Bellee, where the trader Canty met us behind the entrance jaws.

"It's gone," he said. "Sold."

In the ebony figure's place was a conventional ship's lady, golden haired and bare-bosomed with rouged lips. Canty was offering her at a loss, the sooner to be rid of her. She was an embarrassment, he said, to the customers, who preferred to see how nature had drawn the image of Jesus on a leaf or the bark of a sycamore.

Back at the waterfront we asked which ferry would take us to the back side of Block Island.

"Tomorrow's run from Stevens dock. Not the death-rigged piece tying at Moore's pier. Unless you're in hurry to drown or be shot. Keep your head down if you ride with the young black."

"That must be him. I knew it. I knew it." Sally was beside herself. She led us along the waterfront, then found rooms for the night, but was far too excited to sleep.

All the next day, we walked up and down the seaside avenue, saw a double-ender come in to the Stevens mooring at noon, discharge two, and take on four returning to Fishers. But nothing landing at Moore's. Nor the following day. Cuff thought someone had got word to the back side of the island that we were waiting for their craft to come in; they were avoiding this harbor till we were gone.

On the third day, we were careless in the morning, rising at eight, and taking an hour in the coffee shop, then ambling the waterfront, looking to hire a fishing boat to carry us out to Block Island. We were going dock-by-dock, refused everywhere with silence or mumbled profanity as if we were asking them to poke a stick in a wasps' nest.

We turned around at the far end of the waterfront and saw behind us a long mast over a narrow hull. Loping back, we found ourselves looking down at God Speed! The boat had been painted green with three red stripes where the black had been. We could see how the figurehead had been sawn away. I called from the dock, and followed Sally onto the boat.

No one aboard. No doubt of it; this was the vessel with boxed stabilizer. The mast was new, no longer with the sliding tip. The mainsail was reefed, the jib spilled and gathered on the deck. In the cabin, bedding was tossed to one side. A few dishes, spoons, and forks were wedged against the wall opposite a tin cup and paring knife. Some clothes were thrown forward.

Sally wouldn't leave. Cuff and I went for cheese and a loaf. We were back, and the three of us eating our lunch when they came into sight on the pier! Our elation turned into the saddest thing. Castle and Sarah, arm in arm, coming toward us when they looked up, and that quickly went slinking away, like children caught at mischief. Twice they looked over their shoulders to see if we were following, then turned up into an alley, out of sight. I could only see guilt and shame in the way they moved, as if we'd come to take back the boat we might accuse them of stealing.

Sally was going after them but Cuff called her back.

"They don't want to see you" he said. Aren't you satisfied?"

The questions slowed and stopped her. She turned and called him "heartless bastard." He said something in one of his other languages, then translated for us: "I may be a bastard, and you might be one too." She came back onto the boat and put her arms around him. There was a long, tearful discussion, and she agreed to return with me to Newport if Cuff would stay on for a time to learn more about the pair she considered her children.

"Not for my sake," he said. "For yours," he told her. "And his," pointing at me.

Whatever he meant by that, we left him sitting on the God Speed's cabin floor on the missing couple's bed clothes, waiting to surprise them if they returned. That afternoon Sally and I were in a coach for Westerly, and the next day for Point Judith, where we took the Newport ferry.

<>

At the boatyard Thrip had company, Prescience Townsend. He froze when Sally, crossing the threshold, told him,

"They're alive. They're on the boat!"

He was trying to show no emotion, turning away, covering his face, clearly dumbfounded, then shifting the subject,

"Can't you say hello? Miss Townsend didn't come all this way to speak to me."

Not to bring us poetry, either. "Leaving poetry to the poets," she said.

But yes, she'd have a word with Sally if she could. The two of them went off on the shore path for a conversation. She'd moved to Philadelphia after all, a place, she told Sally, where an independent woman didn't lack for variety, a place where there were still some Quakers who lived the creed in full.

They came back to the house and Prescience was no easier on her Newport cousins than before; the ones, she said, who finished their cabinets with more care than they finished their children; sixteen sired by John Goddard, thirteen by Job Townsend Senior. Prescience was reborn in a service that could best be practiced in Philadelphia.

TWENTY-ONE

IS HE A TRAITOR? IS HE A JEW?

Leaving Sally and Prescience to their Philadelphia chatter, I was in the ale house with Thrip again. Better to show no fear of the town than cower in the boatyard, waiting for the victors' new authority to proceed against us. William Ellery was there glaring, to see us still walking free; Samuel Hopkins of First Congregational sitting with him, holding his abolitionist tongue in that company, along with two Sabbatarians.

The former Constable Withers was there too, no longer serving because Newport had no money to pay him. Several mariners with no ship and no coin stood at the bar nursing the last inch of ale in their mugs, waiting for one of the sitting gentlemen to pay for another round.

Of all things, they were lamenting the loss of Newport's Jews, not the social loss, but the blow to Newport commerce. In particular, the man whose circumcision had been delayed until he found freedom in Newport when he'd changed his name from Don Duarte to Aaron Lopez. They were marveling at this man who came with nothing in 1750, and twenty years later owned 30 ships, with an interest in 50 more. There were sidelong glances at me.

Also lamented, Moses Hays, driven here by the Lisbon flood. He'd refused the Patriots' loyalty oath until the Christian imperative was deleted. Why were the tavern eyes turned on me? Only six families of our eleven hundred Jews left; the ambitious of the next generation had left our struggling port for New York, Boston, or Charleston, and William Ellery chuckled at his conceit: "We could have better lost a better sort." Not quite original.

"We've still got the mahogany polishers," a toper said.

"But not John Townsend. He's in jail."

"Give over."

We went home to tell the visiting Prescience her cousin John, town treasurer since the French occupation, viewer of lumber, a pillar of the Newport Meeting, master craftsman, who built the Governor's furniture, was rumored in the jail meant to be holding us, the Warren yard traitors.

"Yes, he is in jail," she said. But the cell wasn't locked and there was no jailer. "He could walk out anytime. Another Quaker mule," she said. As town treasurer, doing time in payment of the town's debt to a man from Exeter, suing. If our insolvent town raised the man's money, John would walk out, his sworn duty done; Newport made honorable by an honorable man.

"An ass," Prescience said. "Wouldn't come out for an hour to buy me supper."

She was really here to pull Sally with her to Philadelphia, full of the saintly ways of Anthony Benezet, the abolitionist in home spun who, she says, won't eat the flesh of any animal, nor accept the service of any bound man. Prescience had been in his sway in Philadelphia, assisting at the Free School. Mistreatment of any living thing brought him to tears, or anger. Even mice and rats deserved grace.

"I hesitate to tell you," Prescience said.

Sally tugged at her arm.

"Well, he found a mouse in a little pillory on his desk, with a sign in tiny script written by one of his students: 'I stand here for stealing cheese and candle ends.' He set the mouse free in his pantry."

<>

Solomon Southwick, still in town, shepherding the *Mercury*'s transition, encouraged the new editor Barber to go after the scoundrels as the Rhode Island Assembly and a town loyalty commission sorted heroes and villains - the patriots, active and passive; the indifferent; loyalists, traitors, spies, men with blood on their hands. The worst should be hanged or exiled, and their property confiscated. Those super patriots Vernon and Ellery had the backing of the whole patriot-pure town this time, making certain that the Inkfinger and the whole Warren yard were on a list for trial.

Threatened so many times, you might think I had no fear of a rope. But it was different before, when supporters were scattered among my antagonists. This time, our country, our colony, our town, thoroughly transformed into once and future patriots. Those men who had lost their livelihoods could easily be turned to violence. Who'd side with a wandering printer working in a boatyard? Sally too, was marked for the courtroom, the woman of no fixed address, two lost pregnancies, and a head uncovered.

<>

Cuff came home holding a journal of his time in New London and the nearby islands, waving it in front of me like the book of salvation – ours. His story began with the return of Castle and Sarah to the boat, and his waking on the cabin floor to see Castle holding a rusty paring knife. Cuff could hear water lapping against the hull, as they went gliding away from the New London dock.

After a brief calm a squall hit which might have capsized God Speed if Sarah hadn't jumped so quickly to Castle's orders, dropping sails to the deck in a wind-tossed heap. They were saved from the storm only to be shot at from the north end of Block as they skirted the shoals, and were forced to stand off the back side of the island until the gunfire subsided.

Cuff discovered the couple and Starboard had been living and working with a family of black fishermen on the back side of the island. The boat had been refitted and painted there, and was used in occasional ferry service between the island and New London. Cuff was looking for evidence to carry back to Newport - a first-hand telling of Castle's story. For a few days he had to be satisfied with silent watching, because Starboard didn't want Castle telling Cuff anything at all, didn't want anyone in Newport knowing the three lost mariners were alive, and the boat intact.

But Cuff gained the fishing family's favor, writing a message for them which could be forwarded to Benin. There was Sarah's suspicion to be got past as well. She seldom let Castle far from her sight. It was an agreement of their marriage-without-ceremony that he wouldn't sail without telling his destination and swearing his return. She understood that Castle had never been tamed, that he was Coromantee, and that given a pistol and canvas, he might kill and sail toward Africa at any time. He'd already proven it.

<>

As patriot dominance settled on the colony Newport's restoration lingered behind once inferior ports, and there was idle time for blame and tattling. Southwick's successor Barber couldn't wait to be part of the game. How easy it is for a man at the case to stray in incremental composition, letter by letter, until a thought, born in honesty sours into slur or libel, pushed in that direction by some felicitous turn of phrase. Barber was green, too anxious to make his mark, and Southwick turned him loose too soon.

The *Mercury*, which had made a modest recovery during the French stay, carrying war information and misinformation, fresh or stale, was reduced to one sheet of news each week. A sorry thing that Barber could afford only this much for a colony and nation at the new starting line. With no merchandise to flog, he could still sell a hot temper.

"Yorktown was the end of the long struggle," he wrote. "but traitors and collaborators walk free in Newport, unashamed and unapologetic." I knew Solomon had warned Barber against me, but hadn't realized the depth of disgust he bequeathed, tied up with that old sore, my "wanton dalliance with the Warren hussy."

The new target of the paper's scorn was another alias - Poser Oevreprowd, a crypto-traitor whose fraternization with the British in our bleakest years, had been disguised in the overalls and leather apron of an ordinary craftsman, pretending to suffer under the occupation's boot, while profiting in subservience that went beyond obedience into employment in the Royal cause. Poser made his appearance in a series of columns under the heading **Jacob's Roost**.

The press drudge Jacob, so childish in his efforts to embarrass me in the past, suddenly had his own column, and all those hours walking the town with the slats hung over his shoulders as the paper's rag-beggar left him eager to settle old resentments. In the *Mercury*'s reduced economy, he'd become a writer by default.

Reading Jacob was unsettling, not just to have him aping me, but to see him so capable of imitation, his column laid out under the image of a regular Chanticleer crowing on a house peak. His favorite villain in the interim between colonial victory and its formal terms was this fictional Poser Oevreprowd.

But surely he knew how to spell proud? And hadn't the French been in town long enough to teach him a little French spelling?' Shouldn't his taunt be 'oeuvre-proud'? One week, made bold by a growing familiarity with his invention, he took a step too far in his campaign to "scrape the British tripe off our plates;" he allowed his Oevreprowd to be turned from a type into a living traitor, "walking among us, taking coffee and ale, morning and evening in our company." As follows:

A reader asks Jacob's Roost, why be so timid, presenting your straw man Poser Oevreprowd. If there be a real one in our town, wasn't he an agent of our reduced circumstance, with blood on more than his conscience? Why wouldn't I name him for exile, jail or hanging? The British hanged the patriot Hale, you say, a boy of twenty-one, while this man lingers to stain our colony into his fiftieth year and more. Your Oevreprowd, who shifted his political tunic, as the opposing danger met him, and still you protect him with an alias? You hold up straw for vilification, while the breathing man struts along our devastated Thames Street, still breaking his wind on the Newport breeze?

Reader, it never occurred to me you wouldn't seize on his name after my bald hint repeated half a dozen times, the spelling of Poser Oevreprowd. Think on it, while I tell you more of our Poser. How, when the British arrived, his patriotic fervor was no more to be seen in these pages. No, he gave up his journalistic pretension, and moved a short distance up our shore, chasing a well-stained petticoat, the color-blind sort of lady, in case you miss my meaning, and took cover as a jack-leg shipwright in a second-rate boat yard. Here mutes and blacks - unclaimed runaways - worked side by side, and the shiftless woman too, building vessels of dubious design for clients in love with speed.

A Poser he was indeed, with no moral anchor. All our meeting-houses opened their doors to him, and on each he turned his back. I heard our renowned Reverend Stiles, now president of the Yale College, plead with him to choose a faith and follow it, but for all the blaspheming from this man's mouth, you'd suppose his god was his own invention. You might even see him sitting with the Jews on their Sabbath. That he should have questioned our ethics is travesty.

The worst has not been told. You recall the British Lieutenant Rush, the peacock sort of officer. At his order, Oevreprowd's boatyard busied itself with a swift craft for the British navy. They spent a full year, building and rebuilding to the Lieutenant's every whim, protected by a cordon of marines as necessary, or their work would have been sent up in patriotic flames. Weeks before the English ran from our port, this narrow-beamed craft was seen under British flag running down the Connecticut coast, carrying who knows what Admiralty instructions written for our destruction.

Now, think again on Poser Oevreprowd, and don't suppose I couldn't spell correctly if I chose, the spellings are here to the purpose.

As if his insinuation didn't offer name enough, laid bare for the simplest letter juggler, a perfect anagram of Prosper Everwood. Poser Oevreprowd, an aping fury taking after the "*back-slider whose this-and-that religion and political extremes were only cover for his employment in the Royal cause, and a debasing attachment to that stained lady of the waterfront. A man who still walks our cobbled avenue, shares conversation at coffee and ale houses, without apology, carrying shame as if it were a badge of honor.*"

<>

Thrip and Sally had sailed up to Providence to take an order from a bay trader the day before the *Mercury* dropped this latest guano on us from Jacob's Roost. Gummee was bunking for a few days with an ale-house chum in the town to be closer to his evening pleasure. Left alone to mind the boat yard, I'd just walked back from town to boil my supper and read the paper when Solomon Southwick came knocking.

A little panicky, looking around the room, he was relieved to find the shipwright and his sister were away. "Barber didn't know the piece would be published," he said. "Jacob told him it was no more than what we'd printed earlier." Even the next day, according to Sol, Barber hadn't read it till the paper was on the street and ferries. "So don't blame him."

"What will Warren do?" he asked me.

"If he's seen it, he's already on his way home."

"Is Jacob in danger?"

"You as well."

"Are you threatening me?"

"Are you apologizing for your new man?"

"For that matter, Palmer, tell me, what part of it isn't true?"

Thrust, and parry, but it wasn't a dagger, or pistol, or the twisting of a libel action that worried Southwick. What court was there to hear it? No, it was Thrip Warren's well-known thrashing arms, maybe destruction of the print shop, or Jacob walking crippled after Warren was through with him.

<>

I couldn't sit still and wait for trouble to come to me. I was in town, walking the waterfront, back and forth wanting to be seen unafraid. Hoping I might see Jacob, ready to rattle his brains, thinking, 'say it to my face, and we'll see who takes a bath in the bay.' I should have known better than to behave like a sailor who owns a bit of the town waterfront, by virtue of his ordeals at sea. I was looking for trouble.

A commotion of men well gone in their cups died away, as they saw me passing by their noisy pleasure in Pitts Head. It was an odd feeling they gave, suddenly silent and fixed on my progress as I went by window, door, and window. Only a dozen steps past, when a crew of them came into the street and followed me, slinking along behind as if their pursuit was a secret. Little to fear from their silly stagger, I supposed, as they fell behind my quickened step.

I turned off Thames Street onto what was left of Bannister's wharf. The stolen timbers left a peninsula of gravel and mud, a narrow spit of the town slipping into the bay. The several men from Pitts reached the shore-end of the ruined landing, and stood watching me. A moment later they formed a line and began a slow march toward me.

It had been a silly fantasy that I might face the town, one man at a time. I met the eyes of one I recognized as a First Baptist kneeler, two from First Congregational, and two others I couldn't place. They closed around me. I turned as someone ran up from behind. A sack was thrown over my head. With my arms pinned to my sides, I was shoved to the ground, my hands and legs held still by four of them.

Someone was at work on my belt and buttons. They had my trousers down to my knees. With my shirt pulled up and my privates shrunken in fear, though not to a useful invisibility, it was suddenly over. Not mutilated, or tossed on a ship, or into the sea. I was tapped with the dismissive toe of someone's boot, and called a "long-nosed devil." By the time I had the sack off my head, the posse of inspectors was off the wharf. They'd had their glimpse of my willie, foreskin intact. Not a Jew, just an ordinary traitor, my time coming.

<>

I went looking for Jacob in his rooms on South Street, and was told he'd gone, moved to his brother-in-law's house. Back at the Warren compound I found Thrip and Sally home. They'd seen the Jacob's Roost column before sailing down from Providence. Thrip already had a pair of pistols.

Sally said the insult was her own business; she had no use for the guns. Neither her reputation nor Thrip's honor would be saved by shooting the mewling coward; Thrip would only condemn himself as a vengeful bully, a killer. She was up and out the next morning before her brother woke, waiting at the print-shop door to berate the newspaper men herself. And warn them away. Neither Barber nor Jacob showed for work.

Thrip and I followed her, and the three of us spent the best part of a day in the tea room across the street, where we could watch the print-shop door. Brother and sister talking it through and through, with the pistols on the table between them. A Baptist preacher, a Sabbatarian and a Quaker elder all took turns with Thrip, counseling a peaceful settlement.

The nervy Southwick, with a nose for trouble, came after us in the tea room, indignant that Barber and Jacob should be threatened for speaking the truth, that the town news should be hostage to dueling pistols.

"Is it still your paper, then?" I asked him.

"Which part of it wasn't true?" he asked me again. He looked at Sally and laughed in his sleeve. Thrip's hand went for one of the pistols. Sally pulled the gun away.

"What business of yours is her life?" I asked him

He said "keep that black poser off the *Mercury* premises, your Mr. Charleston and his bogus Block Island journal. Did you think Barber would print that?" Everyone knows your three Africans drowned.

"They didn't drown."

"Prove it."

No progress there. What use asking why his man Barber would libel the boatyard whose naval cunning was a Newport treasure? And why make a target of a woman with a clearer conscience than his own? Why doesn't the *Mercury* promote a new town wharf? Why doesn't it call back the merchant princes and their fleet - Malbone, Bannister, Redwood, Taylor, and the grand magnate Lopez himself with his clan, Rivera, Levy, Seixas?

"Purer conscience than my own?"

Yes, I answered. And I suppose the *Mercury*'s readers are more interested in the loyalty commission and inspectors of the community foreskins. Another day went by, with Thrip's anger still on patrol across from the *Mercury*'s door. Jacob hadn't come out from behind his brother-in-law's door where two cousins were coaxing him to accept the shipwright's challenge.

<>

Meanwhile Thrip has a commission from Providence, a quick river boat with the cutter lines he favors. No more floating bananas, no more shallops, but long-narrow hulls again, with enough canvas above to keep a crew jumping for speed or survival. What does Thrip care if the ocean-going trade has moved off to Boston and Philadelphia? If someone wants a bay cruiser or something to dare an up-river reach without fear of grounding, Warren is the man they come to.

While the town nurses its anger for collaborators, he has new confidence in me, knowing I'm a life-in-chains to his sister; that if she wanders, I'll always follow, outlasting her traipse and return. He can still admire that much of a fool for his sister, and nobody knows the heart behind her wandering better than I.

With Castle gone, I'm the one chosen to fit a mold station in place when Thrip's busy with something else, though he knows I'd go back to the saw-pit without complaint. Sally still suspects I'd rather be 'spelling' again, but her brother wants me permanently in the shop, and that's where I mean to stay as long as I'm alive and out of jail and I can pull a draw knife to a clean touch. "Smooth as a baby's ass" is his compliment. I wish Sally could accept that I find more pleasure in shaving a board than setting type.

<>

"Bring them home," Sally begged Cuff, and just to oblige her, he was off to Block Island again, risking himself once more in the cross-fire of that front and back island feud.

"Tell them we don't care about the boat," she said. "We want them here. They need to come home." With Cuff gone, we had no news of the loyalty commission meetings, no warning of the visit of two hefty enforcers, who stood in the boat-house doorway with a young black between them, confirming "that's the one," not even looking at Sally.

"The woman who fixed it for you to run?"

"For me to go on the boat with the English;" trembling as he pointed at her.

Thrip lowered his musket as the visitors backed away with this new piece of evidence in their case against the Warren yard, waiting for a hearing. Yes, Sally told us, she'd assisted the boy's unsuccessful run, not to a British ship, but along her freedom trail to Massachusetts. In the meantime, his owner had been killed in a forest skirmish. Now they promised the boy's freedom in return for his testimony against Sally.

They didn't know they were about to be left with the empty pleasure of recrimination, without their resident Jezebel, that Sally would soon be gone. She was only waiting for the signal from Prescience that Mr. Benezet in Philadelphia was ready for her assistance in his Africans' school.

I'd been sharing her bed. She had come to think of us with quiet detachment, as if she were off to one side, watching us from a corner of the bedroom, lying beside her reformed speller, maybe a little surprised, at the peaceful picture we made. One night, both of us content to a stillness, she told me half the women in Newport were unaware they could know pleasure from a man, and the rest thought the indulgence locked the gate to Heaven. She was leaving at week's end, she said after giving me the gracious way of her. If I were doomed to the eternal bad dream, this wouldn't be the reason, I was sure of that.

"Don't follow me to Philadelphia," she said

She left us before Cuff returned from Block Island by way of New London and Providence. He'd been trying to convince the publisher of the *Providence Gazette* that his evidence, brought home from Block deserved a column in his paper. Exclusive to the *Gazette* because the *Mercury* wouldn't touch it. Copies of the paper reached the Newport dock on the same ferry that brought him home.

I was at the town landing to meet him. Along with the newspaper, he had a package almost as large as himself, wrapped in brown paper tied up with twine. He refused my help carrying the thing though he struggled with it all the way from the pier to the Synagogue before passing it through the door to the Chazan, who must have known it was coming, because he said nothing.

"Read the Gazette," Cuff told anyone who would listen.

TWENTY-TWO

THE TESTIMONY OF CASTLE QUANT

A Brief Relation of the Freed Man Castle Quant - His life from Guinea to the present as told to, and clarified by Mr. Cuff Charleston of Newport.

I came to the ocean in a small boat, sitting beside my mother. Her neck was tied to my aunt's neck. I was four years old. If there is more in my head behind this, it is hidden from remembering. Everything else of my earliest times was told me by the lady in the stone prison (Cape Castle on the Guinea coast) and the man Kalika. He did not know me until we were chained on the slave boat. I was put beside him to stop his caterwaul.

My mother and aunt were taken on the first big ship leaving the prison not long after we come there. I was called Castle Quant. The keeper lady watched me and the other children on the beach until she judged us old enough to run off. I was seven years there, when she suspected the idea, and put me on the ocean ship. Right away on the ship Kalika sent me bent over in the dark, one end of the room to the other, said tell everyone we would jump in the water first chance. Drowned, we would fly back to our villages. From my face, Kalika said, I was Coromantee, and brave to jump, so first to be home again. No. I could not believe it, but if we stay on the ship, Kalika said, we be eaten.

The Captain guessed our plan. He put nets outside the rails, we could not reach the water. So Kalika says, we will not eat. He knocks over the white man who pulled us on deck for the bath. Clarke's man beat Kalika's back raw. When I would not eat, the metal throat was put in my mouth and food poured in. I wore the iron collar and was chained to Kalika, who said I was his kin, though he be Ashanti.

The days to the far island Jamaica, I don't know how many, was a sick time from the twisting, pushing up and down, side to side, in a circle. The food poured in me and it poured out. At Jamaica island, we were all taken off, men with the women, more than a hundred, and there was a run for the choice of us. Kalika grabbed hold of me and would not let go. We were knocked to the ground, and left over when the rush and grab was finished.

The captain had to carry us to Carolina and Newport. His first man whipped my back, left and right, till both his arms was tired. Where we stopped for barrel wood is where the printer man came on the ship, always with his mouth open and lips pulled back over his teeth, and the woman Sally fat with a child. She comes below at night, humming and washing us with her own water and blood rag. No more salt water on our tenders.

Kalika said don't be fooled, she is the Captain's woman come down to make us quiet for the white people. Not true. She is a kind woman full in loving but too close. At Newport, we had to go bare and pull our ass wide. Kalika killed the black boy who poked his ass, and was killed himself. I was put on a ship for the hot islands again, but the Quaker Mr. Job Townsend comes to take me off. He said he will show me the woodworking, and you will teach me white speaking. One day I will be free. For all this I must be happy, and how could I run away? So much put in front for me, they say, how could I run away? Three times? That's what you want to know with your writing it down can't write fast enough. And why don't I come home with you right now?

Mr. Charleston, you are for always with the white people and call it free. I cannot be free without I take a mind to run. No matter where, or studying this people's letters. All the places I go walking horses for the Pequod people, carving Mr. Townsend's pretties on his drawers, laying the wood on Mr. Thrip's cutters, everyone say they give me freedom, but I am stolen so they can't give me the first thing. Teaching me? How many learnings do I need?

Mr. Townsend put me to live in the attic over the printer. Everywhere in the house in the street, he is looking at me his lips pulled back. Coming in my door, studying my business. Bzzz bzzz laba laba, Mr. Townsend and the printer, their mouths always going about me and my improvements.

I run again it was another bad wandering, the Indian people used me in the far woods all crooked hearts, and worse they could threaten was send me back to Rhode Island. I don't know what Mr. Townsend gave you to pay them, He didn't have to give them a thing.

Mr. Townsend says if I don't like furniture I could go to ship making. Whatever I want. Another giving. Sally is a good-heart woman, but smothering, let me get my breath woman. Sally helped me run. I can tell you that because Mr. Townsend wants his guilty clear of me, and won't come back on her. Sarah comes to my bed, and from then we are only for each other.

Mr. Thrip Warren trained me up from ready hands to knowing hands in every part of ship work. If there was a trick to it, he won't be still until I know it. I didn't have to ask him to let me run a boat he forced my hand to a tiller before I knew ought of a come-about, not the first turning. And everything he taught me was another part of me owing that couldn't be paid in monies, my forever owing. And I never asked to come there, so who was owing?

I asked if he could teach me to sail to a place I couldn't see. He taught me the stars and the rise of the sun from the sea with the North Star for steering. Too many numbers to hold all of them in my mind. It was put in the paper that Mr. Warren could as well give me keys to the rum and write me the be-gone papers, making trouble for everyone with an African. Sally thinks at last I am happy and will not be such a fool to leave the island again.

Then the people going bzzz bzzz laba laba about Mr. Warren building a boat for the English before I stole it and sailed it into the ocean with Sarah and Starboard.

(Here a part of the boy's story is missing. *Editor*)

Mr. Warren says go right along by Connecticut, don't need anything but a clear day and your eyes. Starboard comes in my ear with his own way. Better he says we sail to the outside island in back, where we find people to help us. Like we disappeared and the boat too. He says if I must I will bring Sarah too. His way is not the way I mean to go with water to drink on the boat and a barrel of jerky and salt fish. I have the compass Sally bought off the printer's boss.

I set north to Providence as the Lieutenant ordered. Went out of sight above Prudence Island and I cut sharp port close to capsizing, putting Sarah's hand in the water, she screamed. We come up straight again and go down behind the island. When we can see our pier again between the islands, Starboard says the Lieutenant is hopping up and down I don't believe it because the haze is against it. We have wind behind and no mind to turning home no one chasing. The British ships all waving their nose rags at our British flag.

At Point Judith we come past the shoals, I steer West for Starboard's notice. He goes under to close his eyes and I ease off to east he never woke to the tack. Sarah is curious. When Starboard come up again, he says "what's that?

"I don't know it," I tell him.

More land rising, and he already has it figured, we're looking at the Martha Vineyard to the side, and the Nantucket Island ahead, sun lowering behind us going full East to crossing the ocean. Says nothing to me he goes below, whispering to Sarah She come up to put this foolishness out of my head. When she couldn't turn me, he come with gentle talk but no gentling he knocks me down out of my wits. When my lights come back, my head is on Sarah's knee, and we are beside Point Judith again, going west along the shore like Mr. Warren told us.

You can drown yourself, Starboard says, but you not taking us with you. He is working his own scheme that all of us be like dead and God Speed gone to the bottom, which might happen anyway because the next morning a storm from the ocean side knocks off the top mast and takes the sheet into the sea we were near blown into the water ourselves No steering nothing we can change about going this way and that or under the water. We all three rolling side to side on the floor until the storm finish.

Crippled so. Nothing but two paddles and the ocean pushing us in to the island. A double-end fishing boat sees our split mast. This is the freedman Jeremy a cod fisher supposing us drowned. Finding different, he throws a rope for pulling us into his cove. Right away Jeremy is generous past expecting anything from us. We are fishermen with him for some days and he helps us fix the boat, new paint mast sails on the God

Speed, which name is now See Something because when they look at us, nobody has a name for it. We get some monies sailing from Block Island to Fishers and to this cove or that on Connecticut and other work that is our own business.

The See Something is tied at Moore's dock. Sarah and I lying in the New London house where we do our own business. A man comes to the boat and cuts off Kalika. Won't have the rude African in New London. So why is he in Mr. Canty's freak shop and he wants twenty pounds English. Easy for me to break the night lock and take him back to the island. I say all right, Mr. Charleston, you take Kalika. Tell Sarah and Mr. Warren our sailing wherever is not for your writing.

TWENTY-THREE

WHAT HAPPENED HERE?

A Quaker returning from a fifteen-year mission in the Indies, landing on the remains of Long Wharf, seeing the devastation, dabbed at his eyes as he walked by the missing pieces of his boyhood, a checkerboard of burned homes and steeple houses. "What happened here?" he asked as if no news of Newport had reached him in the last decade.

Blame and retribution? Who knows the history of another man's conscience, who's wise enough to sort accommodation from collaboration? Was anyone listening when our Continental General Washington said, "all had a right to choose their side?" Someone writing in the new *Mercury* proposed banishing all those who prayed at the same time for their husbands' defeat and safe return. That would be more than half the women in Newport.

Urging the town toward retribution, the *Mercury* flaunted Pennsylvania's black-list of four hundred and ninety guilty of high treason, and New York's tally of a thousand to be tried and sentenced. Fines, confiscation, banishment, hanging? In the confusion Jacob came from behind his family's gate, and found his voice again.

We're told that Poser Oeverprowd, who warned mortal consequence for those favoring the throne, may now be heard in Pitts Head in praise of General Washington's 'sensible moderation' in healing the wounds of war, and the General's advice that 'all had a right to choose a side.' Will we be so easily charmed to impotence in dealing with our traitors?

I was on my way to silence Jacob for good when I was grabbed in the street by Chazan Touro, pulled into the synagogue, and warned of a gang gathering in Pitts Head with more than just my foreskin in mind. They'd have my neck this time, he said, and without trial.

I supposed Touro would take me to a back door from which I could slink away in the night to the boat yard. Instead he led me up the steps of the bimah. He raised a trap door, lit a candle for me and pointed to a ladder leading into the opened earth below. When I climbed down I had no intention of running from men whose faces I knew. I wasn't thinking of escape, but at last a chance to experience this for myself, the Jews' secret passage of deliverance.

The Chazan handed me a crust and canteen of water, and I stepped down into a space scarcely big enough to turn in. This gave into a tunnel that would require a crawling progress. I stood there for a moment, wondering at the Chazan, so alert to the town's mischief, baffled by his concern for me. "Don't try anything stupid," he said, sounding more like a jailor than an angel of deliverance.

Hearing something slide across the door overhead, I took it as the signal to set off on hands and knees, pushing the candle in front of me through the tunnel, framed side and ceiling with oak timbers. The ground rose and fell as I struggled along, bent here into an S, there into V, where the excavation twisted to avoid rock.

At the end of the tunnel another ladder to the surface. Standing beside it, the ebony Kalika threw his engorged silhouette on the wall behind, scowling over my genuflecting position in his second grave. I was up the ladder, pushing against the door. It wouldn't budge. A rung broke under my foot, and the next beneath it, all the way down.

Wriggling back through the tunnel I was thinking I'm not waiting with you, Kalika, until, exhausted, I stood again under the bimah. Reaching up, it was as I feared; this door was barred as well. No ordinary confinement this, in captivity to the Jews.

I knocked and called. No answer. On the ground again, I let my back slide down the wall until my knees were tight against my chest. The candle was guttering and soon out.

Cramping, rising, cramping, I imagined hours passing as I wandered between panic and freedom. Sorting the future-dueling pistols...did twenty paces mean ten each?...I'd be close enough to see Jacob's trembling hand...he'd take the first shot and miss, helpless...then I was on a ride-away to Philadelphia, visiting in Sally's rooms.

All the while, buried. Was this the way Touro meant to keep my odor from the town's religious nostril? No, I couldn't believe it; the Chazan was a gentle man, with a mind for a difficult text. The first to welcome me in Newport. Something ran over my foot.

I slept, woke and slept, pissed against the wall, held back the other. Cursed the Chazan, thanked him, cursed him. 'Thanked him for his advice to forget the duel. I feared I'd slept through a Sabbath, and another day might leave me too depleted to make myself heard in the synagogue, remembering the Chazan's words: "Newport, the fresh continent's heart, moral and immoral, mercantile engine, courageous, mean, sinning and repenting, suffering all persuasions, the more to prosper."

I heard a sliding overhead, saw light, and heard the Chazan calling.

"They're gone."

"What day is it?"

"Day? It's not morning yet."

Amused by my racing clock, he sent me into the shadows behind the synagogue with a cryptic goodbye. "Wandering souls like yours may save us all. Be safe, Cotton."

<>

The following evening, I gave Jacob his choice of Thrip's pistols, proposing dawn for an end to his newspapering career. "In the orchard on the North Road, behind the powder stores."

"I don't have to meet you anywhere," he said. "There's a law against it." He knew as well as I in those weeks there were no laws in place but those usurped and enforced by any man's whim.

He took one of the pistols in a hand already shaking. I had no experience of handguns, though full confidence in the outcome. I had no second. He had the belligerent brother in law, and lucky for him because the next morning he was too nervous to prepare his own pistol. He was all all for twenty paces each, assuming there'd be two wild shots and he could curse my traitor's vanity, a cursing that began before we turned our backs, and walked apart.

The brother called to me from behind a tree, "You traitor bag of shit wind. This is where they'll bury you, Inkfinger."

On the about-face, Jacob was all jelly, the barrel of his gun moving in noticeable circles. His hand was still moving when he fired, the tip of his barrel was still making a little orbit when his ball struck the flesh of my calf. He didn't know he'd hit me as I trained my pistol on his chest, now a moving target. His chin fell, he stood sideways to me. His brother-in-law called, "stand up." He couldn't, collapsing to the ground. I never fired.

Whose victory? Mine, with herb poultice on a painful leg? Or Jacob's, back at the type case, thankful, I expect, that Barber would no longer print the work of Oevreprowd. The duel did nothing for my reputation, and Jacob was boasting in Pitts Head that I'd limped away, a wiser man.

<>

I was limping along the waterfront when one of the self-appointed posses of retribution knocked me down. My hands were tied, and I was marched off to be locked in a loft. I was held there for two days until they got the service of a man from Providence, another willing to put wool over his head and take the mallet, once again the appearance of a legal proceeding for a matter already decided.

In the stone holding-house beside the slave pen fifty or more were waiting to see me tried. Along with Thrip I was charged with working for the enemy, for hypocritically professing loyalty to the colony. Tried and exonerated by the English for conspiring to steal their cutter, now to be tried for building the boat in the first place, and it was my neck they wanted first.

I could see Ellery and Vernon in the front, and a half dozen more from Second Congregational standing together, as many from First Congregational. Several Quakers too, who were pretending to an unbroken patriotic allegiance. Sabbatarians, Presbyterians, a few of Murray's followers, the Baptists well represented, and the usual topers who could be drawn from the pub for any bit of sport. I recognized the editor of the *Gazette* and several other faces from Providence, a Brown and two Wantons. All there to watch my humiliation and hear the foregone verdict; only my sentence in question.

The judge was calling for order to a drumming cry of "Guilty! Guilty!" As he read the collaboration charge there was commotion in the doorway.

It was Cuff Charleston pushing through, coming forward against hostile voices. "Get back boy."

"What court is this?" he asked the first one standing in his way, repeating the question to any who moved to stop him until the one under sheep's wool must have wondered himself. Someone had the answer:"This is the court that is." He had it right, a people's court of no legal standing, the less to be honored and more to be feared. The judge said "let the boy speak."

"That's no boy," Vernon told him. "That's the Quakers' five-tongue African."

"Well let him use one of them," the judge said, sitting back in his chair, waiting to be amused.

"The boy Castle told me to write this for him," Cuff said.

"They give Mr. Warren shame about me, and then going bzzz bzzz laba laba about he was making a quick boat for the English. He didn't want it. His plan was the Lieutenant Rush would not try the boat first. But I would drive it, Sarah and Starboard to go with me. We would steal it. We would take it to Fishers Island to hide away and paint the boat again beyond anyone knowing it. We would dress it in new sails that would not drown it. Wait there, Mr. Warren said, until the English be gone from Rhode Island."

Back and forth it went in my court room between "lying Nigger" and "honest black man," with the judge rising to leave without verdict, when the first grievance against me gave way to another.

"Antichrist! His signs were all over."

"Deny it, Inkfinger!"

"Swear it!"

"He sat with Jews,, Baptists, Congregationalists, anybody."

Yes, with all those mentioned and six more. Even with the Anglicans in Trinity. The assembled faiths of beleaguered Newport waited for my testimony, ready to pounce on a lie.

"It's the whore's brother," someone called as Thrip walked in and stood beside Cuff who was looking at me, disgusted that I had nothing to say for myself. I pushed free of the two holding my arms, walked up to the judge, turned and said, "Yes!" in a voice that would carry through the windows to the crowd outside.

“Yes!” again, “and hasn’t it been a wonderful free ride since the Anglicans lost control fifty years ago - when Bishop Berkeley discovered this jumble of beliefs. Enough of them, he said, to make a man of reason puke. But before he left he called this the most thriving place in all America. Is it such a riddle that wealth and welfare followed from free consciences?

“In dreams I’ve been taken to unforgiving places where I wouldn’t care to spend eternity. And I thank the god who might repay my mistakes with that long nightmare, that it wasn’t one of us who shot our witless messenger of free thought. And whoever hit me from behind on Thames Street, you weren’t the first to arrest me. Before I was your prisoner I was a captive under the Synagogue.”

“You wrote the idiot’s blasphemy," Vernon attacked me

“If reason is blasphemy, call it what you like. They were a Frenchman’s words copied on the signs by a Quaker lady. So, Mr. Vernon, and Mr. Ellery standing there with you, I sat in the balcony and watched the two of you kick open the pew door, and march out of your church when your pastor told you to render unto Caesar. Is your faith the one I should follow, to be renounced when it threatens my purse?”

The rustling room grew still.

"And Mr. Brown beside you, visiting from Providence, here to see me judged. Maybe hanged. He and his cousins took public money meant for a colonial navy and built privateers with it. Is this the patriotism that should have moved me?”

I pointed to a Sabbatarian who had left Newport a Tory and was now returned a Patriot. He left the building before I could praise the wisdom of his new choice.

“I see three men of Trinity here, home again after a time in the near country. If they never declared a side, are they here now to claim victory and condemn collaboration.?”

I called back one of Bannister’s black warehousemen, who was heading for the door, reminding him that his master said he’d give up his religion before he’d give up his slaves. “A faith for me to follow?”

There were more shuffling feet as I began to move toward the door myself, not quite finished with all the hypocrisy in the room. “If there was a Jew,” I said “who ignored the Non-Importation Treaty, weren’t there merchants in First Congregational who did the same, two of them standing right here? If there's a man here pure in faith and patriotism, let him raise his voice, or just his hand."

Two soldiers home from mountain paths in Pennsylvania and Virginia, men who had come through British musket fire, raised their arms, but maybe thinking of the blasphemies that sustained their long march, pulled them down again.

TWENTY-FOUR

THE "SEE SOMETHING"

Jacob had nicked a bit of my shin bone. The leg still ached two years later as I rode South on leave from the boatyard for a while. My mount was a pacer offered by the Spring Street stable, a young mare that needed gentling according to the hostler. I didn't tell him this was more than one of my trips to Philadelphia where Sally, a favored assistant to Benezet, accepted my autumn visits if I rented a room there, my own bed a required, if fictitious, scruple.

I'd be away two months or more in Virginia if the horse didn't go lame or kill me first. I'd learned to let my feet swing free of the stirrups for blessed intervals of stretching. When discomfort passed to ease in the saddle, my mission came to the fore. Not the next visit to Sally, who'd long since forgiven me for the foolhardy duel. When she learned that my pistol had never fired she called me a damn fool, the accusation softened by a fondling hand and an invitation to watch her work with the African children for a few days.

Our time together, more a horizontal indulgence than may have been best for our election in eternity. I'd stay until it became a concern of Mr. Benezet, and propriety split us again into our separate colonies. I was coming her way once more, but thinking beyond our reunion to the difficulties of the pike between Philadelphia and the Potomac, and the Appalachian foothills where a solitary rider was at risk in camp and on the road. This and the problem of finding a printer in Virginia who'd accept the argument carried in my saddlebag.

There was ample time on the long ride to consider again my rebirth in the synagogue's tunnel. The underground discovery of my usefulness to the Jew and his brotherhood, and the conscience of our reborn country. If I was free to wander and sample, he'd be free to worship in his temple; my unpunished indecision, the complement of the safety of his clan. With Newport my instructor, and Kalika as my witness. Now, if asked, 'What religion?' I'm sworn to answer 'All or none.'

<>

I found a stable off Market Street, walked to Sally's rooms, ready to surprise her. I needn't have worried about my reception. She pulled me inside, prepared a tub in the middle of the floor, and tended to my journey's grime and pain with a warm washrag and slow hand. When she was finished, we carried the tub to her back window, poured the memory of the road into her yard

She was in a hurry to get me to the waterfront before dark. We hired a two-seat, and arrived at the docks just in time to see the slim craft with missing figurehead, her latest name on her transom, SEE SOMETHING, skimming away to the north side of the harbor mouth, ignoring channel buoys, her mast and canvas quickly going out of sight, speed and mischief running together once more.

Castle and Sarah, sailing with contraband. Their cargo, lately hiding under the floor of Benezet's school house, and delivered to the waterfront by Sally the previous night, two runaways from New York, now under the deck for delivery to a cove high on the New Hampshire coast, where a chain of friendly hands wait to guide the way to Canada. By Sally's count it was the craft's seventh freedom flight. She knew that chance ran against such a scheduled thievery, the See Something back at the Philadelphia docks every June, waiting for Sally's next passenger.

We watched the gray sail disappear in the mist, then sat to plates of mackerel and fried potato from a harbor stall. Much to say, but how to explain without insult. Was she in such a hurry to meet someone else? For my part, how to tell her, it was only for one night because I had business waiting in Virginia.

Her hurry was that I should see Castle, Sarah and their water-dart, maybe for the last time, before it fell over the horizon. We finished a schooner of small beer between us, then back to her rooms where her demand for candor would put any deceit to rout.

You've found a new lady in Newport?

No such thing.

With us it was no struggle to find the next harmony. While we fumbled, she asked, "What's in your saddle bag this time? You've written something? About me, is it?" "As if she still feared all my experience was just rehearsal for its description. Never mind that I'd been building boats with her brother all this time, and never hoped to leave him.

No, I assured her, what she and I did together could not be written. Of what worth, anyway, the futile approximation of the thing at once so common and so rare; the contradiction could only pall in the descriptive mixing. But why let my tongue run on when all she'd wanted was a murmured 'no.'

She crossed my lips with a scolding finger and gave my hand the helm, where once more we could sail out to find the wave that would wash us back to shore. We were scarcely breathing easily again when I sat up. "What are you become?" she said, "Can't you stay a while longer?"

TWENTY-FIVE

ESCAPE

I was wandering away from her question to the man with a first name for his last, Henry, Virginia's hero of the Revolution, determined to have all America tithe to faith, to make it the law of the land. I was leaving in the morning

If I went to Virginia, she said, it was the last place I'd go.

But I rode down the coast, as certain of my errand as any Woolman going north, message ready, fairly burning its way through my saddle bag. I was impatient to see it issued from a southern press, addressed to every yard and parlor, every court and congress.

<>

As witness from Newport, Rhode Island, seaside haven and nursery to three-hundred ocean ships, whose trade has been a marvel of the continent, its fortune on display, where a citizen found his belief anywhere he chose. This was not the colony's business and should not be the concern of any government.

Here in Virginia the law is "one Sunday in four in the pew," with the state in your pocket for a mandatory offering. Now, set free from British tyranny, and ready to make common cause with other colonies in a binding constitution, beware of a dangerous resolution. It comes in the innocence of holiness and the humble cunning of the serpent offering fruit.

Your revered Patrick Henry, once Governor of Virginia and would-be Governor again, a champion of your rights, is leading you in error. By a stroke, he would send you from freedom into spiritual jail. He says you must be ridden under the crop of a universal religious fee, that by the new constitution you should pay to be guided on your way to Eternity.

Listen to the wise men who give his cause the lie, to Washington, who warns you that a sectarian bias would forever prevent an orderly muster, and who calls on the Grace of Providence in public address so that no man's faith is slighted; open your ears to Jefferson who edits his Bible to answer the world he sees; to Madison who says, "conscience is the most sacred property of all." Thus strive for a perfect separation between civil and religious matters?

Can there be a Sovereign who is part God and part Governor to save you from your own reason? Government, the partner of Heaven? The notion mocks itself. Newport's rabbi said it for every man there, 'Newport is the fresh continent's heart, moral and immoral, slave and free, its commercial engine, courageous, suffering all persuasions, sinning and repenting, the more to prosper."

When asked, what is my faith, I answer freely:

All or none.

<>

Richmond, Virginia – We report a midnight escape of the known political agitator and blasphemer, Cotton Palmer, lately of Newport, Rhode Island, from the jail in Winchester. He was taken up in that town a week earlier. This master of the alias was distributing a pamphlet libelous and profane. For all his cunning he could as well have been preaching abolition or atheism.

Of all places, the troublemaker offers that lawless and irreverent town of Newport for our example, Newport, whose sorry sea dogs are out of all work but checkers and ale. Where preachers scold their congregations for profiting on the blood and bondage of the African. There is no question of authorship. Palmer set his own name to the work. No bail had been set for this sly friend of abolition. Just as well for the prisoner. The jail was being watched daily by friends of our defamed Governor Henry. They hoped to see the man hanged.

<>

It wasn't much of a jail they put me in, more like an overnight accommodation for sobering up, with bars of oak on the window. In fact,

I heard the sheriff tell his deputy to open the cell when the ruffians outside went home, even to return my horse along with tack and saddle bags.

Once free, I turned the mare east, close by the Charlestown Road at Berryville. My antagonists would assume a run to the north, but I made straight for the Shenandoah, crossing the river at Shepherd's Ford and hacking up through thick woods to the Appalachian ridge where I could watch for pursuit from east or west from a perch in a tall poplar.

I meant to wait until the commotion in Winchester died away. After a day, with my urine red from wine berries and stomach aching from over-ripe field cress, I finally stunned a squirrel with a well-aimed stone, and was recovering a normal digestion on the flesh crisped over a camp fire. Secure but for the nighttime howling of coyotes.

Planning a morning descent east into the Fairfax grant, I put up for the night, leaving my horse tethered a good distance from my high perch where two limbs made a seat, and I could lean back with feet dangling to either side of the trunk.

The moon was up; I was dozing when I heard dogs again. They'd found my horse, and had begun to circle. Their master shouted, "Sing Maggie! Sing Blue," and then I saw them coming, baying at my scent, my mare following behind. A minute more and the man was looking up at me.

"It's you," he said.

The dogs, frantic, waiting for the rifle blast. The gun was cradled in his arms, his eyes steady on me, as he thought of his options. Take me alive with the trouble of escorting me off the mountain and back to Winchester; shoot me and keep the horse for himself, maybe be accused of murder and horse theft; or simply take the horse and pretend he'd never seen me.

Supposing the long delay had worked in my favor, I was preparing to climb down. The man took aim at me and fired. I slumped over, still held aloft in the crook of the tree, legs dangling again. The panicked horse went racing through the underbrush down the mountain to the east.

The vigilante, his work done, and with no apparent interest in the horse, began his descent to the west, back toward Winchester. I rose from my opossum slump and climbed down from the tree, but remained on the ridge two days, waiting for the news of my death to spread through the region.

I was long enough in the valley on the east to learn that my mare had been corralled, unclaimed in Aldie, and would go to auction for the benefit of that village. A man from nearby Haymarket had bought the tack and saddlebags, whose contents were recognized as the dirty laundry and scribbling of the man who libeled Patrick Henry. My orphaned credo eventually made its way to a sympathetic printer in Baltimore who published it surrounded by the heavy black line used for obituaries.

I crossed the Potomac into Maryland, then Pennsylvania on my way to Sally in Philadelphia where, for us, well-met and farewell were as predictable as the coming and going of the ocean tide. From Philadelphia the same ocean road carried me home to the town that had so nearly been a dead nation's cemetery. I paced the deck and heard it sung, as if from the new country's crow's nest, carrying across the water to that stubborn shore of steeples and statehouse - *"Newport Rising!"*

END

Made in the USA
Middletown, DE
08 September 2018